Light of the World

Book 3 of Light the Ark Series – A Christian Fiction
Thriller

James Bonk

Storming Strongholds LLC

Dedication

" **A**gain Jesus spoke to them, saying, 'I am the light of the world; he who follows me will not walk in darkness, but will have the light of life.'" -John 8:12 RSV

***

To those who fight back.

To those who speak up.

This book is to everyone who takes a sledgehammer to the gates of hell.

Contents

Books By James Bonk

Light of the Ark Series

1. Light of the Ark

2. Shadows of the Ark

3. Light of the World

- Isaiah and the Sea of Darkness (standalone prequel)

More Fiction

- Christian's Look Back at Life

Stay up to date on new releases and email exclusive content: https://hello.jamesbonk.com/signup/

Chapter 1

Suffocating Stars

The forest swayed in the gentle breeze. Matthew looked up as the bright star light flickered through the canopy. He focused on the light. Each twinkling star was like its own lighthouse, drawing in his gaze.

As he stared, trees disappeared, as if stepping aside to give him a better view of sky above. The bright lights pierced the black void.

But the emptiness of space wasn't a void. Matthew looked up, curious. To his amazement, the darkness remained, but he felt a difference. A new pulse from the horizon creeping into view. The former void of space was no longer black because of a lack of light, but a consumption of it. As if a black hole broke free of its circular confines and spread like an ink, clouding the clean water of the night sky.

At first, the new darkness weaved between the shimmering stars like shadows filling darkened corners of a room. But as it encircled a star, it slowly pressed into it from all sides. Each surrounded star slowly faded as its light fought the shadow. Matthew looked on as the new darkness pressed on, spreading across the sky. The unrelenting contagion took over the sky, one star at a time. It was patient, as if enjoying the silent penetration and suffocation.

Soon there was more darkness than light as the blanket pulled over the visible universe.

Matthew brought his eyes back to Earth. The forest that had once surrounded him now faded away, one tree at a time. Each tree withering to a twig before falling into dust. He noticed the fading trees matched the stars. As the darkness strangled the life of each star, one-by-one, a matching tree on the Earth lost its life. Matthew spun, looking around himself. He now stood in the middle of a barren plain. A circle of empty ground where there were once trees continued to expand around him. Moments ago he felt the cool breeze, heard it rustle lush green leaves, but now the air had a rotten, sulfur-like smell as it blew away the black ash of the withering trees.

He turned his attention back to the sky. The new darkness was covering the last of the stars. The bright night sky was gone, the blanket of hungry darkness now fully pulled over.

Matthew stood in the silent, pitch-black night. He turned, looking in all directions for a sign of life, but nothing.

There was no light.

He stood alone in the silent darkness.

Then, a noise.

A faint rumble in the distance grew, gradually turning into a roar. It was raging rapids all around him, a deafening noise of standing in the middle of a powerful waterfall. Then, in the pitch-black night, he felt it before he saw it. The roaring water hit him, shoving him off his feet.

He didn't need to see it to know what it was. He'd seen this before. The sea of darkness from his vision. The same sea of darkness that haunted, yet encouraged, his grandfather, Isaiah.

But now, there was no floating Bible. No family waiting. No safety from the rising black waters at his waist as he tried regaining his footing.

Waves erupted from the water, like geysers to the heavens, and came at him from all sides. First, from below, hitting his chest. Then, from behind, then the side, crashing down. His feet skidded on the wet ground below, struggling for balance, but with every inch of success, the waves seemed to grow stronger, larger.

They crashed down on him, then countered with an upper-cut. Like giant arms from an unseen bully, they pushed his head down, smacked his body left and right. It toyed with him as the pressure built and the waters rose.

The suffocated stars flashed in his mind. The darkness slowly surrounded them, gradually squeezing the life away.

The sea of darkness kept rising. He felt three hundred and sixty degrees of pressure crushing him.

Then, amid the struggle, he felt something in his right front pocket.

The light from the artifact shone through his jeans pocket, like a seam of perfect light, the small piece of the Ark of the Covenant, making its presence known.

Soon, he felt a second piece in his left pocket.

Then another in his back right pocket. And yet another in his back left pocket.

Each pocket shone brightly, but Matthew still couldn't breathe. The water tossed him left and right, pummeling him in the vicious darkness.

And then, without knowing why, he felt himself gather each piece and bring his hands together, squeezing them tight.

In an instant, the pieces melded together, and he held on to them for dear life.

A split second after he gripped the Ark, as if he squeezed a trigger, a brilliant light flashed in the sky. Like shot from a cannon, a new star flew across the sky. It was bigger and brighter than any of the previous stars.

Through the chaos of the waters, Matthew looked up and watched it soar up from the horizon toward the highest point in the sky.

As it reached its zenith like a firework, it erupted in a dazzling explosion of white light. But the center point didn't fade as the light expanded. It grew stronger.

In what seemed like a millisecond to Matthew, the explosion brought the former stars back to life–a flame thrower reigniting candles. As the sky lit up, the water that suffocated Matthew evaporated. Matthew stood, still holding his small piece of the Ark as the barren ground turned green and trees sprouted, shooting up in a burst of life.

Then it was over. Everything was back, brighter than before.

But as the immediate growth and revival ended, so did Matthew's life.

He lay clutching the Ark.

Dead.

That is when Jeremiah woke up.

His dream ended as the world renewed, life restored, but his best friend died.

Ever since J accepted and felt God enter his heart, ever since he laid his hands on two of his dying friends, bringing them back to life, and ever since he walked through a door of light that transported him across the globe, he stopped dreaming of the train and being devoured by a dragon.

His new nightly dream saw the darkness through Matthew's eyes. As if J were Matthew, he felt the fear of the blackness eating the stars in the sky and the intense pressure of the water crushing him.

And every night, the dream ended the same way, with Matthew's death.

***

Matthew pulled his truck into the garage and took a deep breath. The girls weren't running out to meet him. He had an extra second to clear his mind before going in. They were most likely watching a movie or playing in the backyard, and whichever one, Matthew was thankful.

As he moved around his truck, he picked up the small recycling bin that overflowed with soda water cans and cardboard boxes and took it to the side of the house. Breaking down the boxes and dumping the cans into the larger recycling bin designed for city pickup, he heard the girls laughing over the tall shadowbox fence. Their laughter put a smile on his face and shifted his thoughts away from the exhausting work day.

Moving through the garage, he put back the small bin and took out his lunchbox and laptop bag from the passenger side of the truck. Sliding the strap over his shoulders, he felt the warm sensation where the Bible inside his bag brushed against his hip. The Bible, containing the hidden piece of the Ark of the Covenant, went with him everywhere.

Before entering the house, he walked to the end of the driveway and checked the mail. After flipping through the advertisements and a medical bill, he found a card from Aunt Millie, the church accountant. The smiley face stickers and crayon unicorns covering the envelope put another smile on Matthew's face, just like the girls' laughter.

This wasn't a formal church letter, such as their giving tax statement for the year. This letter was from his oldest daughter's, Beth's, newest pen pal. For a school assignment, Beth had written to her Grandma Mary, Matthew's mother, starting a regular exchange of letters. A series of letters between the two gave Beth a fun way to practice writing. Soon, Mary recruited Aunt Millie to join the conversation.

Something shot across Matthew's vision and he looked up from the colorful envelope. Trees blew in the wind. Down the street, a couple walked two dogs. Then Matthew saw what caught his attention: a car roughly one hundred feet away was at a stop sign, now beginning to drive again. A giant black shadow moved with the car. Its edges flowed like dark waves, an opaque water moving as if part of the car. Matthew knew the shadowy figure wasn't with the car, but attached to the driver inside.

The car passed out of sight. Matthew stood looking down the street, then turned to walk up the driveway and into the house.

Looking through the living room windows, he watched his two daughters, Beth and Lyn, run barefoot in the yard. Their joyous play pulled him like a magnet. Normally, seeing their dirt-black feet made him cringe. It usually meant a new, freshly dug hole was somewhere in the yard that he'd have to refill. Every time he mowed the grass, he'd notice the dirt patch until the grass regrew. But seeing their smiles quickly made his thoughts of a perfect lawn melt away. He gave their cat, Porkchop, a scratch behind the ear as he napped on the top of the couch and went to the door.

"Mmmmm, I smell mud pies," Matthew called out as he slid open the sliding glass door.

"Daddy!" Both girls called in unison as they ran up to hug him.

"Wait, I don't see any! Did your mom already eat them all?" Matthew asked. He flashed a look at Liz. She gave a mock laughing expression without looking up from her laptop.

Make-believe mud pies were their current favorite game. It drove Matthew nuts, repeatedly filling the holes and trying to get the girls to the bathroom without leaving clumps of dirt on the floor and black smears on the white walls. To Matthew's surprise, Liz grew used to the dirt-filled time out back, and even encouraged the free, unstructured play.

"Mud pies have been canceled." Beth said matter-of-factly.

"WHAT?" Matthew exaggerated. "You mean no watery hole that you splash in and scoop out mud? No, no, no!"

"Pink unicorns don't eat mud," Lyn said as she put her index finger on her head like a horn and ran towards her sister.

"How was your day, hun?" Liz called out as she typed. She was propped on her elbows, laying on a soft gray blanket in the shade of an oak tree, working on her latest fashion blog post.

"It was alright." Matthew replied, his voice flat. "Better now."

Liz stopped typing and looked up at him. "Again?"

Matthew nodded. "All day. *And* on the way home. *And* again, at the end of the road just now."

"You can't stay quiet on this," Liz said, closing her laptop.

"Come on, Dad!" Lyn pulled at Matthew's arm. "It's freeze things!"

"Freeze tag unicorn." The older Beth corrected.

"Freeze things!" Lyn belted.

"Freeze tag, but you have to run like a unicorn." Beth explained.

"How does that work?" Matthew asked.

"Like this!" Beth said as the two girls bent down and took off on all fours, mimicking a horse's neigh as they trotted in circles.

Matthew laughed and shook his head.

"Well, how can I say no to that?" He said as he unbuttoned his dress shirt and kicked off his shiny black shoes.

"I don't like this, hun," Liz said, putting a hand on his shoulder.

"I don't either," he replied softly, "but what can I do? They're everywhere and it's like they know I see them. Every time I watch them, someone looks at me like I'm crazy. I've been avoiding our staff meetings lately, and that seems to only add more work from all the follow-ups."

"Talk to your father, please? Promise me you will." She had her laptop under one arm and the blanket over her shoulder as she moved into the house. "I'll get dinner going."

As Liz slid the door closed, Matthew looked through the door and towards the front of his house. Through a window he could see down the road. The little red dot of a stop sign seemed to wink at him from the distance, like a beacon across dark waters.

He pulled his eyes away from the stop sign as Beth slammed into him with a giggle.

"You're frozen!" She screamed before running away. The two girls laughed.

"Unfreeze me!" he called to Lyn.

"No!" she cried out, laughing as she followed her sister.

"You can't talk! You're frozen!" Beth laughed.

Matthew stood silent, holding back his smile and trying to push down the thoughts of the demons he now saw regularly. They loomed in and out of his vision ever since the shadow above Nancy Pawly, the one that came out in the courthouse, put him in the hospital last spring. He could still see the menacing red eyes of that overwhelming shadow when he thought of it. That first shadow he saw differed from the others he saw day-to-day. The daily ones varied in size and shape, and seemed weaker than the large red-eyed monster, but all contained an endless black color and feeling of cold, as if void of life and warmth.

Lyn ran by and smacked his leg, unfreezing him.

"Yes!" he cried out.

He took off and spent the next thirty minutes forgetting about the pressures of work, his supernatural visions, and the Ark he carried daily to keep the demons at bay. He enjoyed his time as a father, running around on all fours, neighing like a horse in socks, slacks, and an undershirt. The game changed occasionally and sometimes Matthew turned into an imaginary zombie, picking the girls up as he ran by and pretending to suck their brains out of their ears. The girls happily accepted the transformation. They laughed when they lost their brains, as long as the act resembled kissing the side of their face repeatedly.

Soon, the trio sat in the shade of the back patio.

"I'm going to have to carry you two to the bathtub." Matthew said as he looked at the girls' dirt covered feet.

"One more game?" Beth cried.

Matthew shook his head as Liz opened the sliding door behind him.

"Time for din–" He started asking before seeing Liz held out his phone.

"It's J. He's called twice already," she said.

"One more game ladies, then I'll call you in," Matthew said as the girls cheered and ran off into the yard. Lyn stomped in a shallow puddle, a former mud pie bakery where the girls had the hose pouring into a newly dug hole. He pulled the phone to his ear as he rolled his eyes, seeing mud splash up on her orange dress.

"You can't cancel a good mud pie," Matthew said into the phone.

"What?" J responded.

"Nothing, just with the girls. What's up?"

"It's them." J said.

Matthew's eyes widened.

"And they've hit the US."

Chapter 2

Different Worlds

Matthew sat at his desk, his face staring at the screen in front of him as his finger hovered over the mouse. To anyone walking by his office, he appeared deep in thought on the latest project, a manufacturing plant planned for the Midwest. The mega-facility would bring manufacturing back to the states, along with thousands of jobs over the next five years. However, for all those jobs to come to fruition, the plant needed to hit production targets, targets that Matthew didn't agree with. The laptop's fan kicked into overdrive as the machine churned through another ten-thousand simulations. He looked away from the countless data points and graphs.

He looked out through his office door, across the walkways and cubicle walls. His coworkers periodically popped up and down from their seats or walked by his open door. And when they did, he saw shadows around them.

The darkness clung to them. In some, the shadow was a wisp of black fog, still transparent enough to see through, but in others, the haze thickened to a weightless black form. The visions brought back the memory of the red-eyed demon that haunted Matthew. But as he watched his colleagues, none were as dark or cold as that monster. Still, he silently studied the black fog as a researcher might study the young cubs of a vicious predator. He hoped to discover a correlation between the shadow and what he thought about the person. But as he secretly observed his coworkers, he realized he knew far less about them than he thought. He saw only their work personality, yet the dark shadows appeared to reflect their spiritual life, or at least some version of it.

A reflection of the unseen. He thought to himself. *And no one is free of it.*

He pulled his Bible closer and felt the first touch of pain flash through his body, followed by a feeling of loving warmth. After the tidal waves from months prior and now seeing shadows nearly everywhere, he never let the Bible, and the hidden Ark within it, out of his sight. It was always in the room with him, preferably within reach.

"Welcome back from your extended leave," the HR person had said. His work suspension ended as the dust from the trial settled. Her ignorantly delightful voice told Matthew that either she was a great liar or she knew nothing about his absence.

Ever since he returned, he'd carried his Bible with him like a notebook. A few people noticed, mainly those who'd witnessed him dive under his desk before his suspension as he hid from an imaginary black tidal wave. But having been back for months, his colleagues were used to him carrying it by now.

Occasionally, Matthew's eyes darted to the Bible on the side of his desk like a person staring at their phone, waiting for an important call. He always ensured the book stayed close by.

"Hey, champ!" Jaden popped out from the hallway into Matthew's doorway.

"Oh..." Matthew said, startled. "Hey." In his surprise, he'd grabbed the Bible and held it to his chest. Now, he slowly put the book down.

"You okay?" Jaden said as he stepped into the office. His hair was slicked back and his impeccably white button-up shirt-sleeves were rolled up past his elbows.

"Yeah... Yeah, I'm good."

Jaden looked at him curiously, but dismissed Matthew's jumpiness and took a seat.

"I can feel the brain power in this room." Jaden put his hands around his head and motioned like his head was growing. "How's our five billion? You hit six yet?"

"No." Matthew said, trying to ignore the shadow hovering around Jaden. "Four and a half is pushing it, and don't repeat that number. I'm going to say three-eight is tops in our next update." Matthew said.

"Three point eight? Are you kidding me? We'll get laughed out of the room. What happened to FOUR-eight?" Jaden replied.

"We never said four-eight. That was the OEM's claim for max output. We've talked about this, Jaden."

"Well, I'm responsible for this contract, and if the client thinks five is possible, then you make five possible." Jaden stood up, his hands out wide. "You said you'd design a new layout to get five."

"I said that I'd try, but did you tell them that their constraints on labor and floor plan are their limiting factors?"

As Jaden questioned the updates, Matthew's mind shot back to comments spoken to him in private before the project kicked off. Trusted colleagues who'd told him to be careful working with Jaden. The project manager recently turned account rep had a reputation for over-promising to bring in bigger clients. He was eager to please, that was obvious. One of Matthew's closer colleagues bluntly said, "He's a brown-noser that will sell you out." The words rang in Matthew's head as Jaden talked. The rumors swirling around Jaden's character were the reason

Matthew took the work on himself, instead of delegating it to a team member.

"What are you going to do about this?" Jaden acted like this was the first conversation regarding the risk of promising five billion. Matthew could remember at least three others.

Matthew shook his head. He wished he didn't see more of the black haze hovering in his office. It was like a scent coming off Jaden.

"The likelihood of hitting five with this design is under five percent." Matthew said, looking down from Jaden and at his Bible.

"That's great!" Jaden called out, sitting back down.

"No, it's not, because once we apply the proper safety factors and maintenance programs, that drops to under three percent. It's impossible to run over designed capacity all day, every day."

"Not impossible..." Jaden raised his eyebrows. "Three percent possible."

"That's not how manufacturing works," Matthew said. "Throughput is only as fast as its slowest part. We can't change that."

"But they came to us to make it work. You have an entire team to figure this out."

"Yeah, and they're working on their own projects. We all have our work and deadlines."

"This is our biggest contract!" Jaden leaned forward. Matthew should have expected Jaden to play his trump card: he held the largest individual contract in the company's history.

"But it's far from our only source of revenue." Matthew replied, thankful he knew enough of the company's finances to refute Jaden. He leaned in, mirroring Jaden's aggressive posture.

Jaden shook his head, standing up and backing away as Matthew matched his posture. The salesman eyed Matthew, and without another word, he left the room. The hazy shadow followed behind him.

Matthew got up and closed the door. Ignoring his growing distrust of Jaden, he told himself he'd do all he could to improve the simulations.

Back at his desk, the most recent simulation blinked a new result, but the same old findings. He typed out a few lines of code and pivoted his data back into a bell curve. He dragged it up to his right monitor and stared at it, hoping for an insight. But the visualization wasn't changing from the countless other times he'd checked it. Taking a deep breath, he rubbed his eyes and whispered, "Lord, help me."

A moment later, an email notification popped up on the bottom right of his screen. The flashing box was normal. He usually ignored it, but his boss's name was under a subject line that caught his eye.

Subject: FW: Not Sure.

Opening it, he skimmed down to see only one line from his boss: *"What's this about?"*

Scrolling down the thread, Matthew saw it was from Jaden to Matthew's boss, written mere minutes after Jaden had left his office.

The last sentence stunned Matthew.

"This is the highest grossing project in our history, but how can we put the customer first when he looks at his Bible more than his work?"

Chapter 3

Intrusion

The next morning, Matthew closed his Bible and walked from his usual spot in the front room, near the windows overlooking the front yard, to the family room at the back of the house. He flicked off the light as he picked up the television remote and sat on the couch.

Porchop, his fluffy gray Chartreux, followed close behind. The cat effortlessly leapt onto the couch and rested next to Matthew.

He sat in the darkness, with the automatic, amber-colored nightlight from the hallway the only light in the room. He looked at the blank TV, not sure if he wanted to see more news coverage of the church attack. In the past day and a half, the story of over one hundred people dead had exploded across the news. Every station repeated the same grisly details of how attendees of the suburban New York church went into Wednesday night service but never left. News anchors couldn't describe the unknown poison in their HVAC system, but from the bodies of those found, it was a painful way to die. One anchor described the boils covering the victims so graphically that his co-anchor shook on screen as if her skin crawled.

Matthew turned his head to Porkchop. The cat cuddled up next to his leg near the Bible on his lap. He wondered if the cat could feel the same sensation Matthew felt when he touched the Bible and the piece of the Ark of the Covenant hidden within its binding.

Either way, you'll be lying here all day. A small piece of him envied the quiet, napping life of the house cat.

He set down the remote without turning on the TV. The thought of attacks on churches ripped at his heart. He'd rather imagine his girls playing in the backyard than turn on the news and face the carnage.

Porkchop rolled over, still pressed against his leg, exposing his fluffy belly as he stretched. He sprawled out like a toddler in his parents' bed unaware of putting a knee into their backs, but loving every minute of being in their bed. Matthew gave a scratch to the cat's chin and Porkchop gave a soft purr of acceptance.

As Matthew petted the cat, he felt the Bible on his lap. He carried a small notebook with it and as he shifted his weight on the couch, the book slid off.

He read the cover: *Joshua 1:9 "Have I not commanded you? Be strong and courageous. Do not be afraid; do not be discouraged, for the Lord your God will be with you wherever you go."*

The words *strong and courageous* stood out to Matthew. He read them over and over. The font of those famous words was three times the size of the rest of the verse in the artistic design of the cover.

The six by four inch faux-leather notebook was J's idea. His friend encouraged him to add the SOAP method of Bible study to his morning routine.

"The SOAP method is easy, and great for getting into the Word," J had said. "S is for the scripture, whatever individual verse that stands out to you. O is an observation within that scripture. What did you notice? A is for how you could apply the verse or observation to your life. And finally, P is for a prayer on the day's reading. Write it out, read it as a prayer, and then keep on praying!"

He smiled, thinking of how passionately his friend spoke of the spiritual growth he went through years ago after implementing the SOAP method.

There was only one problem with Matthew's version of SOAP. After enjoying it a handful of times, he'd stopped doing it. He carried the notebook but hadn't made a new entry, let alone opened it, in weeks. Until today.

With the lifeless TV in front of him and the purring cat at his side, he flipped through past entries, taken from readings in the Book of Isaiah and other books of prophets. The horrific attack on the New York church took on new light as Matthew skimmed his notes on Babylon attacking Israel.

Is our country following Israel's footsteps into exile?

Matthew sat in silence for a moment, thinking of the Book of Isaiah, and then of his grandfather, Isaiah. He remembered his grandfather winking at him and then flashing a quick half-smile.

Matthew flipped back a few pages in his notebook and read over a verse he had recorded weeks prior. *Psalm 91:5-7: "You will not fear the terror of night, nor the arrow that flies by day, nor the pestilence that stalks in the darkness, nor the plague that destroys at midday. A thousand may fall at your side, ten thousand at your right hand, but it will not come near you."*

He observed how these words could apply to his own life, how he could find comfort in them during the unsettling times that surrounded him. He couldn't help but feel a sense of fear and uncertainty about the future, but the words of the Psalmist reminded him he could trust in God's protection. However, a seed of doubt crept into his mind. The terror *had* come near him. It put him in the hospital with only an unexplainable light saving him from the sea of darkness and the red-eyed demon. And the terrors weren't just close to him. The result of the trial wrecked his family's church, the church his grandfather and father devoted their lives to building and used in serving others.

His mind raced, but soon he set the notebook aside and rested his hands on his Bible. The power of the Ark helped calm the thoughts that ripped at his peace.

After a series of deep, calm breaths and asking God to clear his mind, he prayed for the families affected by the recent church attack. He continued his prayer, asking God to protect his family, for guidance in his difficult work situations, and for the Holy Spirit in his own spiritual growth. As Matthew prayed, a sense of peace washed over him.

He opened his eyes and saw Porkchop, still at his side, now lazily cleaning his paw, and the television in front of him. The black screen patiently waiting, yet eagerly calling for Matthew to bring it to life.

Matthew smiled at Porkchop, giving him another scratch, and then he turned on the TV.

Immediately, a burst of sound rang through the house. He quickly turned the volume down as the noise cut through the quiet house in the pre-dawn hours.

On the screen, the latest update on the church attack came to life. He watched as the reporter described the ongoing investigation and the growing fear among the community. Matthew couldn't help but feel a sense of sadness and anger.

Evil, he thought to himself. *Evil is out there, and it's moving, whether I like it or not.*

As the news continued to quietly play, Matthew opened his Bible again and flipped through the pages. He landed on the book of James and started reading. The words on the page spoke to him, reminding him of the importance of faith and works. He knew he needed to do more than just pray for those affected by the attack. He felt the Bible calling him to act.

With a newfound resolve, Matthew closed his Bible and took a deep breath.

He raised up from the couch, but a flicker of light caught his attention. The nightlight from the hallway up the stairs went off, then on, casting eerie shadows across the room as if a shape passed by it. Matthew's heart rate quickened as he listened for any unusual sounds, the footsteps of his daughters or wife, but nothing came. He couldn't shake the feeling that he wasn't the only one awake in the house.

Goosebumps rose on his arms as the temperature dropped. The once warm and cozy couch in the comfortable living room now felt like an icebox.

He shot a glance at Porkchop. The feline was on its feet, back arching, and hairs on end.

Matthew slowly stood, his heart pounding in his chest. Tiptoeing up the stairs, his eyes scanning the darkness for any signs

of movement. At the top of the stairs, he saw it. A shadowy figure standing at the end of the hallway, just outside his bedroom
door.

"Hey!" Matthew whispered, trying to keep his voice steady yet
low enough to not wake the girls.

The figure didn't verbally respond. The dark shadow stepped
forward, coming into the light of the amber nightlight.

Matthew gasped as he saw the two red eyes in the shadowy
haze.

It held his gaze and a shiver shot up Matthew's spine. The
demon watched him, then looked towards his room and then to
the girls' doors before turning back to him. It eyed him as a hawk
looks down on a mouse. A moment later, the haze dissolved.

Matthew stood alone in the dark hallway, his chest heaving as
he caught his breath. A soft amber glow illuminating one half
of his body. His other side, dark.

Chapter 4

Haunting

Matthew, Liz, and the girls arrived at his parents' house a couple of hours before lunch. Matthew rubbed his eyes, feeling like he'd been awake a full day already.

His mother, Mary, was standing in the front room, watching the news. She clicked off the screen as the girls burst through the door and hugged their grandmother. As she held them, she shot a watery-eyed glance at Matthew and Liz.

"Your grandpa is out back, girls. I wonder which of you can grab that big man and hold on to his leg the longest?" she said.

The girls cried out in enjoyment as they ran towards the back door.

"I'll go with them. Hey, Mom." Liz said, giving Mary a quick hug before following the girls.

As the girls left the room, Mary wiped her eyes and motioned to the TV. "I can't believe it. So senseless."

"They see it as their purpose." Matthew shook his head. "But yeah... It's bad, even for them."

"And at a church service!" A look of disgust washed across her face. "All those people, all those families..." She picked up a cup of tea and a tissue, then walked to the kitchen. Matthew followed.

He walked to the edge of where the kitchen turned into the back living room and looked out the windows to the backyard. Zech was playfully pretending to walk as Liz and Beth each clung to one of his legs. Matthew smiled as his dad went to the ground and began tickling the girls. They ran away screaming, but looked back, beckoning their grandfather to give chase.

"Mom." Matthew spoke back toward the kitchen.

"Yes."

Matthew turned but jumped back in surprise.

A black, shadowy figure stood in between him and his mother. It watched him, then turned to his mother, then looked back to Matthew. The red eyes seemed to penetrate his soul as his body went cold.

"Matthew? What's up?" Mary said.

Matthew blinked, and the evil figure was gone. He now looked at his mother. She paused, watching him, as she held a chunk of ribs in between a slow cooker and a cookie sheet already half-filled with more ribs.

Matthew stood in silence, shocked by the instantaneous appearance, and then the vanishing of the ghastly figure.

His mother eyed him curiously as she finished the transition from slow cooker to cookie sheet. She put the cookie sheet into the oven and grabbed the towel, cleaning up around the slow cooker.

"Hey, I'm excited about the women's conference next month. Did J tell you that Ashley is joining?"

Matthew nodded, slowly gathering his thoughts again. "Yeah..." he said. "Liz is thinking of bringing the girls now since you, Millie, her, and Ashley are going."

"Yes. The hotel has a lazy river! Perfect! Millie and I will float with them for hours."

"I thought you were supposed to be going for the speakers and all the breakout sessions?" Matthew asked.

"Oh, we'll still attend a fair amount, but I'm not missing a girls' vacation with my granddaughters." Mary smirked as she walked past Matthew towards the back door.

A knock came from the front door.

"You mind getting that?" Mary asked as she went into the backyard. "I have some girls to play with."

Matthew nodded. Before he turned, he saw his father plop down in a lawn chair, exaggerating exhaustion toward the young girls.

Matthew walked to the front door, but the person at the door slowly opened it before he got there. He paused, wearily, as his mind ran through scenarios of the red-eyed demon or New Christians sneaking into the house.

J stuck his head through the threshold.

"Hey!" J said, stepping through the door. His open arms held a small box.

"Hey," Matthew replied.

"Your dad said to come over for lunch. And I needed to drop this off."

"What's that?" Matthew asked.

"A new microphone. Your dad refuses to get a new computer even though his PC is older than us. But we're making it work, mainly off my computer."

Matthew and J walked through the house and towards Zech's office.

The updated room looked more like a command center than the office of a humble North Florida pastor.

"Wow," Matthew said as he walked in.

"Yeah. This is now the most high-tech real estate in our online-only church," J said.

Since losing the court case, Zech and J led a transformation of the church. The damages owed to the plaintiffs effectively bankrupted their church and parent organization. The ruling meant foreclosure on their magnificent church building and losing nearly three-fourths of their congregation. Furthermore, Zech laid off the small, yet mighty church staff, unable to make payroll. Regardless, Zech kept on preaching, much of the staff still volunteered, and the congregation who remained were engaged more than ever.

With help from tech savvy church members, the Light's church had quickly pivoted to online only. For a couple of months, they used a free version of a popular meeting software. After the free version's time limit cut off Zech's first online-only sermon, he shortened his sermons to be clearer and more concise. He and J made a game of trying to end their first few online sermons as close as possible, but not *over* the limit. Matthew once heard Zech and J laughing about their *Price is Right* time limit - who could get as close as possible without going over.

However, the free version of the software also had an attendee limit.

That's where the women leaders of the church came in.

Eight weeks of online sermons with a consistent number of viewers quickly changed when Mary, Liz, and Millie began posting the meeting link to their social media accounts. The online waiting room exploded, quickly filling up the two-hundred-and-fifty-person limit to the free version. The limit prompted dozens of direct messages to the three women from their online friends who could not join.

With a nudge from Mary, Zech paid for the unlimited corporate version the next day and soon saw double digit growth in each of the following weeks.

"God was finally using social media for good!" Zech mused as he thanked the new viewers each week.

Through figuring out the technology, Zech's office underwent a technology makeover. The corner room in their house went from an ancient desktop tower computer and basic monitor into a beautiful wooden desk with a high-powered laptop. Previously unused space near the doorway now held two cameras on tripods. A wall with artwork and family pictures transformed into three huge flat screen TVs. The family pictures now shifted above, in between, and below. The room recorded and streamed all their messages and provided a conference room. Matthew thought the once-simple room now resembled the Bat Cave more than a preacher's office, but he loved it.

"Afternoon, J," Zech said, walking into his office. "You got another new do-hickey?"

"The new microphone do-hickey? Yes, Pastor." J laughed.

"How you like the new setup?" Zech turned to Matthew.

"Love it. I mean, each week the stream looked a little better, but I didn't know all you two have done behind the scenes," Matthew said.

"Not just us two. Even without a church building, donations and volunteers are the lifeblood of our congregation," Zech said.

"Amen," J echoed.

"And tomorrow we finally get both cameras working. Get ready to see different angles!" Zech said as J pumped his fist.

"What?" Matthew laughed.

"Nothing. Just something we've been trying to get right for weeks. We're going to look like news anchors." J said as he set the microphone down on the desk and gave Zech a high-five. Matthew shook his head as a smile broke on his face at his dad's and friend's enjoyment.

"Okay, enough tech. The ribs are done! Let's eat," Zech said.

For the rest of the afternoon, they ate, played games, and enjoyed the time together. They even got to see Matthew's oldest brother, Luke. The simple video call on Mary's cell phone gave Zech and J the opportunity to transfer the small screen to the giant flat screens in Zech's office.

Matthew heard his sister-in-law, Helen, laughing as Mary brought in Beth and Lyn. The girls strutted in front of the cameras for their aunt like they were in a fashion show. Soon the girls' older cousins, Nina and Xavier, had their dad's phone on the other side.

Matthew tried getting a word in but couldn't compete with four kids excitedly talking together.

The sun drifted lower in the sky and Matthew thought about how his day turned around. Not long after waking, he was staring at a demon, but now, hours later, he was laughing with loved ones and waving to family members hundreds of miles away. He thanked the Lord for all he had in his life.

"I'll catch you guys later." J patted Matthew on the back and nodded to Zech before walking out. Matthew heard him saying goodbye to the girls on his way out. The kids' video call was finally ending as he overheard his niece say her dad's battery was dying on the other end.

With J leaving, Zech and Matthew stood together. Matthew finally pulled his father aside.

"Hey Dad," Matthew said, "can I talk to you?"

"What's up?" Zech said, turning to Matthew.

Matthew thought for a moment as his dad eyed him casually.

"There's something..." Matthew paused, and Zech's casual expression shifted into concern. "There's something I need to tell you."

"Go ahead." Zech patted Matthew's shoulder and took a seat on a nearby couch.

"You know how months back, during the trial, when I was... seeing things." Matthew said, as he followed Zech to the couch.

"Yes."

Matthew looked out the back door, a sliding glass door that overlooked his parents' backyard. The view was mostly dark, with a faint hint of the sunset still clinging to the expanding darkness.

"I still see them."

"The shadows?" Zech asked.

Matthew nodded as he continued to look across the darkening backyard. He closed his eyes as he spoke. "It's not always the same one from the courthouse and hospital. These are different, but somehow still... Still *evil*. I see them everywhere. At work, the store, down the street. They latch on to people, follow them like they have hooks in them."

Zech blinked, taking it in.

Matthew opened his eyes. He looked out, trying to see the last rays of sunset light, but they were gone. The entire doorway was a deep, unsettling black.

"When's the last time you saw one?" Zech asked.

"The drive over." Matthew said, paying less attention to his father as he watched the darkness. There was something unnatural about the night sky. His mind shot back to the tidal wave that attacked him in the same backyard he looked at now. That wave came like a raging storm cloud, but the darkness outside was more like a void.

Matthew shook his head, looking away from the dark outside and back at his father. "Wherever people are, sure enough, there's one of those horrible clouds."

"Give me an example." Zech inquired, leaning in. Matthew looked back toward the glass door and the empty darkness outside. Something about it held his attention.

"The exit ramp... That busy intersection as you get off the interstate on the way here. It had dozens..." Matthew lost his train of thought. He stood up, walking towards the glass door. Looking at an angle, from side to side, out the door, he tried to see lights from the neighborhood. He couldn't see any. No back porch lights from neighboring houses. No streetlamps illuminating strips between houses. Everywhere, black.

"Son?" Zech said, standing up and moving to Matthew's side.

Matthew stood inches from the glass door and investigated the darkness. He felt the temperature drop.

Zech looked out the back door with him.

"Pretty sunset." Zech said, as he followed Matthew's eyes. "I'm glad it's back, especially after all the recent storms."

Matthew couldn't see the brilliant pinks and oranges painted across the horizon. Instead, the haunting red eyes of a demon took shape in the darkness that filled his view. The same demon from earlier that morning, from the tidal wave, and courthouse months before. The memory of dropping lifeless in the courthouse hall flashed before his eyes. He remembered the limbs reaching out in pain from the sea of darkness. If it wasn't for the brilliant flashes of light, and Liz's prayer, he never would have woken up in that hospital bed. The darkness would have pulled him into the enraged, pain-filled sea of darkness.

The eyes floated mere inches outside the door. They mirrored back his stare, and an outline of a body formed. It reflected his every move, mirroring him yet taunting him at the same time—Peter Pan's shadow but mischievousness replaced with malice.

"You said it wasn't *always* the same one from the courthouse. Have you seen that one?" Zech asked. The two men stood shoulder to shoulder, but their views of the setting sun were drastically different.

"It was in my house this morning, right outside our bedrooms." Matthew said as he turned to his father. His father's face tightened, and they locked eyes. "And right now, it's on the other side of this door."

Chapter 5

From Desire to Destruction

The next morning, Matthew set up the girls with the Kids' Church recording in their playroom while Liz poured the coffee. After confirming the girls had their snacks and water bottles, Matthew joined Liz on the couch. She moved a small table in front of them and opened their laptop for streaming Sunday church. Moments later, Zech came on screen and welcomed all the virtual attenders.

The church lost everything in the legal battle with Nancy Pawly. She ruthlessly went after the church, representing the families of those lost during Isaiah's actions. She framed Isaiah, the Light family patriarch, as a murderous zealot who killed a dozen men because of distorted religious beliefs. The four men whom he had saved—Matthew, J, Zech, and Paul—along with anyone acquainted with Isaiah, were aware that Isaiah had taken those lives to protect his loved ones from a gruesome fate orchestrated by Terrence and his followers.

Despite Isaiah's noble intentions, his actions killed twelve men to save four. The math didn't add up. As a result of the devastating vehicular carnage and Nancy's exceptional legal skills, an eight-figure ruling was issued, resulting in the complete dissolution of the Light's North Florida church and most of their international parent organization, Lost and Found Ministries.

All Isaiah built, all those churches with their pastors, staff, and followers, now without a home.

The sale of their land and church building to a private retail developer paid most of the debt. Zech said their property appreciated substantially in the past twenty years, and they received fair value for the high-tech audiovisual equipment. The building now sat abandoned, mostly cleared out, as it awaited a future date with the wrecking ball.

The legal fallout also put a stop to funding local charities and missionaries around the world, including Matthew's brother, Mark, in Eastern Europe. Thankfully, Mark managed the savings from his finance days well and could still support his family.

Matthew blew off the steam from his coffee as he sat next to Liz. He watched his father give a welcome address and a few announcements on local Bible studies and group meetups.

Overall, the announcements were minimal, given no church building or staff.

Zech then introduced today's worship, a recording from one of the few Lost and Found Ministry churches that survived the ordeal.

As the video began, Matthew felt good sitting next to his wife. A moment worshipping next to her without the girls immediately on his mind was the peaceful situation he felt he needed.

Even if it was through a monitor and a far cry from being in person.

Before learning the family secret to protect the Ark of the Covenant, he would have liked a virtual-only service. Frequently, he'd tried to convince Liz they should avoid the drive and simply watch from home, but now he missed being in person.

Worship ended, and Zech came back on the screen.

"If I can get this to..." he fumbled with the controls, his eyes darting away from the camera and around his own screen. "Here we go." He looked back into the camera. "For today's message, my favorite pastor and speaker, outside of myself, of course," flashing a sly smile as he continued, "has a new way of looking at the fall before Babylonian captivity. Remember, last week we discussed Josiah. He was one of the few 'good' kings and he reformed much of the detestable activity, but the books of Chronicles and Kings mention how Israel had already turned too far from God, and that *His* wrath was coming. Here is our own Pastor Jeremiah."

Zech clicked a few buttons and J soon came on the screen. He sat at the same desk as Zech, with the camera at a slightly different angle. Matthew smiled, thinking anyone on the tech team must have cringed, but how happy Zech and J were for their own do-it-yourself recordings.

Matthew sipped his coffee and put his arm around Liz as they settled in to hear this week's message.

J welcomed all the virtual guests and encouraged those on social media to share the link. He spoke about how each share that popped up in a friend's feed helps to spread the word by leveraging today's technology.

Then he dove into his message.

"God uses those at their lowest points, people beaten down by the world or other circumstances that do not know what to do next. Often in the Bible, God comes to someone's benefit at a time of weakness. It may be a time of self-doubt or lack of faith. A classical example is Moses. When we think of Moses, many of us visualize Charlton Heston defiantly telling Pharaoh to let his people go and then leading the people out of Egypt. I can see the glorious scene of Heston raising his staff and God parting the Red Sea. But remember the Bible version, the real version, not Hollywood's. We jump from baby Moses in a reed basket to Moses murdering an Egyptian. Then he gets called out by a fellow Israelite and runs away to the wilderness for forty years. And this wasn't the forty years wandering the wilderness *after* leaving Egypt, this was forty years *before* being called. Not one but *two* different stints, each forty years of Moses's life, bookend the great exodus of Egypt.

"The first forty years, he's a shepherd out tending the flock, when God comes as the burning bush. Moses begs him to send someone else, he legit begs. He says he is not the man for the job because he's not a speaker. God is ready for Moses's response and suggests Aaron, Moses' brother. Moses drags his feet a bit more, but eventually the two go to Pharaoh and kick off the Exodus.

"Now here's an extreme way of looking at it. God called a murderer. Moses committed murder, then he went on the run in the desert for forty years. God called this man to come back to his people and lead them to freedom. I have a strong feeling that, while in the wilderness, Moses did not know what he wanted in life. He was fine being a shepherd. That is *until God* gave him a new desire."

J paused a moment and then looked down, shuffling his papers, as he smoothly continued his message.

"Gideon, another example, a timid man in the time of judges. When God calls him, he is so unsure that he asks for God to

prove multiple times that it's really God! First, an angel joins
Gideon under a tree, which is crazy enough, and also very reminiscent of the men who traveled to Abraham, but when Gideon
asks for a sign, the angel puts out his staff and cooks a meal with
it." J held out his hands and exaggerated a look of amazement.

As J's message flowed, Matthew once again missed being in
person. He knew J's impression with his facial expressions and
arm movements would have drawn laughter.

"I imagine that in God's eyes, Gideon, like so many of us that
are astounded by his glorious actions, must have looked like a
baby ecstatic over a game like peek-a-boo. 'Hey, where'd you go?
There you are! Amazing! How'd you do that? But wait, can you
do it—you can! No way!'" J laughed at his own impression of a
baby. "But once God shows Gideon the miracle, Gideon jumps
to action and begins taking down the poles of false idols. God
gave him a purpose, and Gideon responded." J looked into the
camera and let out a breath. "But if you know this story, you
know that's not the end of Gideon's doubt. Removing some
poles, that's one thing, but taking on the enemy army?"

J switched his voice into a timid impersonation of Gideon,
"Uh, hey God... Uh, I'm not sure about this, but if you can make
dew come down on this sweater, and *only* this sweater, nothing
else? Oh, you can... Well, how about now you make dew come
down on everything *but* this sweater? Oh, you can do that too...

"Soon, Gideon is obeying God by sending thousands of soldiers home. He's willfully reducing his army *through faith*, before the big fight. And then once God tells him to reduce his army, God tells him not to fight with modern weapons of the day, but with jars, torches, trumpets, and screams. But Gideon has a purpose. He has a desire to see his purpose fulfilled."

J turned at his desk and looked at another camera. As he turned, he popped a broad smile, mimicking a television anchor starting a new report. Matthew laughed and Liz looked at him, confused.

"They've been planning a cut like that for weeks." Matthew laughed. "You should have seen them yesterday. They were almost giddy about it."

"I heard when they told your mom. They were giddy." Liz laughed.

J continued. "God uses us at our weakest. Think about it," he paused. "How has God used you at low points?" He gave another brief pause. "Our weakest... It's funny when we think of stories. The hero's weakest moment is usually a launching point. The hero can't see it at the moment, but the audience does. Think back to times in your past." He paused a moment, giving the audience time to think. "It's like you were on a trampoline, at the bottom of the jump. You're primed, legs bent, muscles ready. And the surrounding environment was there to help you. The springs of the trampoline extended, ready to recoil and unleash their potential energy to shoot you up. Your legs shoot out as the trampoline recoils, and *whoa*." J threw his hands up as he looked high above the camera. "You're flying."

J pivoted back to the first camera. "Anyone thinking about our church's situation right now? We're all watching from a computer somewhere, *not* in person! We are at a low point regarding community. No conversations in the rotunda, no bumping into a friend as you wait for a cup of coffee. Our youth group still meets weekly, but it's at a quarter of prior attendance. The 'Ladies with Hats and a Bible' group are a fraction of what they once were. We are losing our community; like Moses, we killed, right or wrong, and now we're wandering in the desert!"

J rubbed his hands across his face, tightly closing his eyes, before looking back at the camera.

"If I'm being honest, this stinks. I was gone for a while before this happened, and I feel like it has been so long since I've shaken some of your hands. It's been so long since I've heard about your kids' ballgame or what school so and so decided on. But think of Moses in his *first* wilderness and think of Gideon *before* God calls. What do they want? What is their desire?" He eyed the camera with a solemn expression. "What is ours?" He paused a moment, just like he would have if he were in person. "Do we even know?"

"The Bible isn't totally clear, but I feel confident that before God came into the picture, Moses and Gideon had no idea! Moses was on the run; he was reacting. He wanted to stay safe, to not get stoned for murder. Meanwhile, I think there's enough with Gideon to infer he simply wanted to keep his head down. Both men are in short-term, survival-based mode." He paused as the camera went back to the first point of view. He leaned in with emphasis. "They had no long-term desire because they feared destruction. They feared the enemy."

Matthew no longer noticed the camera angles as the message pulled him in.

J continued. "It hadn't dawned on me until recently rereading Exodus and Judges, but now I can't miss it. *If* we're in the short-term, *if* we stay in the flesh, and *if* we don't have God, just like Moses and Gideon, then we *should* be afraid. They had things to fear that they avoided until God showed up."

Should I be afraid? Matthew thought as he leaned in towards the computer screen.

"You okay, hun?" Liz asked.

"Yeah," he said reflexively.

But he thought, *I am afraid.*

"Want more coffee?" He grabbed Liz's cup and headed to the kitchen. He stood at the pot, thinking about J's comment: *we should be afraid.*

His mind raced as he examined his own situation.

If I told you, he thought to himself, *that a demon is going to haunt you, that it will knock you unconscious and try to pull you into a sea of darkness and despair, that a brilliant light from your dreams would appear, and the Ark hidden in your Bible was the only way to stay safe, what would you do, Matthew?*

Matthew topped off his and Liz's coffee, warming each cup up, as he thought about his answer. He looked out from the kitchen, peeking at his girls. Kids' church was over, and Beth switched on Veggie Tales. He nodded in delight that she obeyed their rule of only watching Veggie Tales after Kids' Church. The two young ladies each sang along to the catchy theme song. Matthew hummed the tune as he returned to the couch and Liz. It lifted his mood as he continued to ask himself the same question, but as soon as he sat, the fear came charging back to his mind.

What would I do? I'd hang on to the piece of the Ark as tightly as I could, and I'd pray.

He glanced at the end table near the couch, where his Bible sat, housing the glowing piece of the Ark.

Liz smiled as he gave her the refilled cup and then pressed play.

"If we're thinking short term, we should be afraid," J continued. "Because as Christians, we know the enemy doesn't want us to win! Thankfully, God has our back, and as His people, we have His blessing. But that doesn't mean we won't experience pain. No, not by a longshot. If we were in person right now, I'm sure we would see dozens, if not hundreds, of hands go up from those who went through horrible experiences before and after being saved. Remember, in the Book of Job, when speaking to God, Satan mentions that surely God has put a 'hedge of protection' around Job. Let's dive into that concept of a 'hedge of protection.' Back to the time of Job, stone walls and wood were expensive, but you could protect your flock with a hedge of thorn bushes. These sharp and dense bushes discouraged wild predators, such as wolves and bears, while keeping in the sheep and goats. Thorn bushes were a great natural protection.

"It's interesting the word choice in Job. For example, Satan, who the Bible mentions as what type of predator? A lion. And not just any lion, but a lion seeking to devour. In his conversation with God, he references hedges of protection that God puts around Job. The very thing meant to keep lions out!"

J paused as he shuffled his papers, turning to the next portion of his sermon.

"The Book of Job is a great parallel to this message–Job was successful by all measures of the day, but God *allowed* Satan to test him. And maybe *ravage* is a better term than test. It's hard for us to imagine what Job went through. Just utter destruction in all areas of his life."

J paused, waving his hand across the desk like he was wiping it clean. Shaking his head, he took a sip of water.

"But in the end, Job got through the destruction of Satan by looking to God for deliverance. He kept his deep faith. Job had an eye on the long-term. He weathered the horrible storm because he knew his desire to be with God in heaven. You can withstand years of pain when compared to eternity. It ain't easy, but it *is* possible."

J took a deep breath and turned to the other camera.

"As a church community, we're going through destruction right now. It feels as if God lifted His hedge of protection and the enemies are coming in. Like mosquitoes, our enemies swarm around us.

"A question I want to leave you with is this: If Job hadn't had such strong faith, would God have let Satan go after him?"

J looked into the camera.

"What will our church become on the other side of this destruction? Well... What do we desire? What do we want? Is it a lovely building? Is it a Sunday School playground for the kids?"

He took a deep breath and stared into the camera again.

"Let me ask it this way: What did Satan want in the Book of Job? To *break* Job. To break him so severely that Job renounced God.

"Well, what is the enemy trying to do to us? Break us.

And to do that, what is he trying to stop us from? From gathering! Think about it, when we want to stay home from a church gathering, you never find excuses to go?" J looked into the camera and raised his eyebrows. "No! We find excuses to *not* go. Most folks stay home at the slightest hint of an excuse. The enemy doesn't stand in our way when we're staying away from the body of Christ. He doesn't object when we decide to stay quiet in our chairs instead of raising our hands during worship. The enemy doesn't drop a sinking feeling in our stomach when we *avoid* speaking the truth in public. No! He drops that feeling there before we speak. The enemy puts resistance in our way.

"Think about this. I want you to go stand in front of a grocery store and tell all the folks that walk by you how much you love Jesus and how *He* is the way and the truth. That only through Him could their lives be saved." J paused.

"How'd that feel deep in your belly? You got scared just thinking of talking to folks in front of your store, didn't you? We get that same feeling when we think about praying for someone in public! We find a reason to *not* read the Bible, to *not* connect with another human, to *not* pray for them. Those sinking feelings are a sign of the enemy getting in our way! He's trying to stop us from spreading the kingdom, from making a close-knit community so he can isolate us and hit us like he did Job.

"There are many ways the enemy comes at us. He might stop us from using our God-given abilities–just think of how easy it is to procrastinate. Either way, it's something we must overcome, and to truly win, we need to know what we desire and be ready for the enemy to punch back. The enemy will fight us when we have our desire. But when he does, and we're following the Word, then we know we're on the right track. We still need to have the deep faith of Job, but we learned from the hint God left us in His book."

The screen faded out and soon came back with Zech. He went through the Sunday offering, giving specifics for how to give through their online platform. Matthew got up and took their empty coffee cups to the sink as Liz went to see the girls.

A moment later, a knock sounded at the door.

Chapter 6

The First Bowl

Terrence

Terrence stood on the tarmac, admiring the sunrise. His finely trimmed black beard matched his black slacks and sport coat that opened to a white dress shirt. He fastened the top button of the coat and looked just like countless traveling businessmen. But unlike most businessmen at an airport, Terrence was not waiting at the gate for a commercial flight. Standing on the vast expanse of concrete outside the small regional airfield, he patiently awaited his private flight while observing the last-minute preparations of his carefully selected team.

Years prior, the New Christians were cautious in their plans, calling off missions days and sometimes mere hours before starting. But now Terrence had Solomon's approval to make the call himself. He smiled as his team loaded their bags and supplies for their first official mission under Terrence's new leadership.

This mission had to be successful for the later pieces to all fall into place. Solomon made that abundantly clear through the weeks of Terrence being confined to a chair and isolated in darkness, reminiscent of how he had left J. However, unlike Pastor Jeremiah, Terrence did not experience liberation through a supernatural light.

"Nobody just disappears!" Solomon screamed into Terrence's face. "I approved your father's plan in Paris to get more eyeballs on our work. I even approved of the coffee shop job. But two *dead* bodies and an American pastor brought into, and then lost, at a safe house?"

Terrence had stood silently in front of the leader of the New Christians and took his punishment.

"Dead bodies don't just walk away. Was that Jesus of Nazareth you brought us?" Solomon shoved a finger into Terrence's chest. "Huh? Did you bring us Christ, our savior?" Solomon slapped Terrence, "No," he said through clenched teeth, "you did *not*."

Solomon pulled down on his suit jacket, snapping it back into place as he hid his rage and straightened his posture. The international businessman who secretly ran the New Christians now spoke in a dignified tone, like he was addressing the floor of the United Nations.

"Forty days," he said as he looked down his nose, looming over Terrence. "You are valuable to the cause, but you must be punished."

Terrence remained silent as he nodded. Moments later, two of his fellow New Christians led him to the same chair that Terrence had strapped J to. They obtained fresh wraps since the previous ones became unusable when they melted off J, as if his skin had reached a temperature far exceeding that of the room. They fastened Terrence's arms and legs to the steel chair.

For forty days of darkness and isolation, Terrence thought about J and the Light family.

His first day out, he asked for a phone and retrieved his Bible. He turned to Revelation, and then he called Jeremiah Grey.

***

Months later, as Terrence regained his strength and mobility, he was back to planning missions. Solomon trusted Terrence, or at least enough to let him try again in Paris.

God won't let me fail, Terrence repeated to himself daily.

It was his destiny to carry out each of the seven missions. And once he did, the world would see what he saw. Observers would notice how far they had fallen into sin and darkness, and how much Biblical-correction they needed to be aware of.

The New Christians supplied him with top talent for the jobs, including former Israeli special forces and Saudi Arabian covert operations people. No longer would Terrence be picking the scraps of a team from local prisons. No longer would he be fighting for extra funds. Now he had everything he needed. Most of all, he had the authority to execute the mission on his terms.

With the team on the plane, Terrence did a quick mental inventory and walkthrough of the plan.

They were ready to make their mark on Paris. He was ready to make his mark on the world.

***

In Paris, there were numerous tattoo parlors, and the New Christians furnished Terrence with a compilation of the top seven highly frequented ones within the Boulevard Périphérique loop, which encircled the city's center.

"The mark of the beast," Terrence muttered to himself as they left the small plane in a private airfield outside of Paris. The temperature was above average for early fall as summer humidity filled the French air like a thick blanket. But the warm weather didn't bother him. In fact, it helped his plan, and in twenty-four hours, they would be long gone.

Terrence's team knew their orders, nodding to their boss before silently leaving the plane, confident in their mission without needing further instructions.

Less than an hour later, each member of the crew found their target. Casually walking into the side alleys or climbing the stairs for roof access, the New Christian terrorists located the bronze tube carrying a specific air conditioner's coolant. They punctured the tube. The hiss of escaping compressed coolant filled the air.

Just as casually, each soldier disguised as a civilian walked away.

Terrence received word from each contact. Seven tattoo parlors, spread across the heart of Paris, lost air conditioning on one of the hottest days of summer.

Chapter 7

Selena in France
Selena - Paris, France

Selena hung up the phone and wiped her forehead. Her broken French didn't help get the AC repair man to come any sooner.

It was two months since she arrived in France, after the pleading call from her mother wrenched her heart and caused her to uproot her life in America. But the call felt serendipitous. In the same week her mother called, her son's day care pulled her aside.

"Selena, I'm sorry. But he cannot come back." Mrs. Rachel, the head of the day care, told her.

"Where else are we going to go?" Selena said.

"Maybe hire a stay-at-home nanny. He might do better in a familiar area." Mrs. Rachel said. She was kind. However, the two-year-old classroom lead, a plump, short woman named Mrs. Devine, was not so kind. The first week, Mrs. Devine seemed like an angel. Her pale complexion and rosy cheeks giving a cherub-like image of a sweet woman. A week later, the ever-patient woman was giving Selena looks and asking uncomfortable questions.

The prying questions turned into an uproar when long-time families began leaving the day care. Combined with Lucian's biting and other outbursts, the sweet elderly woman went off like a struck match.

"That boy needs a father figure! He needs some discipline!" Mrs. Devine shouted from the classroom door as Selena picked up Lucian.

"That's enough, Sue-Ann." Mrs. Rachel said, turning to Mrs. Devine and trying to keep her voice low. Other parents moved in and out with their children. Selena wanted to run around the corner and knock Mrs. Devine's teeth out, but she could feel the other parents' eyes watching her, judging her.

If I catch that woman outside these walls... she thought to herself as Lucian stuffed his head into her shoulder. His biting problems hit epidemic levels, and now they were leaving their third day care in as many months.

"I can't afford a nanny." Selena whispered to Mrs. Rachel. "Is there anything else we can do?"

"I'm sorry, Selena. Try calling a local church, or the college. Young education majors are great babysitters."

"I need more than a babysitter. Please." She reached out and grabbed Mrs. Rachel's arm.

"I'm sorry, Selena," Mrs. Rachel said again as she tried to wiggle her arm away, but Selena squeezed it, as if letting her go was letting go her son's chance at a normal education.

"Selena, I'm sorry. You're... You're hurting me!" Mrs. Rachel forcefully ripped her arm away. After a disturbed glance to Selena, she turned, moving to engage with the other incoming and outgoing parents.

Selena closed her eyes and held Lucian in her arms.

"It'll be alright, baby," she said. As she opened her eyes, she saw Mrs. Devine glaring at her. Defiantly, she held the woman's gaze, trying not to wilt like a dehydrated flower. She would have held the stare longer, but Lucian started fidgeting. When he released a high-pitched cry, she broke off the stare and quickly turned to leave the building.

She once again felt every other parent's judging eyes locked on her.

She was used to the stares; most of the time, people stared at her bright blue tattoo. A dragon reaching up from under her shirt. Glares at the artwork she helped design didn't bother her. But she never got used to the same people's judging eyes when she was with Lucian. The stay-at-home moms with their luxury SUVs. Their children talking about their next Disney vacation or playing ball with their dad. All these parents who never worry about things like working two shifts to pay rent and childcare costs, constantly finding care for her son, and being a twenty-eight-year-old widow. They ignorantly stared, and Selena wanted to rip their eyes out so they'd never point their judging eyes at her, or anyone else, ever again.

She loaded Lucian in the car and they went across town to her lawyer's office.

***

"In your situation, I recommend the annuity." Her appointed lawyer, Clark Thomas, said.

Selena took offense to the 'your situation' comment but dismissed it as she tried to understand what was happening.

"Why?" Selena tried forming a question but didn't know what to ask.

"This is a large, lump sum settlement, and thankfully Lucian's father clearly named you as his beneficiary."

Despite her efforts to avoid acknowledging Lucian's father, Selena couldn't help but recall the numerous instances of mistreatment and turmoil that characterized their relationship over the course of five years. These included frequent late-night arguments, multiple breakups and reconciliations, and even periods of his incarceration.

She knew he cared for Lucian with his whole heart. In his last few months of life, Lucian's father was even attending religious meetings a few times a week.

"We're going to make a better life," he'd swear to her. "This is a fight I can win!"

When he didn't come home for days, she'd assume all the same lying and drinking led to another arrest. When the officers knocked on her door, she nearly threw Lucian's toy car at them. She was so angry Ignace was in trouble again, and these cops just kept locking him away.

But they had unexpected news. Her long-time on-again, off-again boyfriend and son's father, Ignace, was dead. One month after he swore they'd have a new life in Christ, she watched his casket go into the ground.

"We will set the annuity up in a trust, then you get a set amount every month sent to your checking account." Clark said.

"Wasn't the settlement over a million dollars? I need that money!"

Clark took a deep breath and leaned over his desk. Selena shook her head and looked away. Lucian squirmed in the chair, and she handed him her phone. The two-year-old knew exactly how to use it, pulling up a kids' game within seconds and pressing the flying objects on the small screen.

"This set-up protects you, Ms. Treble. A lump sum can be a lot to handle at once. But once it's gone, it's gone for good."

"You want to give me thousands when I'm owed millions?" Selena stared at the man, confused, as he watched her from across his giant wooden desk in his three-piece suit.

Just like all those parents... She thought. *No idea what it's like.*

"Ms. Treble, I'm going to level with you. I've been doing this a long time." Clark Thomas's mostly salt in his salt and pepper hair spoke to his years in the legal profession. "I didn't want your case."

Selena pulled back as Clark continued.

"When my partners took the distribution of this settlement, my heart sank. Sure, the money is great, but huge windfalls can sometimes bring more harm than help." He took a deep breath and sat up straight in his tall, black leather chair.

"How often do you think lottery winners go broke?" he asked.

Selena shrugged.

"Seventy percent of the time." He said with a solemn expression. "Seventy! And do you know what happens when people go broke after thinking they have the world?"

Selena shook her head.

"Most go right back to the low-income life they had before, usually with enormous debts or bankruptcy." Clark locked eyes with hers. She could see his eyes water. "And some of them commit suicide. My father won the lottery when I was fifteen. He killed himself the week before I graduated high school."

The sound of popping balloons rang out from her phone like gunshots in the otherwise silent room.

"I recommend this, not to be rude or assume your situation. Despite the media's attention of rare cases, many single mothers and their children cannot overcome the adversity. Do you have parents nearby? Family or close friends to lean on?"

"I don't need—" she started, but Clark cut her off.

"Well, as someone about to receive a multi-million-dollar legal settlement, in my opinion, someone you trust is exactly what you need. I also recommend you go get a financial advisor."

Selena remained silent.

"Take the annuity. Think of it as another job, except you don't have to go to work. Many people take the lump sum, buy a house and a new car. They pick up the tab for their friends, and they feel great helping family pay their bills, but your family doesn't always have your best interest in mind, or that of your child. And that's not even mentioning the drugs and alcohol that acts like a cancer in their lives. I recommend you keep working, but sure, dial it back. It'd be great to spend more time with your boy here, but don't *act* rich. Learn to budget this cash. Give, save, spend, and let it be a blessing, not a curse. Make a new start."

Selena reluctantly agreed to the annuity, and the same week the settlement money flowed into her account, her mother called, begging her to come help her in France.

She begged Selena to help her get sober.

With the new cash, Lucian's daycare problem, and a memory of overhearing patrons at the bar Selena worked at talking about the benefits of French-style parenting, she quit both her bartending jobs and moved to France.

***

"They said they're coming!" Selena called out across the parlor. "So shut up and quit hassling me. This isn't my job anyway," she said under her breath.

"Quand?" one of the other tattoo artists called out.

"I don't know when. They said they're coming," Selena called back, then stopped and spoke in French. "Je ne sais pas."

She wondered how many people would leave the parlor after feeling the thick blanket of humidity building in the shop. Outside felt like an oven, but with the moving air, it was better than inside the small shop. As she set up her station for the next client, she heard a knock on the door.

A tan-skinned man in coveralls and a neatly trimmed, thick black beard stood at the door. He smiled as she approached and held up a toolbox.

Selena thought of how familiar he looked.

Chapter 8

Pouring out the Bowl
Terrence - Paris, France

Terrence stood in the doorway, smiling and waving at the approaching woman.

"Je suis là pour le climatiseur," he said with his best French.

"The air conditioner?" The woman blurted out.

Terrence cocked his head. He spent hours practicing French with his father and other New Christians. Now this woman talked like she was straight out of New York.

"Oh, sorry, I mean, désolée. La air... Conditioner..." She struggled to find her phrase in French.

"Yes, I'm here to fix the air conditioner." Terrence said.

"Oh, thank God," she blurted out. "You'd think after a month it'd get easier."

"Eventually, it will. I promise," Terrence said with a convincing smile.

"You're American?" she asked. "I'm Selena." She extended her hand.

"Yes. Well, sort of. My parents were French immigrants, then American immigrants. I somehow found my way back here." Terrence lied, using his prearranged cover story and reaching out to shake her hand. "I'm Pierre. Can you show me where the unit is?"

"Pierre, you look awful familiar. Where abouts in the US?"

"Down south—" he paused. He could recite where his pretend parents lived in France but blanked on this simple question.

"Southern California. Moved back to Europe as soon as I could afford it." He lied, trying to pick a place as far away from where he'd grew up in North Florida as possible.

"Okay," Selena said without another thought. Turning, she pointed to the thermostat and a vent above it. "It won't stop blowing, but the air ain't cold. And ugh, sweat is not your friend when you're trying to draw Tweety Bird flying on someone's back."

Terrence furrowed his brow, unsure how to respond. "I bet..." he said.

"Oh, don't worry, the bird came out grand. I watched those toons as a kid, and I felt like a kid with a coloring book."

Terrence looked at the thermostat. "Where's the air handler?" Terrence asked, knowing exactly where it was when he punched a hole in the coolant line before.

Selena shrugged.

"Hey Jess, where's the air handler?"

A woman with a small black and pink unicorn tattooed on the side of her forehead looked up from a customer. She shrugged. Terrence noticed the unicorn's horn on Jess's face. The red tip dripped blood, like the artwork pierced her skin.

"I'll find it. Back door?" Terrence pointed to the back of the narrow shop.

Selena nodded.

Terrence found the outside unit and quickly patched up the hole and recharged the refrigerant. He then moved back into the shop and found the small closet that housed the inside unit. Unscrewing the cover, he removed the air filter and placed a small magnet attached to a half-liter cartridge near the inner coils. Confirming the magnet was secure, he removed a cap on the cartridge. Replacing the filter and then the cover, he moved back to the thermostat.

Selena hopped up from her chair and met him. He turned the unit back on and smiled at Selena.

"You're good to go. If anything else happens, please let us know."

"I think I know where I remember you from. Did you know a man named Ig–"

"Sorry!" he interrupted, putting up his hand. "Lots of calls in the area and such a hot day."

She pulled back at his abruptness. She felt cold air from the vent and forgot all about her question.

"Stay inside for the next few hours. Enjoy the cold air!" Terrence said as he walked out the door.

The staff and remaining clients cheered. They were all smiles as the cool air flowed out of the vents.

Terrence stopped a moment and looked back in through the parlor's window, observing his plan unfold. "Comfort," he said to himself softly, no one else within earshot. "Yes, you enjoy your comfort as you disgrace your body. Your comfort will end in the pain you deserve. The ink will bubble off your sinful body."

The air vents slowly filled with the custom-made toxin. No one could hear, see, or smell it, but with every breath, the poison seeped into each person's lungs. As the toxin built up in their lungs and worked its way into the bloodstream, it'd flow through the entire body and take irreversible hold. Within hours, the immune system would trigger its response and severe boils would cover the body, including the inside of the mouth and airways.

The painful boils would not cause death, though. Suffocation provided the awful tipping point from life to death, as the breathing pathways swelled and filled with fluids, blocking all airflow.

Terrence looked at his watch. Approximately two hours of incubation, ten minutes of painful boil growth, and five minutes of choking to death.

He turned from his vantage point outside the parlor's front window. He sidestepped a passing woman, and with a friendly nod, made room for her to enter the shop. As long as she stayed inside the shop for at least twenty minutes, taking normal breaths, she would be dead in approximately two hours.

Terrence disappeared into the crowd, smiling as if taking a relaxed Sunday stroll. His mind imagined the newscasts and images of the victims. The people who would mourn, but they would not understand the pain required to reteach this world. A correction is painful, yet necessary. It would take pouring out all seven bowls, and maybe not even then, but he knew that one day they would all praise him, they would all thank him. He would show Solomon, the leader of the New Christians, what he could do with authority. He would make his father, Terry, proud. And most of all, he envisioned God smiling down on him.

As he walked toward the safe house, Terrence sent a group text to the six other New Christian men who posed as repair men: GIP. Their motto, God Inspired Power, confirmed to the group that Terrence finished. Soon, GIP texts began rolling in. All seven of them.

A van pulled up, and he casually put in his toolbox and took a seat. In minutes, he was miles away from the poison.

Back at the safe house, the team celebrated their success. Then, he gathered a few chosen members in a small room to enact phase two of the first bowl. This piece of the plan deviated from the seven bowls, but he assured Solomon it was necessary.

"Begin Lazarus," he said to the men.

The professionals nodded and left the room.

Chapter 9

Foreign Aid

Mark Light - Odessa, Ukraine

Mark Light kissed his wife, Grace, and hugged his daughter, Joy, and son, Noah.

"Can I come?" Joy asked with hopeful eyes. In an instant, Noah was behind her, smiling with his eyebrows raised at the thought of joining their father.

Mark paused, considering their request more seriously today, and his kids sensed it. Joy bobbed up and down on her tiptoes, her smile growing wider.

"Please, please?"

Given the turmoil in the region, he never took them on supply drop-offs outside of the city. He and Grace agreed to keep them inside city limits.

"No, no, no!" Grace called from the kitchen of the two-bedroom apartment. "Today is home school day."

Joy and Noah's shoulders fell as they trudged back to their seats at the wooden table.

Decades of wear had turned the edges of the sturdy wooden table's color from a deep cherry into a light tan. The table came with the apartment, and like so many other things in their cramped living space, had been passed down or resold over and over.

"Oh, really?" Grace said. "So, you don't want your World War II lesson on the beach? I suppose we'll stay in all day."

"No!" Joy perked back up.

"I understand. The beautiful beaches of Odessa aren't Normandy. Maybe we should stay inside all day," Grace joked.

"Love you." Mark smiled as he kissed his wife goodbye and patted his kids on the back.

The morning air was crisp as fog clung to the streets of Odessa, Ukraine. For the past two years, Mark and his family made their home in the midst of rising political tensions and turmoil. He wasn't exactly planting a church, because he never considered himself a pastor, but he liked to think of himself as a modern-day John the Baptist. He was laying the foundation for revival in the community. And had his own piece of the Ark that empowered him daily.

Zech had introduced Mark to the crate, and as Zech opened the wooden box encased in green leather, the amber glow waited for Mark. The faith to believe in a piece of ancient artifact being a home for God on Earth wasn't difficult for Mark. He'd been a believer his whole life. Nevertheless, following his firsthand encounter with the Ark, which involved being shot and captured in France alongside J and Lucas, and the subsequent miraculous healing and unexplained transportation to the US—a challenging experience to explain to his wife—he swiftly developed an unwavering conviction in its power.

The small groups he was developing in the Ukraine were sprouting, and he knew soon they'd need a larger space. The growing community of believers couldn't keep meeting in restaurants and apartments.

It was hard and draining work, but every time he baptized a new follower, he felt the Holy Spirit wash him clean, renewing his energy and commitment. Days like today also helped him recenter. He always figured out how to make time for the donation drop-offs. The time and effort to gather the supplies reminded him of a long-ago message his father had told him.

"Coming to church each week, or doing any sort of service for your fellow man out of love, is like a restaurant owner putting the salt and pepper shakers back in the center of the table each night," Zech said.

There was no normal church service in his area and this servanthood to the poor helped him gain focus. God was the owner, and he was the messy table that needed cleaning.

He closed the tinted glass hatch to his truck bed's topper and began the long drive to the impoverished outskirts of the city. The blue Chevy rambled along, and he smiled as he rolled the manual window crank to let in the cool air. Grace ridiculed him for the old beater with manual brakes, no power steering, and crank windows, but he loved it. It brought him back to learning to drive with his father. Every time he had to push harder than expected on the old-style, non-ABS brakes. He remembered blowing a stop sign on a small side street behind his parents' house. He was terrified at the moment, but never forgot the unexpected force required.

The winding drive through town led him to an ocean of tents. The tents stretched under an overpass of the highway, alongside a nearby lake, and down a narrow field in between. He pulled off the exit and parked his truck. It sputtered and shook as the engine cut off.

A few heads popped up above the tents and moved toward him. He made this donation run weekly and developed relationships with some of the more permanent residents in the area.

"Privet!" Mark called out as he saw two men approaching.

"Your accent is terrible," the taller man said, his own English laced with a thick Russian accent.

Mark laughed. "Oh, come on, Petro. That was the best one yet!"

Petro shook his head, a stern expression on his face.

"What can we do for you, Mark?" a shorter, stout man said, with only a hint of Russian accent.

"Lead small group Bible studies, Nikolai?" Mark replied.

"No." Petro snapped in his deep voice.

Nikolai shrugged.

"I'm hopeful, fellas. One day. One day." Mark smiled. Nikolai returned a grin as Petro kept his face implacable.

"In the meantime, Nikolai, can you ask Mr. Friendly here to help with these boxes?" Mark said.

"Yes." Petro said, grabbing the ragged cardboard box out of Mark's hands.

Mark and Nikolai caught eyes and smiled at Petro's engagement.

"What do you have this week, Mr. Light?" Nikolai asked.

"Pocket Bibles, canned food, blankets, and–"

"Socks!" Petro shouted as he popped up, holding plastic bags of tube socks.

"That's the first time he's smiled all week." Nikolai said, as others began gathering around.

"Back up, Igor!" Petro shouted as another man approached the box. "Bread line, bread line!" He shouted as he motioned for the newcomers to form a line.

Igor growled at Petro, but Petro's resolve won the moment.

Igor sidestepped into the forming line, cutting off others.

"Vernut'sya! Vernut'sya!" Petro demanded. "End of the line!"

Igor looked toward the three-person line forming, then angrily at Petro, but reluctantly agreed.

Nikolai and Mark placed the other boxes behind Petro as he began tossing bags of socks at folks in line. He faked a toss to Igor, who dropped the tattered blanket he held wrapped around himself as he extended his hands. Igor's expression turned to rage and confusion, but Petro laughed as he tossed him a bag, and the man's face lit up.

"I think your visits are the only thing that brings him joy anymore." Nikolai said to Mark. "Or maybe it's how he torments Igor with everything you bring."

Mark smiled. "Any word from his family?"

"I'm afraid not. Ever since the war separated them, he hasn't heard from his wife or daughter."

"I can't imagine."

"This place is growing. More and more of our people dislodged from their lives." Nikolai said. "We can't get them out of the country fast enough."

"How about Blake? He's still coming by, right?" Mark asked.

"Yes, one family per week." Nikolai nodded, but a frown formed as he looked out to the field and pointed. "But look. All new arrivals."

Mark stepped away from his truck to get a better view. "Whoa," he said as looked over a new section of tents.

"Dozens of people. I counted at least fifteen children, six women." He paused and shook his head. "The heartache grows faster than the hope."

Mark clenched his jaw. "Can you make sure they get a few cans and blankets?"

He turned back to his truck and pulled out a stack of plastic water bottle cases.

"And some water?" He grunted as he set the heavy load at Nikolai's feet.

Nikolai nodded.

"I'm going to take a walk, talk to some folks. Any prayer requests, my friend?" Mark asked as he moved to the passenger door of his truck.

Nikolai scoffed, "sorry, Mark. I believe in reality, not filling your holes with imagination."

"Hmm," Mark opened the door of his truck and grabbed his Bible off the seat. "So do I."

Nikolai didn't notice the glow of the binding as Mark held it between them.

"You are a professor of mathematics, an educator, right?" Mark asked.

"Was..." Nikolai looked down. "Before all this."

"Then you know probability." Mark reached out, putting his hand on the shorter man's shoulder. "I don't think this was all a roll of evolutionary dice. Either an infinite number of assumptions take place to make this world and life exist, or... there's a God who made it all, and loves you like crazy." He smiled at Nikolai, whose eyes remained focused on the ground. "And you *are* still an educator. No war will take that away."

Nikolai called out as Mark turned away. "How do you keep your faith? Look at this," he motioned to poverty all around them. "You see the horrors of this world, yet you keep believing in your God?"

Mark turned back and held his Bible close to his heart. He felt tiny cuts of piercing pain shoot through every cell in his body, followed by a warm, loving sensation that calmed and strengthened him to his core. "Because I died, Nikolai. And my God, *your* God, brought me back to life."

He locked eyes with Nikolai, then turned and walked into the sea of tents.

"Mark!" Nikolai yelled.

"Yeah?" Mark said without turning back.

"Be careful. Some of those new folks don't look so savory. May not like your message!"

"Challenge accepted!" Mark called back and held his hand up, waving.

As he approached the tents, three children kicked a small plastic ball on a patch of grass. Mark walked up slowly, savoring their innocence, despite the camp's inhabitants of homeless and refugees. He squatted down, watching the kids' soccer game and keeping an eye out for their parents.

His phone buzzed in his pocket. Pulling it out, he smiled as Lucas's picture lit up his phone. It was of the two of them on their flight back to Europe. They each held up a finger, like a team posing after a championship, as in, "We're number one."

The inside joke originated during their one-way flight to Europe, following J through the supernatural portal that transported them from captivity to a courtroom in America. They only needed one flight, and with both being Christ's followers, they knew of the one way to Heaven, through Jesus.

One way.

"Hey, buddy." Mark answered.

"Mark, you must run." Lucas shouted in his French accent. Mark could hear him gasping for air.

"What? Like exercise? Are you on a run?"

"They killed us. Remember! Now they want to finish the job. They're coming for me now, and each Light! Me and each Light!"

"Lucas, what are you–"

"Get to safety! Get out of your house, wherever, get safe. They're–" Lucas stopped. Mark could still hear him panting. "You're next." He said in a low voice.

"Lucas!" Mark screamed into the phone. He heard noises on the other end, a rustling as if Lucas dropped his phone, followed by a struggle and shouts in the distance.

"Lucas!"

The line went dead as Mark brought his phone down from his ear and looked at the screen, only to find that the call had barely lasted a few seconds. Soon, app icons floated in front of a picture of Grace, Joy, and Noah. His family smiled at him from the picture.

Through the screen, he saw the reflection of two men walk up behind him.

"Mark Light?" A gravelly voice said in a Russian accent. It wasn't Petro or Nikolai. He didn't recognize the voice.

He held up a finger to give pause. "Great to hear from you. Yes, more food and water." Mark pretended to be on the phone, forcing his voice steady. As he spoke, he quickly clicked a family group text and shared his location, then texted: Help Lucas.

Slowly standing, he slid the device back into his pocket. Turning around, he smiled at two men that towered above him and easily outweighed him by fifty pounds.

"A rugby match in town, boys?" he jested. "I'm partial to American football myself, but must respect the–"

A lightning-fast fist slammed into Mark's cheek. He stumbled back and fell to one knee, dropping his Bible. He rubbed his cheek and opened his mouth as if screaming in pain, but held back his voice. Only a soft grunt escaping.

Two large hands, the size of bear paws, grabbed him and jerked him up, slamming a knee into his midsection. He felt a painful crunch in his ribs before being dropped. His face collided with the cold ground and dirt flew up as he gasped for air.

"More of soccer fans, eh?" he struggled to say before a swinging black book connected with his hip. Extreme pain shot down his leg as he rolled over.

"Ay!" Nikolai called out from a distance. "Get off him!"

Petro heard Nikolai's shout. He stopped passing out blankets, dropping them at Igor's feet and rushed up behind Nikolai.

"Ay!" they called out as they ran to Mark's aid.

The attackers turned to see the two running at them. One pulled a gun and shot it in the air. The loud bang rang through the camp, silencing all side conversations and causing the playing kids to run into their tents. Mark could hear children crying.

The man with the gun pointed it at Nikolai and shook his head no as he locked eyes. Petro and Nikolai stood motionless, raising their hands to their sides.

Mark took advantage of the distraction. He held his breath as he rolled onto his belly. He grabbed his Bible from the dirt and shot up, at first hobbling but soon trying to sprint between tents. However, it was more like the gallop of a wounded horse than a thoroughbred.

The one with a gun held his position as the other brute took off after Mark.

He took a good angle through the tents and caught up quickly.

Mark turned at a large tent and found himself pulled off his feet. The attacker swung a clenched fist, holding a short knife, and planted it straight into Mark's stomach. The killer wrenched the knife, ensuring he tore through flesh and hit vital organs.

Mark's eyes bulged at the pain.

"Let 'im go!" A plastic crate slammed into the man's head and Mark dropped.

Igor stood ten feet away, holding another plastic crate, a ragged brown blanket draped over his shoulders and bright white tube socks on his feet.

Igor screamed at the attacker. A mix of Spartan warrior and wild animal fury came out of the man. His eyes held a mad stare as he swung his arms like windmills, picking up and throwing more plastic milk crates and other nearby debris.

The attacker reached an arm inside his jacket, attempting to pull a gun, but Igor's use of random objects as weapons pelted the man.

Mark looked at his belly. He felt blood trickle and a pinch of searing pain, but to his amazement, he saw his Bible. The two-inch thick book took the brunt of the attack. His fingers glided over the book and felt a thin slit that shot through both sides of the hardcover and every page. The book dampened the impact and reach of the knife, but blood pooled on his shirt. The Bible had saved his life, but without immediate medical care, the wound would be fatal.

Once again, Mark blocked the pain and got up. This time, he took the offensive before running. He clutched his Bible tight and swung it at the back of the man's head. He had to swing up to hit the giant's head. Igor's attack kept the assassin off balance and as Mark swung, the giant tipped over, as if weightless. An invisible repulsion sent the attacker flying, his face smacking against the hard, cold dirt. The man grunted in pain.

The swinging motion had torn his wound further, causing blood to run from Mark's stomach.

Igor stood looking at the man.

"Thank you." Mark softly spoke as one hand went back to his stomach.

"You're welcome." Igor said in a deep and powerful British voice. The Patrick Stewart-like voice surprised Mark.

"I've never heard you talk before."

The giant stirred, a grunt escaping his throat.

"You should go," Igor said.

Mark nodded and took off toward a large drain in between the overpass and lake. The brute got back to his feet. He glanced at Igor, who'd run out of objects to throw. Igor shrugged and stepped back. The giant shot him a look of hatred, then took off after Mark.

"Good luck, young man," Igor said.

Chapter 10

Domestic Terror

Luke Light - Atlanta, Georgia

Luke's phone buzzed as his family stepped out of their black SUV.

"Have you heard from Mark?" the text from his father read.

Luke typed back: No, what's up?

His father didn't immediately respond, but another text came in, this one from his kids' youth pastor. Luke read it and then caught up with Helen and the kids.

"Want to grab us a seat?" Luke asked. "Text about a quick board meeting before church." He held up his phone.

"Oh, you think they'll announce Tyler leaving?" Helen replied.

"What? Tyler isn't leaving. He loves his role."

"He's been distant lately." Nina, Luke's daughter, replied.

"No way." Luke shook his head.

"Who told you there's a meeting?" Helen raised her eyebrows.

"Unknown number." Luke replied.

"Unknown?" Helen looked skeptical.

"The system they use for group announcements has new numbers whenever they make a new group or change a setting."

"I bet it's the new youth pastor!" Xavier entered the conversation.

"You three are nuts." Luke laughed. "I'll be sure to tell Tyler how devastated you were at the thought of him leaving."

Helen shrugged with a smile. "I'll grab our seats. Have fun, kids."

Luke walked with Nina and Xavier. As they went into the youth hall, Nina hugged him goodbye and Xavier gave him a high-five. Luke caught Xavier's hand and pulled him in for a hug.

He continued out of the main building that housed the sanctuary and youth hall, and out to the smaller strip of offices beyond. Most people never saw the aluminum overhang and sidewalk that led to the original worship building. The huge street-facing structure of the main building and surrounding trees blocked the older building from view.

The former house converted to church was now offices for the staff. The head pastor and church staff all had an office within the building, with one room reserved for working sessions and meetings.

Luke walked in, surprised by the silence inside. Usually, at least one of the elders, if not three or four, would be in conversation. He glanced back at his phone and confirmed the meeting location. He was in the right spot.

Even in the quiet, he was familiar with the building, having attended monthly board meetings for the church since his appointment years ago. Typically, budget decisions, staff salary, and which outreach programs to focus on dominated the meetings. But ever since the legal ruling against Luke's family and their sister church in North Florida, things had changed. The Atlanta church of Lost and Found Ministries was one of the few churches that survived the consolidation. The church's steady tithes from the North Atlanta, Buckhead, and Marietta areas were desperately needed income that couldn't be ignored. Plus, the successful local and international missions were the most consistent and impactful work in nearly the entire global church organization.

While the Atlanta church kept many items intact, there were more cuts and even more unhappy members.

To Luke and the head pastor's dismay, one person cried out "Cut 'em off!" in the middle of church service during the announcement of cutbacks. The rumors of the North Florida branch bringing down the entire ministry were hot on the congregation's lips.

"I hear their pastor isn't all there, in the head, ya know?" Luke had overhead in the rotunda. "Talking about covenants and holding up some fake gold."

Still, Luke had many conversations with his head pastor, Jason, and with his father, Zechariah. The church was slowly getting through the tough times, one ordeal at a time.

Luke walked through the empty hallway and peeked into offices. The lights flickered on as he passed by the motion detectors. When he saw the meeting room empty like the rest of the building, he pulled out his phone and texted Pastor Jason.

He didn't notice the small red light as he walked into the room, but under the conference table, a lethal device signaled its armed status with a silent blinking light.

Luke took a seat in one of the black leather chairs. He pushed himself away from the table as he felt his phone buzz.

Eager to see Pastor Jason's response, he was let down to see it was a notification. His daily Bible verse reminder. He pulled it open and read the verse: 1 Corinthians 10:13, *No temptation has overtaken you that is not common to man. God is faithful, and he will not let you be tempted beyond your strength, but with the temptation will also provide the way of escape, that you may be able to endure it. -RSV*

He smiled, thinking about the tough times at his family's church, his own local branch, and the parent ministry.

As he thought about the verse, he remembered his Bible and notebook were still back in his black SUV, snug in the pocket of his driver's side door. The glowing piece of the Ark of the Covenant hidden in the binding. A present from his father, Zech, to Luke and his brother Mark upon the trial's conclusions months before.

He stood up with a renewed vigor as he looked out the window, through the trees towards where his car rested in the parking lot. As he got up, the chair shot back harder than he expected. The well lubricated wheels glided smoothly on the hard floor.

Luke approached the window as the chair rolled through the doorway. It passed through an invisible beam of light, triggering the device under the table.

The explosion ripped through the building, blowing apart the doorway and hallway, disintegrating the black chair in a ball of flames.

The concussion wave blew out the window in front of Luke and launched him out of the building. Flames burst out of the windows as the roof of the building blew open, then fully collapsed. A giant smoke cloud rose into the sky from the decimated building.

Flames erupted and spread, feeding on the wooden fuel and melting plastic. A wave of immense heat enclosed the building.

Luke lay on the grass outside the building as the fire raged on behind him. The explosion had ripped off strips of flesh from his back and burned the remaining skin.

He didn't move.

Chapter 11

Strangling Stars

Matthew

Matthew peered out the window and noticed J's red Jeep parked in the driveway. The doors and windows of the car were removed to enjoy the cooler-than-normal fall weather.

"Hey, we were just watching you!" Matthew said, opening the door.

"We recorded that one," J said as he came in, his head hanging low and his voice softer than normal.

"The new camera angles were great. Only made me a *little* dizzy." Matthew smiled. But J stopped after only a couple of steps into the house and looked at Matthew. His face was pale and solemn.

"What? I was kidding. They didn't really make me dizzy."

"No... No, it's not that." J took a deep breath. "Have you heard from Luke, Mark, or Lucas?"

The expression and serious tone on J's face gave Matthew pause.

"No. Only that random group text from Mark hours ago. I don't think he's replied to any of our responses."

"Your dad called on my way over. He said Grace called your mom... Mark never came home from his donation drop this morning. I called Lucas, but he's also not responding, which is unlike him." J turned away.

"Mark has lost his phone before. Maybe just out of service or battery died?"

"Atlanta. Luke." J turned back. Matthew's eyes widened. "Your brother is in critical condition. He's on life support." Matthew's jaw tightened, his face tense. "Pastor Jason, from Atlanta, called. An explosion destroyed an entire building. Luke was in it, or at least was before being thrown from it."

Matthew felt his heart collapse, like a black hole in his chest sucked up his vital organs.

"Wh..." Matthew couldn't get the question out.

"He's at the hospital, and your parents are already on the road." J replied.

Matthew nodded. They stood in silence for a moment as Matthew took the horrible news in. J watched his friend, debating whether to tell him one more thing.

J cleared his throat. "Matt, I think I know what's happening."

Matthew looked at his friend.

"I've been having a dream."

"The dragon?"

"No, this is new, and I've had it every night for weeks. I'm almost used to it now, but all this... The attack in New York, Mark and Lucas missing, the explosion in Atlanta... It's starting to come together in my mind, to parallel the dream."

Matthew directed them to the dinner table, each took a seat.

"In the dream, there's a night sky. It's a beautiful night. I feel a gentle breeze and hear the leaves rustling from the surrounding trees. Up in the sky, a gorgeous blanket of stars. The kind of sky that is a hundred miles from any city, you know?"

J smiled as he recounted the opening of his dream, but then his face flipped to a frown.

"But then something happens," he continued. "A dark, cloud-like thing creeps into the night sky."

A chill ran down Matthew's spine as he imagined all the black clouds of demons that haunted everyday people.

"I couldn't tell if it was always in between the stars, or it came from somewhere, but it was like a thick black ink. It moved through the night sky, surrounding the bright stars, and one by one it blocked out their light." J shook his head. "No. It didn't just block the light. The darkness somehow strangled the life out of each star, growing stronger with each one it put out."

"And you think this dream mirrors what is happening to our family?"

J nodded, "I do."

Matthew leaned up in his chair and rubbed the back of his neck.

"But that's not it. As this happens in the dream, I feel something in my pocket, in all my pockets. The Ark is there, one piece in each pocket, all four of them. I pull them out and it's just like the ones we each have in our Bibles."

"Four of them," Matthew said.

"Yeah, and I can't help but think of you three Light brothers, plus me. Four of us, and we each have a piece. Your dad told us there is usually only one piece at a time, but at various times, he felt the Spirit move and he knew the crate would have another piece."

"He said that once he gave you yours, it was like he already knew another piece was waiting there, for me." Matthew nodded his head up and down.

"He said the same thing about Luke and Mark. That he prayed for years about passing down the Ark to Luke, then Mark, and then to us. He never felt it until Terrence showed up and Isaiah saved us. Then, after the court case and everything that happened to me, Mark, and Lucas in Europe, he said *he just knew*. He said the Spirit told him not to let Luke and Mark leave town without taking them to the crate, that their piece would be waiting," J said.

"I don't understand it," Matthew said.

"I know, four pieces. Five, if you include Zech's, the one that started it all."

"Not just that, but why now?"

J looked curiously at his friend.

"What do you mean?"

"It's been in our family for what, a few thousand years? And even a generation ago, Isaiah passed one, *one piece*, down to my father, but as soon as he and your dad, Micah, figured out how to protect it, your dad died. It's all repeating."

J's eyebrows furrowed.

"J, your dad was close to the Ark holder before he passed. Now, the number of Ark holders grows, and it seems like evil is fighting back in proportion."

"It's almost like you're saying Satan is picking us off. Like my dad didn't die of a blood clot, but because he was there to help Zech," J said.

Matthew's face was like stone. "Maybe. If your dad's stay in the hospital was anything like mine... God had to intervene. I can't describe the horrors I saw."

"So, why save you and not my dad?"

"I don't know, but you say you had four pieces in your hand, right?"

J nodded.

"Didn't you give a sermon once about the parallels of the Ark and the empty tomb?" Matthew asked.

"Yup. That was your dad a couple of years ago. I'm trying to encourage him to give it again."

"Each piece we have is like a cherub's wing. Four wings extended over the cover of the Ark, just like the two angels sat at the ends of where Jesus's body was supposed to be," Matthew said.

"It marks God's place on Earth, his dwelling..." J said.

They both thought in silence for another moment until J spoke.

"There's more to the dream. The four pieces. I slam them together and it creates a new light that blasts away the darkness."

"That makes sense! At the center of the four wings is the Ark, and jumping to the New Testament, it's the empty tomb."

"Life over death!" J said.

The smile on J's face soon faded as the final part of the dream replayed in his mind.

"But there's one more piece of the dream. How it ends."

Matthew sat back in his chair.

"The light, whatever it is, doesn't just kill the darkness. It kills me, and then I see–"

"Uncle J!" Beth and Lyn shouted as they sped around the corner and slammed into J's chair, hugging him.

"Girls, girls." Matthew tried wrangling them. He looked back at J expectantly.

"Uh," J stuttered, unable to continue with the girls present.

"And then?" Matthew asked as Lyn turned and hugged her dad's leg.

"Oh..." J snapped back into focus after watching the young girls hug their father. "Uh, it wipes out everything around me. Like a bomb exploding, the trees, water, all that, poof."

"Like it cleans house?" Matthew asked.

"Yeah," J shrugged and Matthew nodded.

"Speaking of cleaning house, I saw all those toys scattered in your rooms!" Matthew turned to his girls. "Was there a toy bomb? If you want to play with Uncle J, we need those rooms cleaned." The girls ran off toward their rooms.

"You still want to stay with me and the girls while Liz is at the conference?"

"Given all this chaos, there's no place I'd rather be."

"Cool, and I'll talk to Liz and my brothers and Lucas." Matthew said.

"Talk to me about what?" Liz said.

Chapter 12

Footsteps Coming
Mark Light - Ukraine

Mark dashed toward the lake, eyeing the oversized storm drain. The giant cylinder sat under the overpass with a stream of runoff water flowing into the lake. He didn't slow down as he crashed into the lake and dove under. Feeling the water sting against his stomach wound, he swam with restrained strokes. The urge to look back ate at his mind, but he kept pressing forward, hoping to get out of sight.

He felt his stomach rip further as he pulled himself from the freezing cold water and up onto the drainage tunnel. Before crawling through, he finally stole a glance back. The heads of the assassins bobbed up and down as they ran through the tents.

He saw they were approaching the lake, and as quick as he could, he crawled into the tunnel and away from view.

A moment later, he heard a splash. He cringed, feeling them close in on him.

Looking down, he saw blood weaving into red streams as it mixed with the lake water coming off his clothes.

You can't stop. A voice in his head told him.

He took deep breaths as he prepared to move again.

"God, help me," he said through gritted teeth as he stood up. Ducking his head, he moved faster through the tunnel, focusing on the light at the other side. Scrambling through, nearly falling out of the other end, he swung out and pressed his back against the concrete wall of the overpass.

A split second later, he heard the sloshing noise of someone getting out of the water. The sound of boots taking careful steps echoed down the rippled aluminum shell of the tunnel.

Mark looked around, *think, think,* he thought to himself. A large runoff ditch rested in front of him. Beyond the ditch, an open, grassy field. He closed his eyes, quickly reviewing his options.

He heard footsteps echo in the tunnel behind him. The sound like the ticks of a time bomb counting down the last seconds of his life.

Mark looked back toward the underside of the overpass. His vision peered over a hundred yards away, past a rocky mesa that kept the tents away from this side, to where he parked his truck. He could run for it, but in his weakened state and unstable footing, the assassin would easily pick him off. Plus, where was the villain's double? He could have gone back to cover Mark's truck.

Past the ditch, he eyed the open field and, far off in the distance, a tree line. The safety of the trees called to him, but he knew they were deceptively far away. Even without pursuers, with his wound he couldn't make it across the ditch and the great swath of knee-high grass to the forest. And even if he could, then what?

Then the realization of what jumping in the lake had meant. His phone was in his pocket, surely ruined by the water. Mark squeezed his fist in frustration.

The steps continued to echo in the tunnel. A tolling of the hangman in his ears.

He figured his last option was that he could cut in front of the tunnel and run for the highway, praying to get picked up before they gunned him down.

Lord, help me. He said to himself as the thought of his wife and children went through his mind.

The steps came closer, and Mark pressed firmly against the wall and slid down, trying to hide himself in plain sight as indecision filled his mind.

The ditch. He decided. *Just hide and figure it out.*

But before he could move, a colossal head stuck out next to him. It looked straight ahead, eyes squinting toward the ditch.

Mark froze, realizing he was only feet away from the assassin's head. If the killer turned to the left, Mark's life would be in immediate danger.

The assassin eyed the ditch, and up at the field beyond, waiting for his prey to give itself away. Soon, he turned to his right, looking up the gravel incline toward the road.

The thought of reaching for the man, to choke him or gouge his eyes out, went through Mark's mind. But he remained frozen. These men were much larger than him; he didn't stand a chance.

But I knocked him down before. Mark thought. When he swung his Bible, trying to slam the book into the man's head. It didn't make impact but the creep's head still shot forward, slamming into the ground.

I never hit him. The Bible repelled him. The stories from Zech, J, and Matthew came back to him, the repulsive force of the supernatural object.

After swinging it, he'd tucked the good book into his back waistband and taken off running. He forgot all about it.

But now with the stories running through his mind, he felt the book push against his skin and welcomed the loving sensation of the Ark as it pulsed through him.

A black pistol emerged from the tunnel and was positioned close to the man's head.

Mark inched his hand toward the Bible, preparing to swing it.

"Ay!" Mark went to stone as he heard a deep voice echo from far within the tunnel. The head and gun turned back into the tunnel as the heavyweight shifted back towards the voice.

Mark heard further commotion, a mixture of Russian and Ukrainian from the unfamiliar voices. But Mark singled out one voice. Nikolai. He could hear his friend screaming at the men, misleading, and distracting them.

A moment earlier, Mark thought he'd be in a fight for his life, but now he heard retreating footsteps.

Thank you, Lord.

He still needed to escape and he needed medical attention for his stomach wound.

My truck. He thought.

He looked back towards the small piece of the tent city, under the overpass, wondering if he could make it unseen.

Then, the sound of tires on gravel stole his attention.

A white van pulled off the road.

Mark recognized it.

Chapter 13

Go Fish

Matthew

"Do you have any threes?" J asked. He leaned over his elbow, putting his face low and smiling at Lyn. Their eyes inches apart.

"Noooo," Lyn giggled.

"What?" J exclaimed. "You just asked your sister for a three!"

Lyn kept laughing. The deep belly laughs only a child could give.

"I can't tell if she's kidding," J laughed. Lyn's infectious laugh brought a smile to his face.

"One of these," J pulled a card from his hand and showed the girl.

"Oh!" Lyn popped up in her seat, trying to hold back a laugh. Beth was giggling now, too.

"Here." Lyn extended a card to J.

"This is a skip. From the Uno deck."

J shook his head and then looked at Matthew. "How in the world do you play go fish with regular cards *and* Uno cards?"

"You just gotta roll with it. Hey Lyn, do you have any skips?"

"This one?" she flashed the skip card.

Matthew nodded and took it, laying down a pair of skips and holding his hands up. "Thank you. I'm out!"

"No! One more game?" Beth pleaded.

"We've already played four, sweetie," Matthew said, playfully closing his eyes and dropping his head.

"Please!" Lyn echoed from across the table.

"No," he said firmly. "How about lunch, J?"

"Yeah! Who wants a knuckle sandwich?" J screamed.

"What?" Matthew said, standing up. Lyn screamed as J chased her toward the couch. Beth jumped off her chair and grabbed Matthew's leg, trying to pick it up off the ground.

"No!" Matthew shouted, hopping on one foot toward the carpet and couch area. "Okay, you asked for it!" He wrapped one arm around Beth, putting her in a headlock, and started tickling her with his other hand.

Laughter filled the room and took both men's mind from waiting to hear news about their brothers.

A moment later, Matthew's phone buzzed. He broke free from Beth and quickly slid away. She moved to double team Uncle J with her little sister. Lyn stacked pillows on top of J, who no longer pretended to be knocked out as he eyed Matthew, eager for an update.

Grabbing his phone, he saw Liz's picture displayed for the incoming call.

"Hey, hun," he answered.

"Hey. I got a hold of Helen. Your brother's vitals are stabilizing."

Matthew let out a sigh of relief.

"Thank God. How's he doing overall?"

"Well, he's still in critical condition, but they're hopeful he'll pull through," Liz said. "He lost most of the skin on his back, but he's alive."

"That's good to hear. Any word on Mark?" Matthew said.

"I talked to Grace; she still hasn't heard from him. A couple of friends drove out to the homeless area and found his truck." Liz said.

"But no Mark?" Matthew asked.

"No Mark. But hun, his truck was still there. He made it out there, and distributed all the donations..." Liz trailed off.

"But?" Matthew asked.

"Sounds like there was a struggle. Some kind of commotion has that place still all riled up. Their friends are trying to find out more, but hun, there was a puddle of blood."

"Where are the cops?" Matthew raised his voice, catching J and the girls' attention.

"Grace didn't know; they called them, but saying a missionary is missing while visiting a known homeless area doesn't get the authorities moving."

Matthew exhaled with noticeable frustration.

"Grace will call once they find out more. I'll keep you posted. I'm sorry, hun. They'll find him."

"Thanks. Talk soon. I love you." Matthew hung up the phone. He turned to give J an update, but his phone buzzed again.

"Hey, Dad. You caught up on Mark and Luke?"

"Yup, your mom's been in touch with Grace and Helen," Zech said from the other end of the phone. "But this isn't about that. Son, could you turn on the news?"

"Okay... What channel?"

"Any channel."

Matthew walked to the remote as J and the girls stopped playing and watched him. He turned on the TV and saw a press conference.

Matthew and J saw a familiar face: Nancy Pawly. The prosecuting attorney that called his grandfather a murderer and led the legal victory, which crippled their church and parent organization, stood confidently on screen. Matthew watched the demonic cloud hovering around her as she answered questions from reporters.

"We need to go straight to Washington and protect our citizens," Nancy said, her fist pounding the podium filled with microphones. "How long will they stand by and let innocent people die?"

"Matthew? You see it?" Zech asked. Matthew forgot his father was on the line and brought the phone back to his ear.

"Yeah, what is this?"

"Our *friend*, Ms. Pawly, is up on a soapbox. She's talking about the recent attacks."

"The New York tragedy?"

"And now the one that nearly killed your brother."

Nancy's voice continued. "I don't see how these incumbents can live with themselves and *NOT* take action to protect our people. This country was founded on religious freedoms. But, I've yet to hear a statement about what your President is doing to find the monsters responsible for these attacks."

"Religious freedoms, huh?" Matthew shook his head.

"Don't buy it," Zech said. "She's turning this into a crisis, and in times of crisis, authoritarians take control. This is a political power grab."

"But she's a lawyer," Matthew replied.

"A lawyer who is positioning herself for office. Jimmy has been keeping tabs on her in the media ever since the trial. She's made countless comments to undermine our nation's leaders. She's setting up a campaign," Zech said.

"But if she protects churches from these attacks, isn't that a good thing? An example of God using bad for good?"

"Would you want her, or one of her allies, given control during a time of crisis?"

"Not a chance," Matthew said.

"Agreed. I've only heard ten minutes of this, but Jimmy and Paul tipped me off. They've listened to the whole thing. She's pushing for a special session of Congress this week."

"What will that do?"

"I don't know, but if she gets it, it'll show how much clout she's got," Zech said. "If it's a public session, you bet we'll be there. Paul and Jimmy are already packing for D.C."

"Okay," Matthew said. "Let me know how I can help."

"Are you with J?"

"Yup. Let me put you on speaker."

"J, turn on your phone!" Zech shouted.

"Sorry, boss. It's in the car."

"Hi, Grandpa!" the girls screamed as they rushed up to the phone.

"Hey, little ladies!" Zech's tone shifted instantly from cactus barbs to a cozy blanket.

"Can you girls tell Mr. J and your dad to look after the church? Your grandma and I are going to be gone all week."

"Yes, Grandpa," Beth said. Lyn turned to Matthew and J, holding out a finger like a teacher reprimanding a student.

"Hey, Matthew, take me off speaker," Zech said. "Bye, girls!"

"Bye!" the girls called out as Matthew pressed a button and held the phone back up to his ear.

"Yeah, Dad?"

"How have you been? Still seeing it, the darkness?"

"Yeah." Matthew's eyes went back to the television and the thick cloud around Nancy. The darkness blocked his view of the people stacked behind her. "There's one all over her right now."

"I thought so..." Zech exhaled. "Keep an eye on her, will you? And tell J to put out feelers for Terrence again."

"You got it," Matthew said.

After saying goodbye, Matthew turned to J.

"You've been watching out for Terrence?"

J nodded. "Trying to at least. Religious blogs and forums are abuzz after the recent attacks. No sign of the New Christians after the New York attack, but there was something in Paris this morning. It looks bad, and it's driving conversations about the bowls of Revelation."

"That's what he always talked about," Matthew said.

"Paris was number one on the map in T's flat. HVAC and skin. It's them."

"Wait, Paris? Lucas is in Paris. You think it's related?" Matthew asked.

"I wouldn't take Lucas to be at a tattoo shop. That's where they hit, and not just one, but seven at once. They used a chemical agent that caused boils all over, even down the throat." J looked at the girls and whispered, "one forum said the victims suffocated as their throats closed and puss filled their lungs. Not pretty."

"That's horrible." Matthew shook his head.

Matthew's phone buzzed once more in his hand.

"My boss is calling..."

Chapter 14

One More Family
Mark Light - Ukraine

Mark slowly pushed off the concrete wall of the overpass, tentatively peeking through the storm drain. The empty cylinder and placid lake beyond felt too good to be true.

He waited a moment, listening for footsteps, but only heard the distant commotion of the tent city.

He crawled past the tunnel opening and gradually hobbled to his feet, hunching over as he moved toward the van. Intense pain shot across his midsection every time he lifted his torso beyond a hunchback-like posture.

The gravel-covered embankment rose to the side of the highway and his feet struggled for traction on the loose stones. As one hand clutched his still-bleeding midsection, he dropped to his knees and used his free hand to crawl up the gravel hill. His Bible was still secure in his belt, pressed into his back. The slow progress gave him hope, but his heart sank as he saw the van start to pull away.

He scrambled up a few more feet, pushing more rocks down the incline as he dug in furiously, trying to wave at the van and keep moving.

"Hey!" he called out, nearly at the top of the hill.

The van crept slowly toward the highway but stopped as a semi-truck roared past. Mark's heart leapt, and the break gave him the last step needed to reach the van.

The driver looked over his shoulder, toward oncoming traffic as Mark's bloody hand slammed into the driver's window.

"Blake!" Mark choked out. The driver jumped in his seat as the red handprint smeared across his window. Mark coughed as he fell to the ground. A muffled crunch of the gravel rose to meet Blake's ears.

"Mark?" Blake put the van in park and jumped out.

"Help," Mark squeezed out through gritted teeth.

"What happened? You need to–" Mark hissed in pain as his shirt lifted, exposing the open flesh wound.

Blake gagged as he saw the open wound.

"Whoa. I'm going to..." Blake jumped to the side of the van and threw up. He fell to his knees.

Mark eyed Blake and then rolled back, trying to get up. He looked down the embankment and saw the two men coming out of the drainage tunnel. The assassins had heard him shout. Mark locked eyes with the one he had knocked over with the Bible.

He swung back toward the van and tugged at Blake's untucked flannel shirt.

"We gotta go!" Mark shouted.

"Yeah, yeah, just give me a second," Blake said.

Mark looked back and saw one man moving up the gravel as the other pulled out a pistol, eyeing him and Blake.

"Gun," Mark choked out. He tugged on Blake's shirt harder, pulling Blake off his knees as he fell back. "He's got a—"

The loud pop rang out as a bullet struck the side of the van, inches from Blake's head.

"Whoa!" Blake screamed. Turning, he saw the two linebacker-sized men. The shooter moved forward a few paces, giving them precious seconds as he re-aimed.

Blake grabbed Mark and shot up, throwing Mark into the open driver's side door. Mark cringed as he rolled painfully over the seat and the plastic center console area, and on to the passenger bucket seat. Blake jumped in as another bullet struck the van inches from the door frame.

Now, both attackers had their guns out and opened fire. Bullets rattled the side of the van as Blake jammed the gas pedal. The back wheels spun, searching for traction. More bullets impacted the van and the driver's side window blew out, spraying glass across Blake and cutting his face.

Tires spun as the van turned ninety degrees, Blake wiping the wheel around. The spinning tires spit deadly gravel back at their attackers, their own return fire. As the rocks hit the closer man, he dropped to the ground. The rapid-fire gravel forced the other assassin to duck, unable to fire at them again.

The tires eventually found their grip and the van shot forward, nearly swiping a speeding car that swerved out of the way.

"My house," Mark said. His vision becoming darker by the second.

"The hospital!" Blake replied.

"No, my house," he insisted before his head gently landed on the window.

"Fine," Blake shook his head, seeing Mark lose consciousness, and he didn't argue further. "It is closer."

Thirty minutes later, they pulled up to Mark's house.

Grace ran outside, tears in her eyes, as she saw Blake help her husband out of the white van. Inside, she pulled out a medical kit as Blake dragged Mark to the couch. Grace organized the kids to get their father comfortable, removed his shirt and propped up his head. They brought clean rags and a bucket. Blake watched in astonishment as Grace spoke, keeping the kids calm while mending Mark. The former physician's assistant washed his wound as he flickered in and out of consciousness. Halfway through the stitches, he passed out. Blake turned away, unable to watch the living room operation.

"He'll need rest, water, and later today, food. Once he's ready," Grace said to Joy and Noah. "Think about how much blood he's losing. He'll need a lot of rest and water to replenish that, plus heal the wound."

Once Grace finished, she stood up and calmly walked over to Blake.

"That was amaz–"

Grace slapped him.

"Where were you two? What'd you get him into?"

"I found him like that! At the homeless village outside of town."

Grace glared at him, then turned to the kids.

"One of us is always on watch. Make sure he has water and find out what happened when he wakes."

Joy and Noah nodded.

"Where did you find him?" Grace demanded.

"At the homeless village, like I said," Blake replied. "He was like that and came up to my van on the side of the road."

"Why were you on the side of the road? Why not pull into the camp like Mark always does?"

"I wasn't sure... I didn't..." Blake stumbled, then seeing a bucket full of blood-soaked rags, he gagged. "I'm not good with blood..." He bent over and put his hands on his knees, breathing heavily.

Grace fumed at Blake's hesitation. She moved to the bedroom and a moment later returned with a shotgun.

"Hey!" Blake jumped back.

"Mom?" Joy asked.

"It's okay, peanut. We protect our family."

She stuck the barrel of the gun inches from Blake's face. "Last time my husband went missing, a terrorist set off a bomb and then shot him. A terrorist group, posing as a religious group, betrayed a friend. He should have died that day if not for the Lord!"

Grace starred down the barrel at Blake.

"You know me, Grace. Mark and I have been working together for months, years. They shot at me too. You see this?" He pointed to the many cuts on the right side of his face. "They blew out the window of the van trying to kill us, both of us!"

"Why were you on the side of the road? No one parks up there!"

"I didn't go down because..."

"Because why?" Grace shouted, pushing the barrel even closer to his nose.

"Because I was scared! Okay? It sucks going into that camp!"

Grace lowered the gun and tilted her head. "Why?" she said calmly.

"I get families out of the country, Grace. There's a war going on. Do you know what it's like to go past border patrols while there's a war going on?"

Grace took a deep breath and lowered the gun completely, but she continued to eye him skeptically.

"A year ago, there were six of us. Now, just me." Blake poked his chest. "Every week, more families are torn apart, and the camp grows. I can get only one out a week, but for how long? How long until I disappear because some patrol guard goes on a power trip?"

"I'm sorry, Blake. By all accounts, Mark died because a friend betrayed him. The good Lord brought him back, and I want my man of God to live out his days."

Blake let out a deep breath as Grace went around the corner and put the gun away.

"Tell me more about what you saw. Who was shooting at you?" Grace asked when she returned and sat near Mark.

"Two men. They were huge, never seen them before. They were chasing Mark, firing at us, and I'm guessing they were the ones responsible for that," he pointed to Mark's stomach. "He couldn't talk much once we got away."

Grace jumped at that.

"Kids, get our overnight bags and supplies."

"On it!" Noah called out, running back to the room he shared with his sister.

"We just got here. And he's still out," Blake said.

"Blake, we've lived in war-torn countries before. Eventually, you are going to upset someone. Ninety-nine percent of the people in this world are normal folks, but every so often you get a tribal leader, a political party, or *whoever* that rages against you like the devil himself. And, you have two choices." Grace turned to see Noah and Joy holding already packed duffle bags. "Good kids, thank you." She turned back to Blake. "You walk into the fire, trusting God, or you stay alive, trusting God."

"Sounds like we're trusting God," he said.

Grace tossed him a bag. "Come on, kids. Let's get your dad into the van."

Chapter 15

Check Your Email

Matthew

"Hello?" Matthew answered.

"Matt, where are you? I need those numbers!" Eugene Simmons, Matthew's boss, hollered.

"It's Sunday, Gene. What's going on?"

"Yes, it's Sunday. The same Sunday we've talked about all week. Jaden and I are in Missouri, and you're supposed to be on the call."

"I was never invited or told about a—"

"You know what, Matt. I'm done with this. Jaden's been keeping me posted. You've been unresponsive and now a no show. We don't treat people like that in this business. You weren't this way before. Everything has changed in the last year."

Everything has changed. Matthew thought as he imagined the Ark.

"We gave you time during that court thing."

You suspended me.

"You were the best analyst we've ever had. Maybe we promoted you too quick."

"Excuse me, Mr. Simmons. I've been working all week to get that plant's output up. I told Jaden the probability, but he won't accept the natural constraints–"

"Yeah, I've heard. He's here. Remember? We shared a flight and I'm not happy with what I'm hearing."

Matthew's jaw clenched as he wanted to scream into the phone, to tell his boss that Jaden had a reputation of selling out his colleagues. He took a deep breath to gather his thoughts, but it only gave his boss more time to vent his frustration.

"And another thing, you have a full team, shouldn't they be running those numbers?"

"We've discussed this," Matthew fired back. "There are a dozen *priority* projects going on now. I'm helping clear the load, but the deadlines aren't realistic."

"That's a leadership problem. You should be able to motivate them."

"Motivation eventually runs out. We're over-working our most productive assets. Just like Jaden's request for the Missouri plant's output, the demand on us right now isn't sustainable. If we don't change, we'll need to add more head count."

"We don't have approval for new heads!" Eugene screamed.

"Well, then get ready to rehire as people leave. Slow down and keep talent or stop once they leave!"

"We're not having the head count discussion again. Remember Matthew, there are no bad teams, only bad leaders."

Matthew felt like he was out of his body. Rage boiled inside him as sweat beaded on his forehead. With everything that had happened - the whirlwind of demons, death, and trials that were trying to rip his church and family apart - now his boss was calling him a poor leader?

J and the girls stopped talking on the couch and looked at Matthew.

Eugene went silent, but Matthew heard voices in the background as Eugene and Jaden talked away from the phone. He could hear his work being discredited as Jaden undercut him.

"It's your choice, boss! What problem do you want to deal with? It's A or B!" Matthew shouted.

"It's never just A or B, and this time it's C," Eugene responded in a bitter tone.

"What?" Matthew said.

"You had such potential, Matt. But you wasted it."

"Wasted?" Matthew screamed.

"You're fired, Matthew!"

Matthew fell silent, his white knuckles squeezing the life out of the phone.

"Security will clear out your desk," Eugene hung up.

Matthew lowered his arm and let the phone dangle in his hand. J and the girls were silent as they watched him.

Then, the rage that filled his heart during the call returned. Matthew gripped his phone, squeezing it so tight the plastic case popped off the glass screen. He turned and threw it towards the wall. He didn't see it slam the couch cushion only a foot from Beth's head. She jumped back and hid under an oversized pillow, a look of terror on her face as she peeked out at her father.

Matthew didn't notice his daughters watching him as he stormed into the bathroom. He leaned over the sink, head down, eyes closed, and hands pressing into the countertop with such force that his skin turned white around his palms. He pushed with all his might, as if trying to squeeze a diamond out of the porcelain countertop.

"What happened?" J asked.

"I got fired," Matthew said sharply, anger in his tone.

"I'm sorry, buddy. I..." But Matthew couldn't hear J anymore. He raised his head and looked into the mirror. His forehead sweaty and his eyebrows scrunched into a V as his jaw tensed, and hovering around him, a demonic black cloud.

Chapter 16

Anger Management

Matthew

"Girls, can you go play outside?" J said as Matthew stared into the bathroom mirror.

The girls went out to the back porch and started blowing bubbles through little plastic wands from two small soap-filled bottles.

"Hey?" J asked softly as Matthew continued to stare at himself.

J looked at his friend's hands. They were clenching the countertop in a vise grip, a mix of white knuckles and bulging veins.

"Hey, Matt? You want to talk about it?" J tried again, but Matthew just stared into the mirror like he was in a trance. J couldn't see the black cloud hovering above him. The large red eyes glowed over Matthew's head. The demon that tried bringing him into the sea of darkness was now floating in and around Matthew, stoking his emotions.

Sweat dripped from Matthew's nose, splashing on the floor of the small half bathroom. J moved his hand towards his friend's shoulder, but in a flash, Matthew backhanded it away.

"You seriously just swatted me away?" J held up his hands in disbelief.

Matthew didn't consciously feel the movement; he just wanted to be alone. He felt a sense of dread and loneliness, like no one in the world would understand what he felt in that moment.

"You have a great resume, wonderful experience. I know this sucks, but I've seen people in worse situations bounce back. Your dad and I coach them. We pray for them all the time."

"Get out," Matthew grumbled.

J stood shocked, watching Matthew's arms and legs tremble.

"Get out!" Matthew screamed and slammed the door in J's face.

J took a step back, disbelief and anguish washing over him, but quickly his face steeled.

"No. I'm not leaving, brother. You stand there as long as you want, but I'm not leaving this house." He turned back to the couch, keeping a view of the bathroom entrance and of the girls out back.

Inside the bathroom, Matthew's muscles violently shook as he tried to maintain balance. He could feel a strength pulse through his body, but it came with disdain for every thought. A sense of hopelessness washed over him, making him feel alone, isolated, and cold.

But he recognized the sensation. These were the same feelings that came over him when the demon tried pulling his soul into the sea of darkness.

"It's your fault," flickered in the back of his mind.

"No," he said. His hands shooting up to his head, as if he could physically hold his thoughts together. He looked in the mirror to see the red eyes over him. The surrounding darkness swelled, filling the room.

"You're killing your family," it echoed.

Matthew opened his mouth like a scream, stretching his jaw as far as his muscles were capable. He silently mouthed the words of a scream: *Get out!* A war raged in his mind.

Outside the bathroom, J stood and paced. He saw the girls playing through the back door and remembered Zech asking about his phone. Trotting out to his Jeep, he grabbed the phone and darted back inside. Seeing the bathroom door still closed and the girls still playing, he stole a moment to check the device.

Missed calls from Zech hovered over a text.

The preview read: *Found him. Hard to watch.*

J opened the message and pressed the accompanying link.

A video loaded with a young man on the screen with his hands tied behind his back. He knelt before a black wall. J squinted at the screen. He looked familiar, but his eyes and face were so swollen and battered he couldn't distinguish him.

A white card flashed on the screen, held in front of the camera by someone offscreen: *He is your watered-down message.*

The first card dropped, a new card legible: *He is dying.*

A third: *Your message is dying.*

And another: *Because we are killing it.*

The last card dropped, and three masked men came into the frame, standing around the tortured man. The physically imposing trio stared down at the constrained young man. Their hands were clenched into fists or holding malicious objects that flashed in the camera's light.

The hostage's posture tightened and his lip curled, his face in defiance of the coming brutality. Then J recognized the defiant expression, and his heart sank in his chest like an anchor into a bottomless sea.

Lucas.

J watched his friend and caught the sparkle of tears forming in the corner of his friend's eyes as he knelt defiantly.

"No," J whispered to himself. His eyes watered, matching Lucas's.

The three men, as if given a silent cue from off camera, took turns punching, swinging, and kicking a prisoner that couldn't fight back.

The video cut out, and J wiped his eyes.

"Matt, watch this. It's Lucas, they..." J walked to the bathroom. "It's horrible."

Matthew, his arm muscles still twitching and clutching at the countertop like he was trying to rip the porcelain off the cabinet below, turned his head to look at the closed door.

In his mind, he heard laughter. A booming voice from somewhere in his mind, enjoying the pain and suffering.

Matthew struggled to contain his rage. His arms shook as he took them off the countertop and held them together, squeezing his hands as his arm muscles tensed. The voice kept laughing.

"We need to help him. They're beating him to death," J said through the door. The screen displayed a still shot of a leg swinging into Lucas's midsection.

"You're weak," the voice in Matthew's head spoke. *"Jobless, worthless, and wasting your time."*

"Stop!" Matthew called out to the voice.

J jumped back from the door.

"NO!" Matthew screamed into the mirror. The world around him went dim as the surrounding darkness expanded like a bottomless pit. He couldn't stop himself from being pulled into the black hole.

"Matt," J called.

Matthew clenched a fist as the turmoil in his mind boiled over. His left hand snapped up, punching the mirror. Shards of glass exploded through the small room.

J kicked at the door, and the hollow wood swung as the latch snapped through the door frame.

"Worthless," the voice echoed in Matthew's mind in between its laughter.

J looked on in shock. "Matt, get it–"

"Excuse me, Uncle J," Beth said. The two girls at his side.

"Girls, let's go outside. Your dad needs a minute," J said frantically as he stepped in front of them, shielding the view of their tormented father.

"But Dad is acting weird," Beth said, a matter-of-fact tone in her voice.

"He is. You're right. And we should give him a moment, huh?"

"No. Mom told us if Dad ever acts weird like this, that he needs a reminder," Beth said as Lyn held up Matthew's Bible. J saw the blinding glow.

Lyn moved it toward Matthew, but he pulled his leg away as if repulsed.

In his mind, Matthew rejoiced as the demonic laughter faded to silence.

"You're brilliant," J said as he grabbed the Bible from Lyn's hands and slammed it into Matthew's chest before he could react.

Matthew shot back and fell against the wall. His hands caught the Bible and held it to his chest. His face returned to normal, a relieved expression forming.

"Feel better, Dad?" Beth asked.

Matthew and J both looked at the girls in awe.

"Mom said you would. I love you, Dad." Beth said as she hugged him.

"I love you, Dad," Lyn copied as she took her turn hugging her dad.

"You need a boo-boo pack," she said, reaching for her dad's hand and examining the bloody knuckles.

"Thank you, sweetie," Matthew said in a hoarse voice. "Thank you, both. I was having a bit of trouble getting out of my head."

He looked from Beth to Lyn, and then to J. "Thank you," he said as his eyes grew watery.

"You're welcome," Beth said as she walked out the bathroom.

"You're welcome!" Lyn repeated as she ran after her sister. "Come on, sis! Bubble quest!"

J raised his eyebrows and looked down at Matthew. "You... good?"

"I am now. That was..." Matthew shook his head. "That felt like hell."

"Getting fired or breaking your mirror?" J extended a hand to help his friend up.

"Both, but..." Matthew stood and looked at the shattered mirror. Countless reflections of himself looked back through the spiderweb-like pattern.

One for each disaster. He thought to himself as he lowered his head and walked out of the bathroom.

"Thank you for being here," he said.

"Always. Here, better use the dark one so it doesn't stain." J handed him a black hand towel from the nearby linen closet. "Get cleaned up, because there is something you need to see."

I've seen enough, Matthew thought to himself as images of the demon, Nancy, and Jaden ran through his mind.

"Any word from Mark?" Matthew asked as he washed his hand and wrapped the towel around the gashes on his knuckles.

J shook his head.

Matthew reached to the side of the linen closet and pulled out a broom.

"I'll start. You watch. It's horrible." J handed his phone to Matthew and took the broom. "I never thought I'd see one of these with someone we knew."

Matthew took the phone and pressed play. He cringed as he watched the men attack Lucas, seeing the dark clouds of demons all over them as their rage turned to violence. But Matthew noticed something. It was faint, but there. He pressed the timeline of the video and moved the timer back, rewatching the men stand over Lucas. The darkness engulfed the men, but as they stood around their captive, Matthew noticed a brightness in the center of the frame. Lucas's chest glowed like a tiny candle in the wind, refusing to go out.

Then the video pulled away as J's phone vibrated for an incoming call.

"Hey, you have a call," Matthew called out. His eyes widened as he saw the name on the screen. "It's Mark!"

Chapter 17

Hospital Bed

Luke Light - Atlanta, Georgia

Luke slowly opened his eyes to the quiet room. His head turned as he laid stomach-down on the white sheets. The soft beeping of medical equipment echoed from the devices at his bedside. The fabric of the crisp, white bed sheets rustled as he tried to move his arms and legs. His body ached and screamed with pain.

As he slowly wiggled, he felt something pulling on his chest and parts of his arms and hand. The fog in his awakening mind cleared and he looked down toward his side. Wires from the sensors dotting his body flowed away from him and into machines at his bedside.

"Good morning," Helen said gently from a single-person Murphy Bed in the hospital room's corner.

"Hey," Luke replied in a scratchy voice. He tried clearing his dry throat.

"There's water." Helen nodded to the Styrofoam cup at Luke's bedside. He struggled to raise his arm, cringing as his back flared in pain.

"I got it." Helen flipped the blanket off herself and helped Luke with the water, holding it to his mouth as he drew from the straw.

"I always knew your family was crazy," she shook her head. "But what have you got us into this time?"

Luke's eyes darted up to see his wife smiling. She patted his arm and then moved to clean up her bed, soon flipping it back up into the wall.

"Your parents were here," Helen said. A split second later, Zech and Mary came back into the room. "Correction, your parents are here."

Mary moved swiftly past Zech and took a seat at Luke's side.

"How are you?"

"I'm okay, I guess. What happened?" He looked around the room.

"The entire office building at Hope of Christ is gone. You're the only thing that made it out," Zech said.

Luke's eyes widened.

"What do you remember, son?" Zech asked.

"Not much. The building was empty, but I thought... I thought there was a meeting. The church's board."

Zech grunted as he looked at Luke's phone on the wooden nightstand next to Helen's bag. "Helen showed me the text and mentioned your youth pastor. You think he sent the text?"

"Tyler? I can't believe he'd... He's a nice guy, mid-twenties, been here for a little over a year."

"How well do you *really* know him?" Zech asked.

"Not as much as I'd like. The kids and Helen liked the rumors of him leaving."

"Leaving?" Zech turned to Helen.

"Just rumors, but when I asked Nina, she said he's been distant, not the same as when he started running the group. The kids say he's been volunteering outside of church and isn't around as much."

Zech nodded.

"I hadn't heard that. Local missions?" Luke said.

Helen shook her head. "No. He's talked about political science at past parent meetings. Local campaigns."

"Running a youth group is not a simple job. Especially at a big church like yours." Mary said.

"But hang on," Luke looked at his dad. "You think Tyler was a part of this? Of the bombing?"

"You get a text from him about a meeting, but there's no meeting, and moments later the building goes up?" Zech raised his eyebrows.

"We don't know if he sent the text or organized the meeting," Luke said.

"With all that's happened today..." Zech trailed off. Luke looked at his dad and noticed he was clutching his Bible on his lap. His father gripped the binding of the battered green leather with both hands. Grey duct tape held the binding in place, and concealed the piece of the Ark, repairing damage from the standoff with Terrence. Luke could tell his father's mind was racing.

"What's happened today?" he asked.

As if on cue, Mary jumped up and pulled out her phone.

"It's Grace!" she said. A smile flashed across her face, but she quickly restrained it.

"I'll join you," Helen said as she stood. She patted Luke's feet through the blanket before following Mary out into the hallway.

Luke looked at his father expectantly.

"You're not the only one."

"Only one?" Luke looked towards the door, his eyes trailing behind his mother and wife. "Mark?"

Zech nodded. "He had a donation drop off this morning. Grace sent friends, and found his truck, but not Mark."

Zech walked to the window. "And there's Lucas."

"French Lucas?" Luke asked.

Zech nodded and pulled out his phone. He pressed the screen, then handed it to Luke. His jaw dropped as he watched the video of Lucas being beaten.

"The New Christians," Luke said.

Zech nodded.

"Mark's alive!" Mary burst into the room. She grinned from ear to ear, teary-eyed, as she hugged Zech. "Someone tried to kill him, but he got home."

"They're leaving the country. If they get to Chişinău, they can fly out of Moldova."

"If?" Luke asked.

Chapter 18

Over and Out

Mark Light - Ukraine

"We're almost there. How's he doing?" Blake asked over the sound of rushing wind through the van's shattered window. Small pieces of jagged glass scattered the floor under Blake.

Grace looked down at Mark. He lay sprawled across the second row with his head resting on her lap. Joy and Noah held a couple of stuffed duffle bags in the third row.

"Still out," Grace said.

"He needs to be awake for us to cross the border. I have trouble getting citizens through without being detained, let alone bloody, passed out foreigners," Blake said.

"What happens when you're 'detained'?" Noah asked.

"Uh..." Blake hesitated, then saw Grace nodding an approval to answer. He spoke slowly as he answered the boy.

"The government around here is going through *trouble* right now. And they don't like people leaving. They think it's someone retreating, unwilling to fight for their country, or worse..."

"Like a bad guy?" Joy asked.

"Yeah, like a spy!" Noah said.

Blake gulped. "Yes. And we do *not* want them to think that, because then you get detained."

"So, what is detained?" Noah asked again.

"When the guards put you in a little room and ask you questions," Blake said.

"That's not so bad," Joy said.

"I've seen people released in five minutes, or..." Blake trailed off.

"Or?" Noah said.

"They don't come out," Grace finished.

"He needs to be awake!" Blake hollered behind him.

"Let's pull over," Grace suggested.

"Not on these roads. Patrols are the same as the border guards. Some are great, friendly folks, and some, well, not so much," Blake said. "How about we turn around and take him to a hospital?"

"No! We don't know who's after him. We must leave," Grace countered.

Blake shook his head as the van turned a long bend in the road. The green pine trees towered next to the highway.

"Uh oh," he said.

"What's 'uh oh?' Why are we slowing?" Grace asked, looking out the windshield.

"They moved the checkpoint up," Blake said. He waved as one of two guards walked out onto the road and motioned for him to stop.

"He needs to be awake," he said softly, forcing a smile for the guards. "I'll try to buy time, but remember, you're missionaries on your way back home. You are going for supplies, then bringing them back."

"We are missionaries, and that'd be great to get supplies!" Noah said.

"Yeah, we preach the message of Jesus to all children of God!" Joy followed.

"We're going to need Jesus right about now," Blake said as he waved at the guard and stopped the van. "Stay here and get him awake. He'll need to speak for your family."

"Pryvit, miy druzhe!" Blake called out as he closed the van door.

One car rested in front of him with a guard reviewing papers. The guard's hostile body language toward the small four-door sedan gave Blake a sense of pity for those in the car, and he hoped his guard didn't develop the same demeanor. The disgruntled guard shuffled through the papers and peered back into the sedan.

"Pryvit," the second guard said to Blake as he approached the van. "Podorozhuyete sami?"

Blake didn't answer. His attention turned back to the first car.

"Vyydy! Vyydy!" the guard screamed as he grabbed the door handle and swung the faded brown door open. Two hands stuck out in surrender, but the border patrol reached in and violently pulled out the elderly man by his jacket.

"Chotyry?" the guard shouted at the old man as he waved for everyone in the car to come out. A couple, who to Blake appeared to be in their late thirties or early forties, slowly came out.

"Chotyry?" The guard said as he raised his hands to his side and let them drop. The papers of the car's occupants flailing in his hand. He pointed to the back seat and down, as if motioning for something under the seat.

The woman cried out and moved to cover the open car door. "Nemaye! Nem–" she cried out before her husband grabbed her and pleaded to the guard in a calmer tone. The unsympathetic guard shook his head and motioned for whatever was in the car to come out.

"Ay!" Blake's guard said.

"Ya, ya," he said, pointing to himself and telling the guard it was just him in the van.

Blake noticed his guard turned his back to the commotion, as if avoiding a difficult colleague.

"Podorozhuyete sami?" the patrol asked again. This time, Blake forced himself to maintain eye contact despite the commotion.

"Oh, yes, I'm alone. I mean," Blake caught himself answering in English and corrected himself, also standing up in a straighter posture as he did. "Tak, ya odyn," he said. Then he apologized for the language slip up, "Ybachennya."

"Ah, English?" The guard smiled. "I am... practicing my own."

Blake smiled and nodded, feeling relieved for his luck with a more personable guard he could connect with. "Very good. That was well done. How long?"

"Oh..." The guard thought for his words. "Maybe one and two years?"

"Nice. And 'one *or* two' years." Blake corrected as he flashed a smile.

The guard nodded thankfully and returned the smile. "So, you are traveling alone. Where? Why?"

Blake's face went pale, realizing his quick answer went against their prearranged story. "Uh..." He stumbled as he thought how to backtrack. The commotion behind him saved him precious seconds as the woman let out a high-pitched scream.

Blake and the guard couldn't help but turn to see. To Blake's horror, a young girl, maybe four or five years old, was being pulled out of the car. The mother screamed as the father pleaded with the guard.

"Chotyry!" the guard said as he pointed to each person and counted. "Odyn, dva, try, chotyry." Then held up the papers, waving them in their face. "Try! Til'ky try!"

"You must have all the right papers, my friend. My partner does not like to see four people, but only three papers," the guard told him as they turned back to look at the van.

"Of course," Blake said.

The guard eyed him suspiciously. "What happened to face?" he pointed at the cuts and puffy redness spread across one side of Blake's face.

"Cat," Blake blurted out without thinking as he shrugged. He stared blankly at the man, feeling foolish for the response as the guard returned a blank stare. Blake could feel sweat beading on his forehead.

The silent moment dragged on forever as Blake wondered what alarms were blaring in the guard's mind, but he forced himself to maintain eye contact and not back off or elaborate on his story.

A moment later, the guard broke his stoic gaze into Blake's eyes and began laughing. "My sister has cat, too. Little devil. Hates me. I give treats but it runs and..." he searched for the words, "it hisses! It hisses at me when I give treats. You believe that?"

Blake let out a sign of relief and nodded along with the guard.

"Cats..." Blake shrugged.

"Let me look and you go," the guard said pleasantly. "Your papers? And I do my checks."

He moved to the van's sliding side door, but Blake stepped in front of him. The guard's head snapped back, looking at Blake with suspicion.

"My papers. I'll get my papers first," Blake said, trying to halt the man before dashing back to the driver-side door. "I'm on a supply run to help our war efforts," he called back.

"Yes, yes," the guard dismissed.

To Blake's dismay, the guard continued to move towards the van door. Blake tried to dart back and grab the black handle before the guard, but he was too late. The guard pulled the handle and quickly rolled the door away.

Blake froze as he waited for the guard's response, but the man stood motionless as he looked inside.

Blake's heart sank. He tried to throw out an excuse, but the words wouldn't form.

"Uh... We're on a supply run... For the war efforts..." his mouth twitched more than spoke. He envisioned himself and the entire Light family being detained, shipped off to an over-crowded holding facility. Rumors said the horrid facilities were in such squalor, they made local prisons look like resorts.

The guard turned back to Blake with an expressionless face. Blake stood like a statue.

"And your papers?" he asked with raised eyebrows.

"Yes. Yes, of course."

Blake scrambled to the driver-side door. His hand paused on the black door handle as he took a deep breath, cringing inside at his mistake to say he was alone. He exhaled and threw open the door.

Empty seats.

He saw the guard through the van, growing impatient, as he waited for Blake's papers. Nothing but empty crates and a plastic grocery bag spread across the floor in between them.

Blake gathered himself and pulled out his papers from the pocket on the door.

Closing the door, he looked out to the side of the highway, towards the dense pine tree forest. A handful of low-hanging branches swung as if a wind gently pressed on them, but the rest of the limbs and leaves sat motionless.

Blake smiled.

Chapter 19

Worth more than Jewels

Matthew

"We have savings. We'll figure it out," Liz said quietly to Matthew as they sat on the couch in the dim evening light.

"Hun, I'm sorry. I..."

"If they don't want you, then they don't get you. You worked your butt off, and they couldn't see the lies. That's it," she reassured him.

"This is just so maddening," he said.

"My work is bringing in more income than ever before, and how much is in savings?"

"Six months, eight to nine if we stretch it," Matthew said.

"There we go. We'll be fine," Liz said as she rubbed his arm.

Matthew looked at his wife with admiration. He couldn't believe the amount of strength she had, even in the darkest of times. Tough times reminded him how truly grateful he was for her.

He leaned in and gave her a kiss on the forehead. "Thank you, Liz. I don't know what I'd do without you. And I'm very glad I married up."

She smiled at him. "You'd manage, just like I know you'll find another job and we'll be okay."

Matthew nodded, feeling a sense of relief wash over him. Yet he couldn't help but feel like he was failing his family. They had already been through so much in the past year with the Ark, Isaiah's death, the trial and subsequent financial fallout. And now, not playing along with Jaden at work put his wife and daughters in the crosshairs of financial struggles.

He stood up from the couch and walked over to the window, staring out at the darkening sky. The trees outside swayed gently in the wind, a calming sight that he wished reflected his racing and stressed mind.

"How about we take the girls with us next weekend?" Liz said. "I know your mom wanted to bring them, and now she's in D.C., but let's do it."

Matthew turned, surprised. "You still plan to go?"

"Absolutely." She stood up. "Ashley is flying down. Millie is joining us, too. And even if your mom can't come, it'll be a great weekend."

"Mark, Lucas, and Luke... You saw the bathroom, it's coming after me too," Matthew said.

"Then away from you is the best play place to be," Liz laughed.

Matthew didn't laugh.

"Okay, too far. I'm sorry. But seriously, the girls will be fine between the three of us. Most of the schedule is a choose-your-breakout type style, anyway. We'll alternate the girls, and you keep your Bible strapped to your heart."

Matthew let out a deep breath and shook his head.

"And the resort has a pool," Liz said as she hugged him. "They'll play all day and sleep like logs."

She kissed him, but he remained stone-faced.

"Hey," she pulled him close and locked eyes, "do you remember when you were in the hospital, when the trial was going on?"

Matthew nodded.

"You remember how my blog and all my social media blew up with all those crazy, hateful comments?"

"Yup." A tiny smile on his face. He remembered how she moved through all the hate with grace. Her determination inspired him.

"Well, I'm not letting whoever this is stop us from living our lives. If we hole up here forever, they win no matter what."

He gave her a full smile, then leaned in and returned her kiss.

"Plus, I wouldn't mind getting the girls away from you," she said.

Chapter 20

Sleeping Dogs Don't Bark

Luke Light - Atlanta, Georgia

"I'll bring them by tomorrow. They'll be so excited to see you." Helen kissed Luke goodbye.

"I'm excited to see them. Tell your mom I said hi," he said.

"Will do. She'll probably come by too."

"We're out too, son," Zech said. "Seems the hearings will take place in a couple of days. Amazing how fast the government works when a post gets fifteen million likes."

"Nancy leading the charge?" Luke asked.

"Yes, that awful woman," Mary uncharacteristically quipped.

"Mom?" Luke said, laughing.

"What? She is. Lying about your grandfather and extorting the church. Now she's all religious and upright, using these attacks for political gain. She's awful." She stuck her tongue out in disgust.

"Paul's got his apocalypse RV stacked with all we need if the world ends," Zech smiled. "Him and Jimmy are already halfway up 95. We'll get a few hours under our belt tonight, maybe Chattanooga, or Knoxville, and then make for D.C. in the morning."

"Thanks for coming," Luke said as his mother bent down and kissed his head. Zech shook his hand, holding it for a while and embracing Luke's arm with his free hand.

The sounds of beeping and other life monitoring devices rang through the otherwise quiet hospital hallways.

Luke wished Helen had brought his computer. He was dying to check his email and connect with his business leaders, not to mention check his growing business's third quarter income, but Helen wouldn't allow it.

"No computer, no work. Not until you're home and healthy," she had told him.

Unable to fall asleep, he looked around the room, wishing he had a book. He pulled out his phone, which thankfully Helen didn't confiscate, and checked his emails. He remembered quickly how much he hated reading emails and books from the small device. He smiled, wondering if she knew he'd try to work from his phone but would give up in five minutes.

"You know me well," he whispered.

He reached for the remote and flipped through channels. His body positioning made watching the far corner of the ceiling where the television hung difficult. Finding nothing but infomercials and replays of Law of Order only helped him lose interest faster. He soon drifted off to sleep.

Hours later, the glow of the TV still illuminated the room when a nurse entered and checked the machines hooked up to Luke. He awoke as she examined the burns on his back.

The nurse shushed him gently as his eyes blinked open.

"It's okay, child. Get your rest."

She scanned the machines once more, making notes on a chart, and returned to Luke's bedside to examine his skin around the IV and replace the saline solution. The replacement bag, full of fresh saline, rocked back and forth from the metal pole. Luke watched the bag, reading the details on the label as the nurse worked. Soon, his eyes grew heavy and closed.

She flipped off the TV and put the remote on the bedside table next to Luke's Bible.

"Getting better every day, praise the Lord. Goodnight, child," the nurse whispered as she left. The door gently closed behind her. Bright lights from the hallway stretched through the rectangular window in the door like a lighthouse into a dark night.

Luke drifted back to sleep.

Sometime later in the night, his eyes flickered, awakening as he heard the door open. He heard footsteps, but, his heavy eyes quickly closed again.

There was shuffling in the room as his mind drifted in between reality and dream. A gentle noise of clips being pinched and released, along with the rattle of the IV bag and pole, filled his ears. He listened to the sounds of the kind woman as she once again replaced the IV bag.

How long was I asleep?

The nurse's body leaned into the bed, common for the night nurse checking his wounds, but the sound of her breath was different. She was a sweet woman whose breath passed over Luke during her checks like a breeze. This was a labored, heavier breath over him.

A different nurse, Luke thought, keeping his eyes shut but his mind coming more awake.

Then the nurse bumped the nightstand, rocking the small wooden tower that held his Bible, and the ancient piece of the Ark inside, and the TV remote. The remote fell and a banging sound pinged through the room as the TV came to light. The famous two-tone beat of Law and Order filled his ears as Luke's eye shot open.

A man stood over him, looking at the TV and then down for the remote. Luke didn't recognize the stranger.

As the man found the remote, Luke noticed the swinging IV bag. A new bag with a new label, totally different from every other bag during his stay.

The man snapped off the TV and turned back to Luke, who quickly closed his eyes and pretended to remain asleep. He tried to breathe normally, keeping his back gently rising and falling as he resisted the urge to jump out of bed. In his weakened state, and facing down on the bed, he was no match for the large man that loomed over him.

He remained still, pretending to sleep for what felt like hours. The long seconds of silence passed. Luke could feel the man above him, watching him. Luke feared he would start sweating as he tried to control his breath.

To his relief, the man moved away, and Luke heard footsteps going away from the bed. The door opened and closed.

Feeling as if the man was still watching from the window, he resisted every urge that told him to jump up and scream, but kept his eyes closed and his body motionless.

Finally, he peeked open his eyes.

The room spun as his eyelids were heavier than ever.

The new IV fluid.

He looked up at the bag.

The emergency call button.

His arms felt like massive concrete poles as he searched. Luke tried to sit up and reach to his bedside, where the red cord came out from the wall. He glimpsed it tied to a nearby plug, moved out of reach.

His entire body felt heavier, and most of all his eyelids.

Fighting the urge to close his eyes, he followed the IV cord as it went from the bag, winding through the bars of his bedside and into his arm. Tape covered the plastic piece housing the needle and the fluid that was knocking him out.

Lying on his stomach, he needed to reach one arm under himself. Seconds felt like hours as he wiggled his arm below his belly.

Finally, the IV was in reach. He pulled on it, but the paper tape resisted. His fingers lost coordination as they tried to pick free the tape. He pulled on the needle again, frustrated as fatigue filled his body. But his hand slid off and lay motionless. The heart monitor beeped slower and slower as the deadly toxin of the new fluid filled his veins.

Luke didn't see the Bible glow next to him as his body felt a flicker of strength pass through from his brain, down through his arm, and to his hand.

His hand came to life and pulled the needle one more time.

Chapter 21

Into the Woods
Mark Light - Eastern Europe

Mark awoke to a woman screaming. He sat up and immediately felt the stabbing pain in his stomach. He winced, his arms going to his midsection, but the motion rolled him off the bench seat in the van. The thud of his fall jolted Grace and the kids, who were just as happy to see him awake as they were cautious about the noise.

He sat up, his eyes darting around the unfamiliar place.

"Hey, hey, it's alright. We're in Blake's van," Grace said, shifting the crate to get him back on the seat. "Can you wake up any louder?"

She peeked through the windshield.

"What do you–" He stopped defending himself when he saw his wife smiling.

"We're at the border check. I couldn't keep you at home, and I don't trust the hospital after Blake said men were after you," she said.

Mark looked around and took in the situation. "Good girl," he finally said, and he kissed the side of Grace's head. Wincing, he tried to get comfortable in the seat and peer out the windows. "I don't ever remember being home."

"Your mind wasn't really there," Joy whispered.

"Yeah, you were out, Dad," Noah followed.

Mark looked down at his stitches and the red puffiness growing around it. "Nice stitches."

"Thank you," Grace kissed his cheek. "You'll need real medical care, though."

"Yeah..." Mark exhaled. "But first, let's get our family safe. Which crossing are we at?"

"M16, northwest to Chişinău," Joy said.

Mark raised his eyebrows and looked back at his daughter.

"What? We study geography, Dad."

"Okay, so then why M16 and not M15?" he quizzed her.

"M15 is closer to the war, which means it gets more refugees and therefore is stricter on searches," Noah said.

"You kids really do listen, eh? Must have an excellent teacher," Mark beamed with pride at the two kids and then flashed a smile at Grace.

Mark leaned forward, looking through the windshield. Blake stood next to a guard, both of their backs to the white van as they watched the other border agent angrily question the occupants of a brown sedan.

"Uh oh," Mark said.

"What?" Grace asked.

"I know that one," Mark pointed towards the disgruntled guard. "Besides what Joy said, he's the other reason we avoid the M15."

"So, what does that mean?" Grace asked.

"It means they are rotating guards, and we aren't passing through. Not if he sees me."

"What? Why?" Grace said. "You've never told us that about M15."

"Well..." Mark hesitated, and Grace's curious expression turned stern.

"I kind of spit on him once," Mark said.

"Ew," Joy said.

"Way to go, Dad," Noah laughed.

"You *spit* on him?" Grace said, her eyes widening.

"Hey, I'm not proud of it. I rode with Chad; remember him?"

Grace nodded.

Mark turned back to the kids. "Chad was Blake before Blake. Well, I rode with Chad to take a family over the border and pick up supplies."

"That's our exact story now. We're missionaries going on a supply run," Grace interjected.

"That's good. But that time, he didn't allow it. Wasn't a fan of missionaries and told Chad and me we were cowards. Foreigners or not, he said we should fight for Ukraine. He shoved Chad and turned away the family. All three kids were under six years old, one a baby." Mark shook his head as a sad expression washed over his face. "They had nowhere to go. I lost it, and didn't want to hit him, so..."

"That's when you came home with a black eye!" Grace started shouting, but quickly returned her voice to a whisper. "You said you hit it on your supply run."

"Well, I did," Mark said as he shrugged.

"Leaving out that a border agent hit you is a big omission."

"Okay, okay. I'm sorry. Thankfully, he let us go after he tried knocking my eye out with the butt of his rifle. I don't know why he didn't throw us in jail. But Chad took the family in, and a week later he disappeared, along with the entire family. I like to think he made it through and helped them set up a new life. But... I think they tried again and ran into *him* again." Mark pointed to the guard as he ripped a young girl from the backseat of the car.

"Kids, did you study what's over the border?" Mark asked.

"The town of Pervomaisc, Moldova. A nice little town, but Russian-friendly so geopolitical tensions are high right now," Joy said, once again amazing her father. "Oh, and we have to cross the Luhan River. The only bridge anywhere close is right past this traffic stop." She pointed past the border patrol station.

"Thank you." Mark nodded to her with a smile. He thought for a moment and looked at his wife. She nodded in return, as if reading his mind.

"We need to go, kids. Now," Mark said as he picked up a bag, trying not to wince as he moved to open the sliding door opposite Blake and the guard.

He opened it gently and they silently slid out. Hugging the side of the van, Mark peeked over the hood at the nearby conversation between Blake and the friendlier guard. When the two men looked back at the commotion, Mark didn't hesitate.

"Go. Go," he whispered, motioning with his hands as he sent the kids and Grace running into the nearby woods.

Mark heard Blake walking toward the driver-side, but then the door on the other side of the van rolled open. Mark took the chance, holding back the urge to scream from the pain in his midsection. Hunched over, he hobbled into the woods as fast as he could.

A moment later, he looked back from a safe distance and saw Blake eyeing the tree line.

Unknown to Blake, Mark returned his friend's smile.

Chapter 22

Congressional Hearings

Zechariah - Washington, D.C.

"And if we don't do something, we're encouraging more attacks!" Nancy Pawly shouted as she beat her fist against the podium. The uproar from the packed crowd in the imposing House of Representatives would drown out her comments, if not for the microphone in front of her.

Zech sat silently, thinking through the implications of Nancy's proposal. Paul sat to his left, frequently clenching his fists or shaking his head every time she emphasized her argument. Jimmy sat to Zech's right, a picture of contemplation throughout the entire session. Paul's and Jimmy's experience building and leading successful businesses gave them a unique perspective on policy. While their faith, friendship, and seats on Zech's church's board gave them a religious perspective that blended uniquely with their marketplace success.

Paul's Shipping Yard was booming, even after the damage caused by Terrence. Zech joked Paul created such a reliable business that he could leave for a year, and it'd grow even larger before he got back. But Paul had no intention of leaving his business for a year, unless it was to defend what he thought was an unheard of and unconstitutional attack on religious freedoms.

"Did you hear her rhetoric?" Paul had shouted multiple times on the drive to D.C. "She's using these attacks to justify going after the Constitution! It's an attack on the Bill of Rights itself." Paul would then gain an audience by tapping Jimmy or Zech's knee or nodding to Mary. "It's the Free Exercise Clause! Every citizen *has the right* to practice their religion as they please, so long as the practice does not run afoul of the 'public morals.'"

That's usually when the soft-spoken Jimmy would chime in. "Or a 'compelling' governmental interest. You know when it comes down to it, whatever she's getting at with all this, she'll make a case that her ideas are an exception. She'll say it's a compelling governmental interest to protect the citizens."

Jimmy's decision to speak was rare, yet typically so profound that even a boisterous friend like Paul would stop and think. The elder man's quiet, yet strong and determined personality had influenced Zech since he was a boy. Zech's father, Isaiah, planted the Lights' church over fifty years ago, and Jimmy was one of the earliest members, becoming one of Isaiah's best friends. Jimmy watched Isaiah go through countless trials of faith, as well as life-threatening attacks on his life and family. The stoic sage, now well into his eighties, kept his mind sharp by operating a portion of his real estate-based business empire. Jimmy gradually taught and handed off parts of the business to his children.

The elderly African American man drove a nice, but used, Lincoln Continental and only donned his custom-tailored three-piece suits for holiday services at church. At Easter service two years ago, Zech was taken aback when he spotted Jimmy entering the church. Jimmy's slow and deliberate stride, paired with his unique Easter attire—a light blue suit complemented by a pink vest, a yellow tie, and bright white dress shoes—made quite the impression.

"Sometimes you gotta dunk on the rookies. Let 'em know you still got it," Jimmy had said to Zech. He smiled as his thumb flipped the lapel of his pastel suit.

With Paul and Jimmy on his church's board, and his wife's kind, honest words at home, Zech felt like he surrounded himself with the smartest, most faith-driven folks he could find. And yet Nancy's fist on the podium seemed to threaten everything.

The volume in the large room died down as Nancy ignored feverish comments and shuffled her papers. She skimmed the notes with patience, as if she were reading in a kitchen nook with a warm cup of tea, instead of in front of some of the most powerful and demanding politicians in the country.

Zech looked around the room. The chamber was filled with plush chairs and sectioned into designated areas for politicians, staff, media, and the public. The high ceiling held intricate architectural details as it covered the vast room and fell to walls adorned with portraits of the country's founders and other prominent statesmen from the nation's history.

He took a deep breath, smelling the polished wood and a hint of coffee. The smell carried in from the nearby refreshment stands in the halls outside the main auditorium-like chamber." And what would *you* propose?" a voice rang out from one side of the aisle that caught Nancy's attention. Its tone was more accusing than questioning as cheers rose from the questioner's section. Zech noticed Paul pump his fist as he mouthed the question, as if he were right in the middle of the politician's section.

Nancy seemed to at first disregard the comment, but a moment later, as the cheers leveled off, she lifted her head toward the questioner. Her confident stance and posture gave the impression she had been waiting for this.

"Oh, that's simple." She stared at the questioner. "I'm happy to be the voice of reason and offer a plan of protection for the large base of religious Americans, most of which make up *your* party, Congressman." She pointed to the man, still standing after he'd blurted out his question. "In fact, didn't your last campaign center on faith and strong moral values? We need these to uphold the Constitution, is what you said. Am I correct?" Zech could see the congressmen nodding vigorously. But after watching her in the trial against his church and family, Zech knew how Nancy worked. She was setting the man up.

"And weren't those the same ads that accused your opposition of trying to tear down the Constitution? You accused your competition of hurting the American public by opening the borders, controlling the school boards, and limiting women's reproductive choices. Yes, I remember those ads."

"And a lack of budget oversight!" The congressman shouted in response, receiving thunderous applause from his side of the aisle.

"I thought so." Nancy nodded. "So, you attacked progressive policies that are welcoming to those in need and understanding of an individual's freedom, a foundational element of our country's Constitution, yet turn around and ignore literal attacks on US soil?"

"No," the congressman shook his head, but his response was inaudible as Nancy kept speaking.

"Chemical warfare murdered all those worshipers in New York. An explosion in Atlanta could have taken more. You argue cross-aisle politics yet ignore the bullets being fired at both sides. Didn't your campaign also mention you spent time in the Army? That you would fight for our country in D.C. as you had overseas?"

The congressman took his seat. Paul's shoulders hunched as he sat back in his chair, sensing what Zech already knew. Nancy was moving in for the kill.

"You ask me what I propose? You're an elected official asking a special guest speaker, and a so-called political rival, what I'd do? Well, Mr. Congressman, I'd protect America. I'd ignore political affiliation and offer suggestions that protect *your* faith-based constituents. I'd prioritize our intelligence resources to find and capture the enemies of life and liberty. I'd protect American lives by keeping them out of the at-risk areas. If you need to hear me say it again, I'd protect Americans by whatever means necessary, because chemical warfare and bombings on US soil, murdering my fellow Americans, is NOT acceptable on my watch!"

The chamber broke out in thunderous applause, starting on the left, but members of the right gradually stood at her passionate response.

A strand of hair had escaped her tight bun during her exasperated speech. She pushed the blonde tress behind her ear and stepped back from the podium, her shoulders rising and falling as she caught her breath and scanned the room. Politicians, media, and the public all stood and continued to cheer. Zech could hardly see the Congressman who'd set up Nancy's passionate response through the commotion, but he made out many members from the man's area standing and clapping their hands. Their expressions mimicking their counterparts on the other side of the aisle.

Nancy raised her hands to cheers. The crowd's applause growing as they accepted their political savior.

Chapter 23

Through the Woods
Mark Light - Europe

Mark, Grace, Joy, and Noah carried their duffle bags and walked through the forest. The soft ground and thick greenery made for a slow journey as they covered the miles of woods between the highway and the river crossing into Moldova.

Mark felt himself growing weaker as the pain in his stomach increased. With every step, he felt the wound in his skin. It felt like his insides were trying to reopen the stitched gash. But as he looked back on his wife and two children, he knew he could keep going for them. They helped him get this far, and if they could do it without complaining, so could he.

To help get his mind off the pain, he began forming a plan.

Once we get out of the forest...

If there are more patrols on the bridge...

If the assassins are waiting at the bridge...

The best way to keep the family safe is...

His mind raced through scenarios.

As if on cue, his son's curiosity vocalized Mark's concerns.

"Dad, who is trying to kill you?" Noah asked.

"Noah!" Joy said as Grace shot him a look.

"What?" Noah said as he raised his hands. "Dad needed stitches. Blake's face looked like he fought a blender. And now we're walking out of the country on foot? I just want to know what started all this."

Grace glanced at Mark. "I'd like to know too. Does this have to do with what happened to you in Paris?"

"What happened in Paris?" Joy jumped on the question.

"See, we all want to know, not just me," Noah exclaimed.

"Okay, okay. Keep your voices down," Mark said. If he were in their shoes, he'd want to know too.

"Remember late last spring, when I went to meet J in Paris?" The kids nodded as the group walked on. "Well, I met a friend of his named Lucas, and found out J was mixed up with some bad folks. They came after him as the three of us talked in a coffee shop. There was a car bomb. It ripped the coffee shop apart. People died..." Mark shook his head. "We somehow survived, but then J's *friends* came in. They wanted J, not us. They shot Lucas, and then... they shot me."

Joy and Noah gasped.

"But days later, I woke up on the ground. J knelt over me. He glowed like the Bible that Grandpa gave me. There's something hidden in it, a piece of God on Earth."

"They shot you?" Noah asked.

Mark nodded.

"So, that must be nothing." Joy pointed to her dad's stomach, where splotches of blood shone through his shirt.

"I wouldn't say that. This hurts," Mark said. "And thinking of the bullet, that hurt. It hurt so dang bad. But then nothing. It was like I was sleeping, wrapped up in a warm blanket, waiting for the sun to come up. Awake one minute, then out. The same thing happened to Lucas. Apparently, once J laid hands on us, we woke up. Healed."

"Dad's a real-life Lazarus!" Noah said in an excited whisper to his sister.

"I have a scar," Mark touched his upper chest, "but I can't explain it. God worked through J. I believe I died, but God brought me back. He healed our fatal wounds."

"So were you de..." Joy began asking.

"In a coma," Noah corrected.

"No. I think I was dead," Mark said.

"What was Heaven like?" Noah jumped up and down as he asked.

"I told you," Mark shook his head and laughed, "I don't remember a thing. It was like I was sleeping."

Mark smiled at Grace; he could see the concern wash across her face.

"I think God pushed pause on Lucas and me, then set up J to press play again. It's unexplainable without God, but I remember the pain of being shot and falling to the ground. I saw boots walk by my face as the light faded away. It was horrifying, but also, I felt a peace, like you get when worshipping and the Holy Spirit is all around you. It was like the Spirit gave a giant bear hug as I went to sleep. The pain of the wound faded, the lights went out, then there was J kneeling over me."

The kids looked at each other, expressions of awe on their faces.

"Dad's like a superhero," Noah said as he nudged his sister with his elbow.

"He's like Lazarus," Joy repeated.

"Yeah, that's what I said, a superhero!" Noah shook his fists and smiled, as if celebrating his favorite team.

"No, Jesus is the superhero. Lazarus was his friend who died, and Jesus brought back to life," Joy corrected.

"Yeah, like a superhero!"

A moment passed as the family walked, then Noah interrupted the silence.

"How'd you get out?" he asked.

Mark laughed.

"Well, if you thought superhero before, get this..." Noah and Joy moved closer to him. Grace kept walking beside her husband. She tried to smile, but concern crept across her face.

"God's the only way I can explain it. J woke up Lucas and me, then walked out of the room. But! When we left the room, the doorway was glowing, and we didn't just go into some hallway. No way. After walking through the door, we found ourselves halfway across the world, in a courtroom with Grandma, Grandpa, and your uncles. We were back in Jacksonville."

"I told you. Superhero!" Noah shot at Joy. "Teleporting powers, superhero!"

Mark shook his head and then noticed Grace. She had drifted ahead as Mark and the kids talked, but now she stopped. Mark followed her eyes. Sounds of cars and the bustle of foot traffic hit their ears. Grace looked through the tree line, over a vast river and at a small town on the other side. Mark turned, and in the distance, he saw the long Luhan River bridge, the only way across the river.

Police cars packed the bridge.

Chapter 24

And Over the River

Mark Light - Europe

Mark's heart sank as he watched all traffic come to a standstill amidst the flashing lights.

"They're stopping every car," Grace said.

Mark observed the activity and ran through scenarios in his mind.

"Another bridge?" Noah said.

"No. Too far, and we're without proper supplies." He took a deep breath and looked around. "We can go through the police, trying to hide in the crowds, or..." he turned and looked at the river, "did we bring any garbage bags?"

"Yup!" Joy said. "But why?"

Mark looked at Grace. She frowned and motioned to his stomach. He shrugged, hiding the pain and lightheaded feeling that was flooding his brain more with every step.

"Okay, kids. It's craft time!" Grace said. "Who can find the biggest branches and longest vines?"

Noah and Joy smiled at each other, then dropped their duffle bags near their mother's feet and took off to examine the nearby trees.

Mark scouted the area, staying under the cover of the trees as he searched for a secluded and less-traveled section of the riverbank. After careful examination, he discovered a hidden cove tucked away from prying eyes. It was a serene spot shielded by overhanging trees, providing much-needed cover.

Grace organized a quick lunch from their supplies. Before eating, everyone came together and prayed, thanking God for the food and health. Finally, Mark prayed over them, asking God to guide and protect them on their journey to safety.

As they ate their unique combination of granola bars, dried nuts, and jerky, Mark and Grace wove the branches and vines into a makeshift raft.

"We could just swim across," she said, eyeing the water. "Save time and get across before dark."

"That water comes down from the mountains to the North. It's swimmable, but very, *very* cold," He looked around for the kids, thankful they weren't in earshot. "Our bags, our clothes, and the kids... The low tonight is in the forties. Let's keep them dry."

She nodded, then noticed Mark failing to knot off the end of the large vine.

"Babe, are you okay?"

He didn't seem to hear her as his fingers attempted to wrap the vine into a knot, but his hands twitched uncontrollably.

"Mark... Mark," Grace called out, trying to get his attention.

"Yeah," he looked up, gathering himself, "what?"

"Your hands... and you're getting pale. We need to get you across and get to a hospital."

Mark blinked a few times and looked up, as if willing blood to flow back into his paling face. After taking a deep breath, he refocused his mind.

"There's a church. If we cross here, we follow the road up and to the left. There's a main road that runs through the center of town. We follow that, and we'll find the church."

"Are you sure?" Grace said as she stood up and looked over the river. "I've never been here. You?"

"I checked the map."

"What? We said not to use our phones. What if they track our location?" Grace looked back toward the flashing police lights. She glared at Mark, a concerned look on her face.

"I had to check, babe. We can't risk you and the kids lost in the woods, especially if I..." Mark trailed off. He looked down at his stomach, his grey shirt showing more blood.

"You and the kids need to know how to get to safety."

"Don't you dare talk like that. We're all getting out of here together."

Mark clenched his jaw. He stood, holding up one end of the make-shift raft.

"I think it's done. Noah, how are the oars coming along?"

Noah held up two large bundles of branches, a huge smile across his face. Multiple pieces of thick circular branches were lashed together on one side while leafy parts extended out on the other. Plastic strips of a black garbage bag wrapped around the wide section.

Mark gave a thumbs up. Noah beamed, put the oars down and checked his knots.

"You think it'll support all of our weight at once?" Grace skeptically eyed the raft.

"God willing," Mark said with an exhale. He turned towards his daughter. "Joy, our bags?"

"Just finishing, then all wrapped up. Literally!" Joy grabbed two parts of the bag and prepared to tie a knot at the top of the black garbage bag that housed their duffle bags.

"Good girl. Can you take out my Bible before closing? I want to carry it."

"You got it, dad," she said as she took out the book and trotted over to hand it to him. He slid it into his back waistband.

He smiled at the happiness the kids held in their hearts. They seemed too innocent to know the danger they were in, but he knew they were brave.

They handled their father coming in unconscious and bloody with the same grace as their mother, He thought to himself.

"Okay, everyone. It's as good a time as any. Let's get across this river."

The kids silently celebrated as they brought the bags and oars over to their parents. Mark looked toward his wife; he didn't need to ask how she felt based on her doubtful expression.

He hated what was coming next, but it needed to be done.

"Grace, you get on first. Keep that end balanced."

She looked at Mark, then the kids, and after a moment of hesitation, she nodded in agreement. The makeshift structure wavered but held her weight. Water seeped through the many layers, but less than expected. Grace nodded in approval as she tried to sit in a way that didn't soak her pants, but ultimately sacrificed one knee to the river's water.

"Oh!" she let out as a gentle wave of near freezing water hit her knee.

"Kids, you're next," Mark said.

Joy went first, her mother helping her balance.

Noah then stepped up and handed his oars to Joy. Mark gently grabbed his arm as he saw Grace and Joy's attention on the oars and the black plastic-wrapped duffle bags.

"Son, if there comes a time where I'm not there or I can't carry on, I need you to be the man of the family. Ensure your mom gets you guys to safety, with or without me," he whispered.

"Dad?" Noah said, matching his father's hushed tone.

Mark locked eyes with his boy, and then hugged him.

"I love you, Dad."

"I love you, too."

Noah got on the raft as Grace and Joy looked back at him.

"Babe, I'm not sure. You're the heaviest one," Grace said. The three of them took up most of the raft, and the chilling water was seeping up to their shoes and pants.

"It looks perfect." Mark gently launched the raft off the bank and took a step back.

"Whoa! No, no, no!" Grace demanded. She tried standing up, but she stopped as the balance of the raft shifted. "Mark, you get on this raft or we're not going!"

Mark pulled out his phone, tapped the phone, and turned the screen toward her. The video of Lucas being pummeled played.

"I know where he is. You three get to the church. Blake is already there. He'll help you to the airport," Mark said.

"We're doing this together," Grace said. "Don't leave."

Mark stood silently, his eyes watering. "Noah, get 'em across. Take a right once over the river, then a left on the main road. You'll find the church."

"Don't you dare paddle that oar, Noah. Mark, get in or we're getting out," Grace said.

Noah looked back to his dad, his face showing the conflicting orders.

"Lead 'em there, son," Mark nodded and Noah soon put his head forward and pushed them out, further into the moving water.

"Joy, stay alert. Use those brains!" His daughter smiled stoically at him.

Grace relinquished her protest and stared daggers at her husband. Mark shrugged and mouthed *I love you* to her.

Grace let out a deep breath and shook her head. She let out the breath and returned Mark's inaudible *I love you*.

"Okay, kids. We have our mission," Grace said. The kids perked up at her acceptance. "See you on US soil, General," she hollered back to Mark.

Mark smiled brightly in return.

"See you there, Captain," Mark replied.

As his family moved further across the wide river, Mark slowly stepped back into the forest. He watched them go until the sounds of the river drowned out their paddling.

He turned and fell to one knee. The pain in his stomach screamed, and now being alone, his mind focused on it. He couldn't suppress it any longer.

"Lord, help me." He felt the Bible secured tightly to his back.

He looked up toward the bridge and the flashing lights in the distance. With a painful grunt, he stood and began walking.

Moments later, he came out of the tree line and approached the road.

The guards jumped back, startled, as the strange man with a blood covered shirt crept out of the woods and lumbered toward them. Many of them pulled their firearms, putting Mark's chest in their sights.

"Ay!" One of them called to Mark as he held up his rifle.

The officer stepped forward from the mix of border patrol and policeman. He eyed the man swaying in front of him.

"I have information about a terrorist attack and crimes against our country." Mark fell to his knees, his voice weak. The loss of blood finally overcame his determination.

The uniformed men looked at each other, a confused expression sweeping through the group. Then one young guard stepped forward, an understanding look on his face.

"English. American," he said, kneeling in front of Mark.

"I need help. Paris. Save innocent lives..." Mark held out his phone. The officer took Mark's phone as Mark fell, face-first, to the ground.

The video of three men beating Lucas played.

Chapter 25

The Times, They are a-Changin'

Zechariah – Washington, D.C.

"**S**omething big is coming. They're going to a special vote," Paul said to Zech and Jimmy as they stood on the steps of the Capitol building. "I've seen it before. An attack on US soil drives new policy. I came up here after 911 and it's the same feeling."

The special session had gripped the nation's attention, causing a flurry of activity both inside and outside the historic building's grand walls. As the news of Nancy's speech and bipartisan support spread, the scene outside took on a dramatic and charged atmosphere. Whirling storm clouds overhead heightened the anticipation and urgency of the political tension as the Press waited to get statements. The dark clouds rolled in, casting intermittent shadows on the immense columns and dome structure, which in-turn, accentuated the somber, yet dignified, atmosphere of the building.

The three men moved to the side of the building as more and more people gathered outside. News reporters swarmed the steps as cameras rolled, capturing every moment. Multiple reporters gave introductions to their camera operators, all seeking to be the first to break the news of Mrs. Nancy Pawly's heroic speech.

"With one fell swoop, she confronted *and* united the entire US Congress!" One woman exclaimed to her camera.

Moments later, microphones extended towards impassioned politicians voicing their opinions and concerns. The comments became a cacophony of fervor and urgency, all praising Nancy Pawly.

The three men's calm demeanor was like an old dog in the middle of a pack of rambunctious puppies. They watched the politicians speak to their favorite reporters. Each side of the aisle playing the information spin game and telling a story to put themselves in the best light.

"What's the only way to keep someone from dying in a church?" Jimmy asked.

"Stack about fifteen Marines around the place and tell 'em if anyone gets through, they'll lose their pension and benefits," Paul said.

Jimmy almost cracked a smile, but the upturned corners of his lips faded to a frown.

"Who needs Marines, if you outlaw church?" Zech said.

Jimmy nodded and pointed at Zech. "Bingo. Keep the people from going to church."

"Holy smokes," Paul said. "You're right, but no way. There's what, half a million churches around the country, they can't close them all. There's no way to enforce that."

Paul shook his head as he eyed the chaos of the reporters nearby. "I mean, maybe in the big cities, but every hillbilly with a gun is going to fight for their religious rights."

The dark clouds swelled overhead, a foreboding backdrop to the unfolding events. Gusts of wind whipped through the area, carrying leaves and debris in tornado-like spirals. The weather seemed to mirror the gravity of the moment, lending an almost surreal aura to the scene.

"I mean, how would that realistically be enforced?" Paul shrugged. "That many churches, even activating the entire National Guard, they couldn't stop everyone."

"Agreed," Zech said, eyeing the crowd amid the growing storm.

"But they won't have to. The people will do it themselves," Jimmy said, raising his phone to show them the screen.

Authorities Warn: Attend Church Services at Your Own Risk.

"Geez, they get these things out fast nowadays," Paul said.

"The government is giving the country an excuse to skip church," Zech said.

The three men stood quietly as they watched the crowd from afar. The massive groups formed and shifted from one politician to the next like a feeding frenzy.

Zech turned away and found Mary approaching. She jogged toward him through the growing mass of people around the Capitol Building.

"Hey! How were Lincoln and Washington?" Zech called out.

"Beautiful memorial and monument. But, more importantly, I heard from Mark. He's okay!" she said.

"Hallelujah!" Paul shouted out as Zech let out a deep breath, as if dropping a hundred-pound weight.

"What happened? Where is he now?" Zech asked.

"See for yourself." Mary held up her phone and a tiny circle of Mark's face that tracked his location moved away from a similar circle with Grace's face. "Grace and the kids are on the next flight out of Moldova, through Germany, then New Jersey, and finally Orlando."

Zech's eyes widened. "They're all coming home? Praise the Lord."

"No, just Grace and the kids." Mary let out a sigh. "Mark is on a different plane... with Interpol. He's going to Paris."

"Lucas." Zech said.

Mary closed her eyes and hugged her husband. "Yes," she whispered in his ear.

Chapter 26

Dreams

Matthew

A sense of hope filled Matthew as he moved around the kitchen and prepared the food. He seasoned the meat, rubbing the tiny flakes on each side. He sang along to MercyMe as he put the tomatoes and peppers on the skewers.

Liz was right, he thought, *we have enough savings. It's just a job. We still have our family.*

Liz and the girls had left the evening before, picking up Ashley and Aunt Millie on their way to the women's conference in Orlando. Matthew looked forward to J coming over for lunch, but he loved the peace of the quiet house. He was still seeing black clouds on nearly every trip out of the house. He didn't want to admit it, but he feared being alone.

What if it came back?

What if he didn't have his Bible?

What if no one was there to pull him out?

He kept his Bible close and tried staying in positive spirits, which was easier after finally hearing from his brothers.

He and his oldest brother, Luke, had talked for nearly an hour. Luke outlining a story that even he wasn't sure to believe.

"I had this awful dream that someone tried to poison me," Luke told him. "I was trying to pull the IV line out, but nothing. It was too strong. The whole thing felt like those dreams kids have, where you're running from a monster, but your legs won't work, and it keeps bearing down on you. Then you wake up and your sheets are all wrapped around your legs."

Matthew wanted to hear about the bomb, the giant explosion that was all over the national news after leveling an entire building. His brother survived with serious burns, but otherwise no serious injuries.

But Luke didn't stay on the explosion. He kept coming back to the dream. "I swear the Bible wasn't next to the bed when I went to sleep. But when I woke up, and the nurse said my IV *fell out*, I mean come on. Something is up. It was a dream, but... wow."

The conversation quickly pivoted when both brothers received a text from Mark. The middle Light brother shared his new location and explained the situation. Outside of Matthew's firing over the past weekend, all the recent death and other horrible news was turning around.

But Matthew ignored the demon that filled his mind days earlier.

J pulled up and rapped on the door as he let himself in.

"Kitchen!" Matthew called out.

J turned the corner, holding bags of groceries.

"We already have everything. What'd you bring?"

"No kids around." J turned and jokingly looked over his shoulders. "What is something we haven't done in the longest time?"

Matthew looked towards the plastic bags and saw the outline of a six-pack. "We are not drinking before noon."

"What are you talking about?" J looked confused, but realizing Matthew's comments, he laughed. "Oh, we're drinking something bad for us before noon. Dr. Pepper!"

Matthew shook his head as he washed the meat seasoning off his hands. "I can drink about half a can until the sugar turns my stomach. It'll be fun."

"Well, make room in that washing machine of a stomach of yours, because that's not all!" J made a drumroll sound and pulled out a tub of vanilla ice cream. "Ta Da!"

Matthew shot his best friend a blank stare.

"Dr. Pepper floats!" J shouted.

"You do this when there are no kids around, huh?" Matthew said, picking up the tub. He spun it to read the nutritional facts.

J snatched it from his hands before Matthew could read it. "Yeah, because your kids always steal mine."

Matthew laughed as he arranged burger patties and veggie kabobs on a large tray. He started walking to the backyard.

"Don't act like you're too good for the Pep. You remember all those summers, we lived in the pool and only came out for burgers on the grill and root beer, or," he grabbed the six-pack and held it up, "Dr. Pepper floats!"

"I remember my dad throwing us across the pool and dunking on my brothers in pool basketball." Matthew laughed.

"Yes! That's what I'm talking about!"

"So good." Matthew nodded as their laughter slowly faded. He set a platter full of food on the side of his simple backyard propane tank grill.

"Last week was tough. Thanks for coming over, and for this," he motioned to the sodas still in J's hand.

J nodded and mouthed a silent *you're welcome*.

For the next hour, the two enjoyed the fall afternoon reminiscing about their childhood. They debated the upcoming football season while J avoided questions about proposing to Ashley.

"You don't have to answer. Your smile says enough. But you know Liz told me to get some answers out of you," Matthew jested.

"Oh, with them two and Millie in a room, there will be no secrets when they come back from Orlando," J laughed.

As they ate, the conversation slowed. Matthew considered bringing up his fears of the demon returning, but as he opened his mouth, J blurted out that he needed to get something off of his chest.

"My dream," J said.

"The night sky one?"

J nodded. "I didn't tell you how it ended. How it *really* ended."

Matthew took a sip of the sugar-filled float and watched J. His friend gathered his thoughts before speaking.

"You bringing the pieces of the Ark together saves everything, except one thing," J said as he leaned forward. "You. *You* die in the end."

Matthew sat quietly. He waited for J to insert a joke, but his friend didn't budge. "It's just a dream, but I had to tell you it all. I have no idea what it means."

"What was your last dream, the one before this?" Matthew asked.

"The train and the dragon. You and Ashley follow me, but it all leads to the Dragon's mouth."

Matthew thought for a moment. "Do you think Terrence trying to kill you in Europe was the dragon?"

"I do."

"But what about Ashley, and me? We weren't there," Matthew asked.

"I thought about asking you to come, but you had Liz and the girls and a full-time job. I would have loved you to come with me, a giant road trip like all the small trips we used to take, just you and me." J shrugged and sat down at the dining table, resting his arms on his thighs.

"I knew you would try to come, but I couldn't ask you to go halfway around the world and leave your family. And then what happens in the dream? No way. That's why I told you I wanted to be by myself, and you know, I think that was right. Once I decided to go, I did want to be alone."

"Then you flew to Boston to see Ashley?" Matthew smiled at J.

"Yeah..." J returned the smile and leaned forward. "There's something about watching your best friend and his family, then going home to an empty house. I missed her." He softly bit down on his lip as he gave Matthew a thoughtful nod.

"If her nephew wasn't there, I probably would have asked her to come with me. Who knows if she would have, but once I saw that kid, it was just like thinking of you. There was no way I could take her."

"So, if your dream warned you about two people that were in danger around you, you left those two people behind. You took it on yourself."

"But that's why I think the dream came to pass. Two people were with me, and they died. Well... almost died. Mark and Lucas died, then came back to life."

"Resurrected," Matthew said.

J pointed at him in agreement.

"Resurrected. If it wasn't for the Ark, for God acting through me, they'd still be dead. I left two people in the US, but in Europe, I still put two people in danger. It was like the dream. Maybe you and Ashley just meant the two people closest to me."

"Now this dream is saying *I'm* going to die," Matthew said.

J locked eyes with his friend. "I think it's saying someone will die. Someone close to me."

Chapter 27

With Us or Against Us

Selena - Paris

Selena watched the jellyfish bob up and down in the currents of the water. The purple, luminescent light of the gently swaying creatures seemed to hypnotize her.

"Must be nice," she mused as she picked at the near-empty box of popcorn. "Your whole life is riding the waves–no paychecks, no family, no dead lovers." She watched Lucian lean against the expansive aquarium glass in front of her, "and no children."

In the days following the Paris tattoo parlor attacks, over a hundred Parisians, tattoo artists and their clients from seven parlors were dead.

The only survivor: Selena.

Instead of seeing the situation as God-inspired lunch break timing, the event depressed her. It meant she lost another job. Plus, all the police and news agencies wanted to talk with her.

Her name was everywhere, becoming infamous to local shops and odd jobs.

"If I can find your grandma, you should be with her. Death and loneliness follow me. You shouldn't be with me." She whispered to herself.

"Viens, viens!" Lucian's teacher called out. All the other chaperons were in a tight circle around the woman, except Selena and Lucian as they drifted behind the pack.

Selena slowly stood up. "Yes, yes! Oui, Oui!" she called out, mocking the woman's excitement. This uppity schoolmaster was getting on her last nerve, but being a chaperon meant a free trip to the Paris Aquarium. Who knew the largest jellyfish exhibit in Europe would be so captivating?

"Float on, ladies and gents," she waved to the jellyfish as she touched Lucian's shoulder and directed him back toward the group.

They turned the corner, but instead of finding the schoolmaster, saw a repair man. She paused, preventing Lucian's advance with a hand on his chest.

The repair man, it was him.

She'd recognize him anywhere. She repeatedly saw him in her mind and tried describing him countless times to authorities.

The AC repair man from the tattoo parlor, now dressed in maintenance clothes, came out from a 'staff only' labeled door.

Another man, in the same attire, slid out of the door behind him.

The two nodded to each other and then walked in different directions.

He came straight at her.

No one took notice of him as he blended in with the crowd, drifting through the onlookers in nondescript tan coveralls and a ball cap.

She thought about running, about grabbing Lucian, and running away from the man. Then, a split second later, she thought she might simply walk by. If she remained casual, he wouldn't even notice her.

But as she took her first step, her eyes couldn't avoid him. The two locked eyes. He smiled a soft, serene smile, but she saw something different in his eyes.

He recognized her, and his eyes widened, lighting up like two bonfires on an otherwise calm night.

"The one who lived," he said with a smile.

"Pierre," she said. Her insides trembled, but she forced a steady posture as she held Lucian tight to her waist.

She moved her hands over Lucian's ear, disguising her movements like she was rubbing his head. "You killed them. You're the tattoo terrorist everyone is searching for."

"Killing is such a strong word. I prefer leveraged. We *leveraged* them for the greater good," he said.

"And here, will you do the same thing here?" Her voice cracked.

He looked around the dark hallway, lit up by the giant jellyfish tanks. "If you mean finding more leverage, then yes."

Her face went pale. Death and desertion once again followed her. She had fleeting moments of happiness in Paris, but this man had shattered her life like falling glass. Every time something good happened, the world ripped it away.

She was happy with Ignace. He was becoming a good father, but then a religious lunatic ripped him away from them. She heard from her mother, claiming to feel touched by Jesus after a conversation with an American Pastor in Southern France. But then once Selena arrived, the drugs came back, and tore her mother away. Once again, missing in action.

"Who are you?" she asked.

"That depends. I could be a friend, an enemy, or a *savior*. That's up to each person to decide," he said.

"What's your real–"

"Mom! I want to see the sharks!" Lucian pulled her arm, his straggly hair bouncing like the jellyfish surrounding them. Selena shot him a look and forcefully pulled his arm, snapping the boy back to her side, and in between her and the man.

"What's your real name?" she asked.

"I told you before. It's Pierre," he smiled a devilish grin.

"Viens, viens!" Lucian's teacher called out from around the corner. Selena didn't budge as she held Lucian tight.

"I'll tell you what," he said as he pulled out two vials from his pocket and handed them to her. "Take these. If you're interested in becoming part of the solution to the horrors of the world, call me once you're back to one hundred percent."

He pulled a card from his pocket and handed it to Lucian.

Selena hesitated, then snapped it up.

"The *New* Christians," she gasped, thinking of Ignace.

"We're different from most groups." He raised his hands at the jellyfish tanks. "If you haven't noticed."

He stepped past her before turning, looking over his shoulder. "You should take those now. It's going to get a lot worse around here before it gets better."

He disappeared into the crowd.

"Viens, viens!" Lucian's teacher stepped back around the corner and stared at Selena. She stared blankly at the woman, then without a word, drank the contents of the vial. She bent down and picked up Lucian, opening the second vial and pushing it in his face.

"Drink," she demanded.

"No!" the preschooler refused.

"Drink it and I'll buy you a whole freezer of ice cream." She pulled him away from the schoolmaster, ignoring the woman's cries to join the group.

Lucian took a sip and nearly threw the vial, but Selena caught his hand before the boy lost it.

"Blah!" he shouted.

"Ice cream *and* a toy. Two toys. Just drink it, baby." She forced it back into his mouth.

"Three toys?" The boy asked, sensing an opportunity.

A hissing noise echoed from the air ducts as dense smoke began pouring from the vents. Screams broke out from the crowd behind them as smoke came out from the tunnel and the thousand gallon jellyfish tank began turning red.

Selena glanced back and saw a red cloud overtake the purple luminescence, making the once calming water resemble an ocean of blood.

"Four toys. Just drink it," she said as she kicked an emergency exit door open. As she moved Lucian through the exit, an oversized woman slammed into her, knocking Lucian from her hands as they both fell.

The frantic woman was the same height as Selena, but outweighed her by at least one hundred pounds, and hardly noticed the collision.

Selena got up and shoved the woman back into the crowd. She struck a group, sending people tumbling like bowling pins. The screams intensified as people ran from the dark tunnels of the aquarium. Parents and children shouted to find their loved ones in the melee as a cloud of thick smoke filled the room.

Selena scooped up Lucian and slid out of the emergency exit. "Did you drink it?"

The boy nodded.

"Show me!" she demanded.

He held out an empty vial.

Selena looked up through the open exit door; the woman she'd shoved had regained her footing and rushed toward the exit. Selena slammed the door shut and moved a patio chair under the handle, pinning the door shut.

"Mom?" Lucian screamed.

"She's dead already."

The door rattled and muffled screams echoed.

"But–""Come on. We have a call to make," Selena said as she held Lucian's hand and hurried away from the aquarium.

In the commotion, she didn't notice the damp spot on Lucian's shirt, where he spit up the liquid from the vial.

Chapter 28

Unfinished

Terrence - Europe

Terrence sat on his couch and watched the news. After two private plane rides, he and his team were back to their home base in Northern Israel. The small team of professionals couldn't contain their smiles, high-fiving throughout the trip home.

After all the setbacks. It's all coming together, he thought to himself, smiling as he drifted to sleep.

The buzzing of his cell phone snapped him awake.

"Hey, Dad," Terrence said as he picked up the phone.

"My goodness boy, it's everywhere. The world is watching!" said Terrence Senior, commonly known as T.

"Two down, five to go. The world will watch us pour the bowls all over Europe." Terrence said. "After all we've been through, we've finally found our place. And the world will see it."

"God will see it, son. No matter what happens with this plan in Europe, and then the US, we have our place in his kingdom."

"Yes," Terrence hissed.

"But I'm calling for more than congratulations. Solomon called today," T said.

"Did he now?"

"Mmmmhmm. That's what I thought too. You bring in all the money through your recruiting, and now you're carrying out the biggest missions, yet that figurehead gets to sit atop it all."

"He's a pawn, Dad. Let him keep tabs on the politicians and make the bribes. It makes life easier on us."

"Hmm," T scoffed.

"I used to not trust you, remember?" Terrence said with a smile.

"That's cause you were a stupid, out of line little boy!" T snapped.

"I was kidding, Dad."

"Well, ain't no time to kid, boy. It ain't normal for that man to be calling me to feel out the missions."

"You think he suspects anything?"

"Nah, but he's antsy. He was impatient. I think he's going to ask you to leave, to hit the US before ending Europe."

"What?" Terrence sat up. "We have *five* more bowls to execute!"

"Quiet yo' butt down. I'm just saying what I think, boy. He's getting antsy, wants more in the US. Probably cause all dem politicians running around after the New York thing."

Terrence clenched his fist. "Our *leader* brings me back after my crew gets murdered, then gives me forty days in isolation, and now he's trying to meddle with our European plans?"

"Mmmhmm, seems like it, boy."

Terrence shook his head. A soft buzz, alerting him of a text message, caught his attention.

Can we talk? Thank you for the vials.

Terrence smiled, then raised the phone back to his ear. "Maybe it's all God's plan."

"Don't you go running back to the US to prove something. First things first."

"You still have the Frenchman?"

"We do."

"Everything in place for the next five?"

"It is. But supplies and plans are nothing without execution. You know that, boy. My best men are watching your French poodle instead of working on the next bowl."

Terrence thought for a moment.

"Kill him and put them on the next bowl," he said without a hint of remorse. "We turned seas to blood. The rivers are next. You keep the bowls pouring, and I'll light the fuse for the greater show."

T grunted his agreement.

They ended their call and Terrence pulled the text back up to get the woman's number.. It rang twice before she picked up.

"How'd you like to go back to America?" he asked.

Chapter 29

In Pursuit of Freedom
Mark - Europe

Mark sat in the plane's seat and felt his stomach, relieved that in two short days of hospital care, most of the redness and swelling were down. He wasn't back to full strength, but he was feeling more like himself for the first time in days.

"How's your family?" Agent Bowers asked from across the aisle of the nimble six-seater plane.

"Good." Mark checked a text from Grace. "They're over the Atlantic now. Thank you for helping them out."

"It's hard to say no to a dying man," Bowers said, his voice crackling in their bulky headset earphones.

Mark expected a by-the-book, suit-wearing politician, but this Interpol agent was the opposite. He wore common day-to-day clothes instead of a suit. Today, sporting brown slacks and a black, short-sleeve button-up shirt. His typical aviator sunglasses now rested in his lap, unable to rest on his ears with the coverings of their headphones.

"I have a feeling you've said no to plenty of people in your past, dying or not."

"Depends on what they're dying of. If they're trying to save lives, it's hard, but if they're trying to kill me, well, those are fun to say no to," Bowers replied in a thick British accent.

The agent gave Mark the feel of a casual James Bond, except more physically fit, his giant forearms exhibit A. The forearms only drummers, handymen, and mechanics developed over a lifetime. Mark felt the agent's elegant accent made him sound ten times smarter than himself.

"Is that why you're helping me get Lucas back? You told me when we first met that your job is more of a handler than a cop. You're the information side, not the arresting side."

Bowers nodded and took his time responding.

"You know," the agent whispered as he leaned over the aisle to Mark. The two men were the only passengers on the small propeller plane. "I trust you."

"Oh really. You trust me? That's why you're flying over a thousand miles and clearing red tape for us to enter Paris and my family to get back to the US?" Mark said as he leaned back in his seat.

Moments of silence passed as the two huge turbine engines hummed from outside the plane.

"I don't buy it," Mark said.

Bowers cleared his throat and faced forward. "Well, maybe I looked you up while you were in the hospital. And maybe I saw your shift from financial services to missionary work. I appreciate that choice. And maybe I investigated your family, their church, their legal and financial struggles, and the comments your dad made about the Ark."

Mark sat up and turned to Agent Bowers. The man didn't flinch. His head was back, eyes forward, and massive forearms resting comfortably at his side.

"You're a Christian, aren't you?" Mark asked, but Bowers didn't reply.

"Yeah, you are. Where are you from?"

"Manchester."

"And your parents?"

"Poland," Bowers said plainly, as if reciting from a fact book.

Mark eyed him, silently trying to draw out more information. Bowers finally turned to meet his eyes.

"My parents left as the Soviets put more and more political and religious pressures on the church. My grandfather knew Bonhoeffer. The man inspired him to dig deep and create a home-grown resistance. But... when my father told my grandfather he was thinking of taking my mother and me out of the country..." Bowers stopped and shook his head. "After all my grandfather had been through, all the secrecy through the Nazi occupation and Russian authority, to see his son and family leave was like spitting at his life's work."

"But he left anyway?" Mark asked.

"Nope. He stayed. Then a nighttime raid killed my grandfather. My mother went to the grocery and never returned. We found out they took her prisoner. Records show she died in a Soviet prison. After that, my father finally left. He escaped with me. I was two years old."

"Wow," Mark said. "I'm so sorry."

"If it wasn't for me being alive, I think he would have stayed. Because, when I was eight, my father killed himself. The guilt ate him alive." Bowers turned back and locked eyes with Mark. "I found him, and ever since I have seen many dying or dead men, Mr. Light. So why am I taking you to Paris? Because any man that seeks to murder another human under religious precepts... I will find him and watch him die, just as I watched my father swing from that rope."

Mark returned Agent Bowers's stare.

"You already knew about the New Christians, didn't you?"

"Your story reinforced what I knew, yes," Bowers acknowledged. "I also know that you should have died in the Paris coffee shop bombing. So, Mark Light, let me ask you a question: Why, and how, are you alive?"

"The grace of God," he shrugged.

"Hmph, I suppose so. Regardless, I knew your story, so it was only fitting you hear mine."

The two men sat in silence as the pilot's voice sounded in their ears. "We're entering French airspace. We'll begin our descent shortly."

"Thank you, Roger," Bowers said.

"Wait, the pilot's name is Roger?"

"Yes," Agent Bowers said.

"So, you could have said, 'Roger, Roger,' right?"

"I don't recommend that."

"Why not? That's great!" Mark exclaimed.

"Roger doesn't like that."

"Affirmative, I don't like that," the pilot's voice crackled in Mark's headset.

"Affirmative?" Mark laughed. "Come on, Roger. You know you were itching to say Roger there."

"Roger doesn't like that," Bowers said again.

Mark pulled down the microphone that reached around his jaw from the right earphone. "He can hear everything we said?"

"Roger," the pilot said through the headset.

"I trust Roger," Bowers smiled. "And like I said, I trust you."

"Roger," Mark said with a nod. He grinned and leaned back as he felt the plane descend.

"Let's go find your friend," Bowers said.

"Roger," Mark said.

Chapter 30

Simple, Effective Chaos

Terrence

Solomon called Terrence, just as T expected. Terrence was all smiles and agreement, acting eager to please the boss. If Solomon wanted Terrence to lead the US mission while simultaneously keeping the European plans alive, then he would do it. He trusted the recruits sent over from the Middle East because he'd recruited most of them. They were loyal to him and once he completed this job, he'd convince them of the actual plan: overthrowing Solomon. Terrence would soon take his rightful place as the head of the global organization. No longer would his place in the pecking order overshadow his abilities.

Terrence leaned over and nudged Selena. She was such an easy recruit, he felt God had placed her with him. Not only did she have all the religious off-putting childhood experiences he looked for in new members, but she was Ignace's girlfriend. As soon as he mentioned adding to Solomon's plan to get revenge on the Light family, he molded her like a piece of clay. She was a godsend, and now she'd help carry out the message to the United States.

"You ready?" he asked.

She nodded.

Sensing her reluctance, he encouraged her.

"What'd you tell me about your son?" he asked.

"That I don't want him to have my life," she said.

"And where is he now?"

"With a friend, back in Paris. You took her son at the aquarium. Lucian reminds her of him. She'll watch him as long as I need."

"Repeat after me. 'He's safe.'"

"He's safe."

"So *I* can change the world."

"So I can change the world."

"Lord, give me the strength to carry out your will."

"I'm still not comfortable with that part," Selena said.

"Traditional religion ravaged your entire life. Your family torn apart. Your son's father murdered." Terrence stared at her with piercing eyes. "You're the perfect person to show the world a resurrection. This world of sin chewed you up and spit you out. But God wants to change that. He always uses those at their worst and brings them to the top. Selena, for the first time in your life, you're about to be on top."

She nodded and took a deep breath. "Lord, give me the strength to carry out your will."

"Now, let me ask again. Are you ready?"

"Yes. But is it really this simple?"

"No. Not always. Some missions are quite complex, with months or years of planning."

"I always thought there was an entire team behind things like this. Someone hacking surveillance cameras and another person causing a diversion for police." She moved her arms around as if pretending to be a ninja.

"There was a team, but now it's just us. You know, it's more about the effect, and with something like this, we're the catalyst. The sheep inside will provide the spark," he said.

They got up from the park bench, and each picked up a duffle bag resting at their feet.

"Just follow your instructions. It's that easy," he assured her as they began walking.

Partly cloudy skies shaded them from the sun as a gentle breeze moved across the sidewalks and streets of downtown Orlando.

"What a lovely day," Terrence smiled. He turned to Selena, his smile turning into a sneer as he nodded for each to begin their work.

Chapter 31

Behind the Scenes

Mark Light - Paris

"We've traced the IP address to this district. They didn't make it easy, bouncing through VPNs all over Europe, but Mr. Light's information, combined with ours, points us here."

The Interpol agent finished the briefing with the Parisian officers and stepped back to Mark. "These men and women are good. I've worked with them before. With them, and maybe a little luck, we'll find your friend."

"And what do we do?" Mark asked.

"It's the best part. We wait," Bowers said as he leaned back in the small folding chair and put his feet up on the card table. Mark thought the feeble table would break under the weight of Agent Bowers's black boots. The table bent but didn't break.

"I can't just sit here," Mark said as he looked across the small warehouse they had taken over. They were only blocks away from the target house. The group of soldiers did a final weapons check as their commanding officers barked instructions in French.

"We can't go with them?"

"Trust me, they're the best in Paris. And you don't want to get in their way."

"We should pray over them before they go," Mark said.

"Just let them work. They're professionals."

Mark said a quick prayer under his breath as the men filed out of the once-abandoned warehouse. He watched them go, impatiently drumming his fingers on the thin table as Bowers put his sunglasses on and closed his eyes. The agent could have been taking a Sunday nap after a large lunch, as relaxed on an undersized folding chair as on a comfortable couch.

Mark continued to drum his fingers on the table as he thought about how long the special task force would be gone. Bowers pulled down his sunglasses, staring at Mark's fingers, then back up at his face.

"Can you stop that?"

"Oh, yeah," Mark said, pulling his fingers off the table and standing up. Bowers moved his sunglasses back up and closed his eyes again.

Mark stood and began pacing next to the table. A moment later, he was humming and tapping his leg, making more noise than the table drumming.

After a few seconds, Bowers once again pulled his sunglasses down and eyed Mark. He watched him pace back and forth.

"Are you kidding me?" Bowers said.

Mark absentmindedly looked up at his companion. "What?"

"Alright, fine," Bowers took his feet off the table and his chair tipped forward. He shot up as the front two legs of the chair hit the ground. "We stay outside their perimeter, which means we stay on this property, blocks away." He stared at Mark like a teacher giving instructions before an exam.

"Let's do it," Mark said. He picked up his Bible from the thin table and tucked it in his back waistband as Bowers instinctively felt the sidearm on his shoulder strap. The brown strap and black pistol rested over a plain white shirt. Bowers left his jacket on the table and walked Mark to the same garage door-like opening that the task force had recently exited.

To Mark's surprise, the streets were quiet. There were no gunshots popping in the distance or shouts from a standoff between the good and bad guys. An engine roared in the distance, the high pitched revving of a motorcycle on the nearby Boulevard Périphérique around the center of Paris.

"Oi?" Bowers raised his eyebrows before turning back to the warehouse. "Let the pros work."

Mark stood in the quiet night, a little disappointed at the lack of action, but deciding that was a good thing.

"We're coming, Lucas," he whispered to the night air.

In the months prior, Mark and Lucas had grown close, visiting each other twice and talking weekly. Mark joked there was nothing like being killed and resurrected together to start a friendship. The plane ride back to Europe from the States was where the two forged their bond. The same plane ride where they took the selfie, holding up the number one with their index fingers. On the flight, they debated theology, the impact of social media on the blended cultures across Europe, and differences in missionaries between the Americas and Europe.

Mark also found out that Lucas's father was American. The man met his mother on a missions trip, and in less than a year, the man moved to France and proposed.

"She told him no the first time he asked," Lucas joked as he told Mark the story. "But he kept coming back. They dated for a few months and my mother said her guard was still up. She wasn't sure about this 'American cowboy' as she called him. Then, once she saw the pitiful flat he rented to be close to her, she told him to ask again."

The conversation turned to heartbreak as Lucas told of his parents going on missions across Africa when he was ten years old. Sitting in the airplane seat next to Mark, he'd drawn a path with his finger in the air, showing the flight from France to Egypt, then their trip by caravan south, hugging the Red Sea and into the Sudan.

"It was their second trip. They wanted to build a church, then a school. I begged them to let me come on this one, but they said we'd be moving down as a family soon enough. My father told me it was like setting up a tent before camping. Once they had a foothold, they'd come home for more supplies and fundraising, then we'd move there. They wrote a letter every week. Sometimes, I wouldn't hear from them. The postal service wasn't reliable down there, but eventually a pack of letters would all arrive together. I loved to see the stack of paper wrapped in a rubber band. I saved all those rubber bands." Lucas had smiled sadly. "But, after five months of what was supposed to be a six-month trip, the letters stopped."

Lucas sniffed. "I always thought that I'd get an entire bag of letters. You know those huge white bags you see behind the scenes at la Poste? I thought, any day, I'll get one of those. Hundreds of letters detailing the wonderful village my parents helped build. But..." Lucas cleared his throat.

"My grandmother was furious. She was, and still is, the most determined woman I've ever met. The government, the church organization, Interpol. She even sent letters and tried calling African governments. Can you imagine an old woman sending a letter to the Sudan government demanding to know where her daughter- and son-in-law were?" Lucas laughed, shaking his head. "I think I was the only reason she didn't fly down there herself. We didn't have any other family to watch me. After a year, we held the joint funeral service. That's when it hit me. The letters weren't coming... I hated that funeral. Hated it. It felt like giving up."

Lucas's words echoed in Mark's ears as he stood in the Parisian alley.

"We're not giving up," he said.

Back in the hospital, when Mark first met Agent Bowers, he'd told him they were going to find Lucas. "We won't give up on him. The New Christians have him, and they have a base in Paris."

Ever since Terrence's father, T, shot Mark and Lucas, Mark pieced together information on the New Christians and Terrence's violent history.

It didn't take much to convince Agent Bowers to rally the troops and fly to France. Now Mark stood in the empty street, waiting to see if the professionals could pull Lucas out of the suspected New Christian's safe house.

"Dear Lord," Mark whispered into the night air, "protect him."

Moments later, Mark resigned himself back to the table, where Bowers already had his feet up and sunglasses over his eyes. As Mark's shoulders dropped in defeat, he leaned back in the chair and stared at the warehouse ceiling, examined the sprinkler system.

They heard a noise from the alley. A muffled scream in the distance.

He sat up in the chair and turned, listening intently, and scanned the entrance to the alleyway, but heard nothing else. A long silence followed as he patiently waited for another vibration in the air.

Just as he questioned his sanity, he heard another sound of a struggle from one of the nearby buildings. He couldn't pinpoint it, but it was enough to jump out of his seat and head back to the alley. He watched and listened carefully, but only engine sounds on the nearby highway echoed through the broken windows and abandon buildings.

Finally, Mark ran back to Agent Bowers.

"Hey, something is going on," Mark said, motioning for the relaxed man to join him.

Bowers looked over his sunglasses with a tired and skeptical look.

"Really. Wake up. I heard something," Mark urged.

Agent Bowers checked his watch. "It's been six minutes…"

"Fine. I'm going into these buildings, Bible swinging. Join me or not." Mark jogged back to the opening and looked around.

Bowers gave Mark a look like a parent gives a toddler. The look of disbelief when the toddler isn't napping.

"Fine." Bowers sat up and followed Mark to the alleyway.

Mark jogged across the alley and down one block. He leaned up against the wall of the building, listened intently, like he was trying to crack the combination lock of a giant bank vault.

Bowers trotted to Mark's side. "What are you doing?" the agent whispered.

"I heard something, a struggle."

"We have no intelligence on this–"

"Shush! You hear that?" he whispered.

"No," Bowers replied, an irritated expression on his face. His British accent was more pronounced in his annoyance. He shook his head and turned away.

Then, from inside the building, a gunshot cut the silence like a sledgehammer. The two men froze, as still as statues, as they waited and listened.

Bowers had snapped out of his malaise and caught Mark's eye. The agent's face now steeled as he quietly pulled the gun from the side holster on his chest.

Mark inched forward to a door, trying to listen. The door, inches from his head, forcefully swung open. The clanging sound of the aluminum door swinging fully open and striking the wall behind it echoed through the alley.

A man shot out like a rocket. His body horizontal, he landed hard, smacking the pavement like he was thrown from a club by bouncers twice his size. The man struck the cobblestones with a thud, a grunt of pain forced out.

The two men stood motionless as a large hand pulled the door shut without noticing Mark and Bowers.

Mark stepped toward the man, who slowly rolled in pain as Bowers kept his gun trained between the door and the man. A trickle of blood came from the wounded man's side. The liquid spread through the bricks of the alley like red chalk outlines around the gray stone squares.

Mark knelt to examine the man as he rolled to his side.

"Where are you hurt?" Mark asked.

In a flash the elderly man shot out a hand, grabbing Mark's throat and squeezing it tight.

Then the two men's eyes met.

"You?" the man wheezed.

"Me," Mark forced the word out through his strangled throat.

T, the man who shot Lucas and Mark months earlier, now lay wounded, looking up at the man he thought he had killed.

Bowers shot forward to Mark's side. He kicked T's arm, loosening his hold on Mark's neck, and pinned him down.

Mark's arm went up to hold Bowers back, his eyes staying locked on T's.

The elder man was still looking at Mark as if he'd seen a ghost.

"You're dead," he said.

"Where's Lucas?" Mark asked.

"He should be dead, too, and soon will be," T said, each word causing him obvious pain.

"God had other plans."

Mark finally broke eye contact and looked down at T's side. Blood soaked the brown shirt, directly under his ribs. Mark could see it pooling in his black jacket before flowing onto the alley's stones.

T clenched his teeth. "I killed you, boy. And I killed your friend. Then I sent men to kill you again," he laughed, wincing in pain. "Now you're here, alive, next to the old man who keeps trying to kill you. Why won't you die?"

Mark's eyes bounced between Bowers and the door.

Bowers stepped away and pulled out a small radio. He stepped back from Mark as he spoke into the device.

"You didn't exactly fail. You killed me. But by the grace of God, I'm back. Lucas is in there?" Mark motioned to the door.

T nodded and took a pained breath. "Just finish me... Do it, boy. You won."

"Do what?"

"Kill me. Be done with it," T whispered as if giving up on a lifelong journey.

Mark looked at him. "Kill you? I'm here to save, *not* kill."

T's eyes went back to Mark, a confused expression on his face.

"Medics on the way. Three minutes." Bowers returned to Mark's side. "They found nothing in the safe house."

"I think they found the wrong safe—" The door shot open, cutting him off. A hulking figure popped out. At first, the brute looked surprised, but within a millisecond, he went on the offensive.

Bowers raised his pistol, but a massive hand shot forward and grabbed his arm. The agent spun, hanging on to his firearm but using the attacker's weight against him as he pulled on the giant's arm. With his left hand, Bowers grabbed the man's jacket sleeve and forced it to the ground, bringing the man down. Bowers continued his spin, rolling over the man as he forced him down, landing on the man's back. Meanwhile, his right hand put away the pistol and smoothly wrapped around the thick neck of the villain.

Within a couple seconds of the door swinging open, Bowers had the man on the ground. The agent's immense forearms now squeezing the life out of the man's neck.

"Don't–" Bowers raised a finger at Mark's comment.

"Shush, shush, shush. He'll be okay." Bowers said, pretending to put a baby to sleep. He gently rested the man's head on the cobblestones.

Another man, in similar black pants and jacket, shot out of the door. He was smaller than the first but still could pass as an NFL lineman. He came out and reached for Mark, but Mark rolled away. As he did, the man lunged forward and pulled a gun. But T stuck out his foot and tripped the man, sending him tumbling towards Mark. The gun skittered across the road.

Given the commotion, the first man found new life and rolled, desperately trying to knock Bowers off his throat, but the agent wouldn't let up. As the pair rolled, Bowers wrapped his legs around the man's waist, hooking his feet over his upper thighs. He pulled the man's legs apart like a wishbone, giving himself the leverage to stay tight on his neck. It worked, as the man's energy once again faded, and his eyes closed.

The second man landed on the pavement near Mark. He reached out to grab him, but Mark shifted away. As he moved away, Mark's sideways movement pulled on the stitches across his midsection and pulled them apart. He stalled and failed to get to his feet, giving the attacker time to crawl towards him. The man got to his knees and brought back his hand, unleashing a haymaker that caught Mark on the side of the face. A blast of pain shot through his face as his body slammed against the hard stones of the alleyway.

A third man now appeared in the doorway. Much smaller than the other two, but apparently quicker on the draw. He pulled out a gun and pointed it at Mark.

The second foe noticed the blood on Mark's shirt and went for the kill. He grabbed Mark's shirt, pulling his head off the ground and clenched his fist. He threw another sledgeham-mer-like blow, but Mark rolled free from his grasp, narrowly escaping it, exposing his back. The attacker aimed another swing at Mark's spine, but he didn't see the glowing book tucked into Mark's waistband.

The man screamed in pain and horror as the Ark's power within the Bible repelled his flesh. His hand seemed to melt away, as if the skin and bones were alive and running from the glowing glory of the Ark.

The man fell back and screamed again, his arm a mangled mess of bone and melted flesh halfway up his bicep. It dripped blood where bone had shattered and punctured the recoiling tissue.

His companion's eyes widened in horror as he watched the supernatural force reshape his comrade's arm. The pause gave

Bowers enough time to get off the now unconscious first man. Opting not to discharge his weapon, Bowers charged him, sending them both into the dark room beyond the doorframe.

Mark heard screams and a loud pop, like a joint popping, followed by choking noises from the darkness. He picked up the second man's gun and dashed into the building while the man rolled in pain and screamed at his disfigured arm.

As his eyes adjusted to the dark interior, he saw Bowers on one knee, his arms wrapped around the assailant's throat and the side of his neck.

"You ripped his elbow out of place?" Mark noticed an unnatural bend in the villain's arm.

"Yeah, but he had a gun. Besides, arm bars are fun. But, this is my favorite." Bowers grunted and flexed his massive arms, squeezing off the circulation to the man's head. His eyes slowly closed, and his body soon went limp. The agent laid him gently on the ground and pulled out zip ties from a pocket.

"Here," Bowers tossed a few to Mark. "Get the other two."

Mark ran back outside. The man with the disfigured arm was already fifty yards down the alley, still screaming as he ran. Mark bent down and zip-tied the first man's arms and ankles. The man's immensely thick wrists and ankles forced him to string multiple zip ties together.

T was still on the ground, looking up at the night sky as if settling into a cozy camping trip instead of bleeding out.

Mark noticed the tactical team approaching from down the alley. He went back to T's side. "We'll get you help. You'll be okay."

"There was only three. You got 'em all, boy," T shook his head and wheezed out a soft laugh. He looked up into Mark's eyes. "I don't understand it. Why you? Why your family?"

"I don't know."

As the team ran towards Mark, he called out, "A downed civilian! He's shot! And three terrorists, two secure here, but another on foot. He's wounded." Mark pointed toward where the screaming man had just turned a corner.

Mark dashed inside.

"You recognize these three?" Mark asked Bower.

"Two large men and one smaller? I saw a video once of an innocent man, tied up and beaten by two large men and a smaller one." The two men locked eyes and then slowly crept further inside.

They turned down a hallway, Bowers kicking open doors and clearing the rooms as they went. The first room appeared to be a snack room with a small table and chairs. Packaged food and drinks were spread across a counter. The next room was a bathroom, and the one after that was empty.

Finally, Bowers darted through a doorway after peering inside. Mark followed closely behind. A tripod with an attached camera was set up just past the door frame.

Bowers checked the dark corners as Mark darted past him.

Under a spotlight and chained to a wall was Lucas. His face was nearly unrecognizable. One eye flickered open, the other too swollen to move.

Chapter 32

Warning

Zechariah - Jacksonville, FL

"They'll be here in a couple hours," Mary said as she put her phone down and reached for her coffee. "No women's conference, no stops at a hotel. Grace said they're not stopping until she gets to our place."

"I understand that. Especially after what they went through getting out," Zech gave a tiny smile. "And Mark back in Europe playing secret agent."

Mary noticed the smile. "You proud of your boys?"

"You bet I am." Zech walked to the sliding glass door that looked out over the backyard. His smile faded into a frown.

"What is it?" She leaned back and put her feet up on the ottoman in front of her chair.

"The last time Matthew was here, he looked out these doors and saw something only visible to him. Something awful."

"He seemed jumpy," Mary blew on the steaming cup and took a sip.

"The demon he saw, it's like a warning only Matthew could see."

Zech looked towards the west; the predawn night sky was still dark. He thought of standing next to Matthew, knowing what his son saw and trying to remember the faint glimpses of the black shadows in his own memory.

Then Zech turned east, looking at the blossoming sunrise light up the sky.

"We seem to have survived, though," Mary said.

"Thank the Lord," Zech said softly.

Zech's phone buzzed on the countertop behind Mary. She reached up, grabbing the device.

"Unknown?" she said, holding up the screen to her husband.

Zech peered at it and then answered the call. He didn't say a word, but listened.

"You don't know me, but I have a warning. A warning you, and your family, should take seriously." a man's scratchy voice came across the line.

"Who is this?" Zech asked.

"I'm a dead man at the bottom of a bucket. I spent my life foolishly trying to dig out,"

the caller exhaled and then took in another breath.

"There's only so far you can dig in a bucket until you hit bottom. Then there ain't no more digging." The voice laughed, then began coughing.

"If it's the same to you, I'd like to know who is threatening my family," Zech said.

"Oh no, no. My threatening days are over. I think God's finally got to me."

"How so?" Zech asked.

"My name is Terrence Shade, *Senior*. My son and I have been tryin' to kill your family for a while now," T said in a tired voice.

Zech's stiff frame seemed to drop, like the words punched him in the stomach. His eye's shot to Mary, who waved him over. He sat near her and put the phone on speaker.

"I suppose you're wonderin' why I called. Well, like I said, I have a warning for you."

"And?" Zech asked.

"We're going to get you, all of you, sooner or later."

"I thought your threatening days were over?"

"Excuse me," T coughed. "My son and the force propelling him. It's still hard not to think of myself as a part of that team anymore."

"And what team is that?"

"Stop with the dumb questions, sir. You all can't seem to be killed. You have the Ark and keep sliding right through our fingers. But my son, he may be rash, but he is the smartest and most determined man I've ever met. I am dang ol' proud of that, sir. But what I've seen, I admit now that I pointed him in the wrong direction. He's a train on the right track, you hear me, but he's full power in the wrong direction!" T exhaled. "God is finally showing me I picked the wrong side."

"And how's that?" Zech asked.

"You know I'm sorry about your friend. What was his name, Milo? Michael?"

Zech's eyes widened and he grabbed Mary's hand, holding it tight.

"Micah."

"Yeah, that's it! I was deep in the bottle back then, but I was at least smart enough to know the good influence he had on my boy. I told little T, I said he needed to go on all those trips and youth groups."

Zech noticed T struggled for every breath. "When Micah died, I tried being the example little T deserved. But I wanted to be better than Micah. Had to be better. I got extreme." T grunted.

"I got clean and got into the word. Even moving that boy to the Middle East, but for what?" he laughed. "I pointed him in the wrong direction."

"What's next, T. Where are we going from here?"

"He's going after your family. There are no more rules. Solomon cut the leash and sent him first class to the US."

"We've seen what he's done. New York. The HVAC poison."

"Nah, we did Paris, not New York. And if you all stay separate, he's going to get you each. Sooner or later, he'll get you."

"How?"

"I don't know. But you need to stay together. There's something different about that boy lately. He's stronger, more determined than even his normal self."

Zech thought of carnage at the Storage Yard. The black shadows that passed from the dead men into Terrence.

"Why don't you call him instead of me? Tell *him* to stop instead of warning us."

"He ain't listening to me anymore. He ain't even listening to the boss man," T coughed. "Zechariah, I called you to say I'm sorry. I'm sorry I brought death upon you and yours. I have much to atone for. If you don't bring it together, you'll all fall, one-by-one your family will die." T kept coughing as he tried to say goodbye, then he hung up.

"Wait–" but Zech could hardly finish the word before hearing the line cut out.

Zech turned to look at Mary. They squeezed each other's hands.

Chapter 33

We Know Him

Liz Light - Orlando, FL

Liz smiled as the girls played on the renovated playground outside of the arena. She glanced at her watch and then hollered to Beth and Lyn.

"Two minutes, ladies!"

"Okay!" they yelled as they played tag around the giant spiderweb-like net. Beth jumped up and crawled to the top as the smaller Lyn tried to keep up.

A moment later, Liz walked up the net and held out her hands, her signal for the kids to stop playing and join her. It took a minute, and a stern look, but the young girls accepted their playtime was over and joined their mother.

"What's next, Mom?" Beth asked.

"I'm going into a session about Abigail. She married King David. And you two are going with Ashley and Aunt Millie."

"Yay!" both girls screamed in excitement.

"We can get Aunt Millie to buy us ice cream," Beth whispered to Lyn.

"Oh no. No, you won't!" Liz tried to hold back her smile. "You already had pancakes, four helpings of fruit, snack bars, and chocolate."

"But Aunt Millie says it's vacation, and it's okay to have extra treats on vacation," Beth replied.

"That woman..." Liz shook her head. "At least save some ice cream for me. Do the lazy river in the meantime."

Beth shrugged.

"Oh really, you better wait for me!" Liz joked as she leaned into Beth, bumping her daughter.

"Dinosaur!" Lyn called out, pointing to a man and woman. They held gym bags and walked parallel to the three of them, also toward the arena.

"Blue dinosaur!" Beth said.

Liz noticed a blue tattoo coming out of the woman's sleeve, a dragon's tail, that reached down toward her wrist. A claw stretched out to her neckline and wrapped around her lower neck.

"I see it!" Beth said, pointing.

"Don't point at people," Liz said, then she stopped in her tracks as she noticed the man.

Where do I know him...

Then she realized it, and spun her head. Taking the girls' hands, she directed them away from the arena.

"Let's say hi," Beth tugged on her mother's arm. "I want to see the dragon."

"Yeah!" Lyn said, still full of energy and wanting to follow her sister.

"No," Liz quickly retorted and brought the girls back to her side, quickening their walk. The girls recognized their mother's tone. They went quiet.

"Quietly now, girls. Do you like hide and seek?" Liz whispered, leaning down to be closer to the girls' level.

"Yeah!" they said in a hushed scream.

"This is like hide and seek, but a sneakier version. Whoever can hide the longest, and be the quietest, wins. Okay?"

"You mean just sit and wait?" Beth asked skeptically.

"Well, what about a pretend adventure?" Liz said.

The girls looked at each other, then nodded in agreement.

"I need you to go to the slides, those tubes ones, and stay inside. You are both top secret agents waiting for your time to stop a crime, but if you talk or come out, you're busted, and the bad guys win."

"Got it! Let's go, sis," Beth said, holding out her hand. Lyn giggled, and both girls ran back to the playground to climb into the slide.

Meanwhile, Liz took out her phone. In the group chat with the other two women, she sent a message: *Emergency, outside now, playground.*

Liz then switched to her camera app. With two fingers, she zoomed in on the two as they separated and began taking small canisters out of their bag. Liz clicked repeatedly, snapping pictures.

They circled the arena, dropping canisters in nearly every garbage can they passed. Soon they were out of view, and Liz looked on, waiting, but nothing happened.

Liz sent the pictures to Matthew, now questioning herself if she was overreacting or if she didn't recognize the person she thought she saw.

A moment later, Ashley and Aunt Millie came out.

"Hey!" Aunt Millie hollered across the long stretch of concrete as she and Ashley came out from the Arena. "Everything okay?"

As they approached Liz, a billowing gray cloud erupted from the receptacle. They ducked, holding their noses as they ran away from the building. Within seconds, gray clouds rose from each canister hidden in the garbage cans.

Giant, poisonous clouds soon enveloped the entire arena. They looked back at the building containing thousands of women, who were now trapped inside a fog of death.

Chapter 34

Friendly Conversation
Matthew

"I'll tell you what," Matthew turned to J. "These past couple of weeks have been a lot. I know this sounds crazy, but I felt like Job. God allowing Satan to come after me."

"It's not crazy. We almost died last year." J held up his hand, showing scars in place of two missing fingers. The wounds from pushing aside Ignace's shotgun, taking them himself instead of putting a hole in Matthew's back.

"And then the trials and courtroom, your job, and brothers. I mean, we're still waiting to hear word on Lucas."

"J, you know I still see them, right? The huge shadowy figures, the demons." Matthew put down his burger and looked across his yard.

"After you were fired, and stared at the mirror like you were burning in an invisible fire, I had an idea." J said. "So, with my dreams and you seeing demons, maybe we should start a hotline?"

"Yeah, paying customers get a picture of the Ark, but the free tier gets smacked with it," Matthew said as J laughed.

"What are you going to do for work?" J asked.

"I could pick up a lower-level job pretty quick, and I thought about asking dad about working for the church."

"Let me rephrase that. What do you *want* to do?"

"About work?"

"You know what, no. I don't just mean work. I mean everything. Life, family, whatever—how you spend your time. What do you want?" J asked.

Matthew glanced towards the end of the patio table, his and J's Bibles sat side-by-side.

"If I'm being honest..." Matthew started.

"*Only* if you're being honest," J replied.

"If I'm being honest, I want to take that Bible, pull out the Ark and go attack every one of those forsaken demons I see. I want to go on the offensive because I'm sick of being beat up. I'm sick of being politically correct as I walked around work with my Bible. I'm sick of these demons and worrying about them around my family. I'm sick and tired of being sick and tired!" Matthew shouted as he nearly came out of his seat.

J leaned back; his eyebrows raised but a wide grin across his face.

"So, go do it," J said.

Matthew shook his head. "You know any openings for demon hunters? I already have the required equipment."

"No, I'm serious. The money will come. I didn't go into preaching to stack cash. I learned how to manage what I had. God will guide you if you commit. Who knows what that demon-slaying looks like, but if you get good at it, and I mean really, *really* good at it, then everything else will follow. Go be so good that no one can ignore you, and then you'll make money with it."

"How in the world am I going to support my family running around with a golden, glowing artifact?"

"By going to smack all those demons, the ones *only you* can see. That's how." J leaned back and then pulled himself forward in an excited gesture. "I never thought about this. You joke, but you have all the tools now!"

He screamed an exaggerate two-tone laugh, first soft and then at the top of his lungs. "Ha, HA!"

Matthew didn't notice the black cloud hovering around him, pecking at his thoughts.

"Brother, what in the world are you talking about?" Matthew said. "I don't need all the tools. I'm exhausted. This last year, these... these hauntings... I just want to rest. Yes, of course, I want it all to go away, but... ugh. I'm tired."

"It ain't going away," J said plainly. "But I think you have what it takes to win. I mean, think about what this world is becoming. We need someone like you who will call out the truth."

"What do you mean, *becoming*?" Matthew asked, his expression growing darker as he questioned his friend.

"I talked to your dad about it earlier today. He thinks the government is going to shut down church services."

"That's ridiculous. You know how many people go to church every Sunday?"

"I do. We review the numbers for our church. But let me ask you, do you know how many people will stay home from church with the slightest push? I mean, you could whisper an excuse and a large percentage of folks instantly put their pajamas back on."

"But that makes no sense..." Matthew's eyes widened. "The attacks. They'll say it's in people's own interest. It's all for their safety."

"Bingo," J replied.

"Thank God for the virtual efforts you all have set up over the years, especially after the trial."

"Agreed, but I'm afraid most places aren't ready for that. You know what happened to our attendance? Dropped eighty percent."

"Eighty?" Matthew repeated.

J nodded. "Now, some came back, and some departures were because of the trial, but more than half of folks never dialed in since we lost the building. What's going to happen across the country if the government closes churches?"

"I feel like that is only the first question. What happens to society if we stop going to church?"

"If only we had a Bible-toting vigilante out there. Someone who could see evil AND had a weapon to fight it?" J smiled as he bobbed his head up and down.

"Hey, you have one too, ya know?" Matthew slouched over the table. "I'm done fighting. All I do is get fired or get my family in trouble."

"Hey man, all joking aside. I've never heard you talk like that," J said.

Matthew rubbed his eyes and keep his palms pressed against his face. The dark cloud went in and out of his mind.

"I just want to be alone," Matthew said in a muffled voice as he pressed his hands to his face.

"What?" J said. "Brother, it's just us."

The demon collapsed on Matthew.

"Alone!" Matthew slammed his hands against the table, denting the aluminum. He shot up and stormed into the house.

J couldn't see what snuck up on his friend, but he watched in confusion as Matthew flung the sliding glass door aside and went into the house.

Matthew caught his reflection in the glass. He saw the darkness that surrounded him.

Chapter 35

Exorcism

Matthew

Matthew felt like his body was on autopilot as he picked up a glass from the dining room and threw it against the wall. It was as if he was seeing his life from the back seat. It was him in control, but somehow, it wasn't.

He was so angry, but for what, he couldn't remember.

How dare he come here and talk like that? He thought to himself, but even in the thought, a small piece of himself didn't believe the question. *Talk like what?*

He punched the pantry door as he walked by the kitchen, leaving a knuckle dent in the wooden shell. Soon, he found himself in the bathroom. The same bathroom where he'd destroyed the mirror days before.

The shards of glass on the ground were cleaned, but Matthew hadn't replaced the medicine cabinet mirror yet.

He peered into the spiderweb of cracks like looking into a black hole. The cracks split him and the demon into countless reflections. He looked at a pattern of repeating images. Him. Darkness. Him. Darkness. The two entities blended, becoming one.

He locked eyes with the triangle fragment of himself and stared.

Red eyes looked back, overlaid with his own brown eyes.

He heard the sliding glass door shut and sank to the floor, a new feeling of terror overwhelming him, pushing him down and away from the door. His emotions twisted from rage to fear.

J walked in and noticed the shattered glass and damaged pantry door. He carried both Bibles, enclosing both Arks within. He approached the bathroom, not sure what to expect.

As he turned the corner, he saw his friend shivering. His knees pulled up to his chest and one hand bleeding at the knuckles.

As Matthew shook, J could see his friend's eyes watering.M atthew curled in a ball on the bathroom floor. He once again felt like he was in the back seat of his mind, he saw the world through his eyes, but somehow watching a movie of his life, as if someone, or something, else drove.

He was so cold.

How could this bathroom get so cold? He thought.

J turned the corner, and Matthew felt a wave of relief upon seeing his best friend.

"Hey, sorry for storming off–" Matthew began to say, but he stopped, noticing he didn't actually *say* anything.

"Hey, J," he said, but nothing came out of his mouth.

"Hey!" he shouted, but nothing.

He felt his body twitch as he tried to stand up, but he couldn't move his legs. He felt like a puppet trying to move its own limbs, but the puppet master was holding the strings too tightly.

A low, guttural laugh came into his mind. The sound was terrifying, echoing in the recesses of his mind like a childhood nightmare coming to life.

He watched as J bent down and tried making eye contact.

"Matt, talk to me," J said as he extended one of the two Bibles forward.

Matthew heard a horrific growl from the same place as the laughter. The sound came from deep within his mind, as if the Earth itself was growling in anger.

"J, back up!" Matthew called out, but once again, the words never formed on his lips.

As the Bible approached, the body parts closest to the glowing Ark within the book now screamed in pain. The burning sensation spread across his legs and midsection.

The growl intensified, like a spring ready to uncoil.

As J extended the Bibles, Matthew's body jumped up and launched over J. Like a gymnast, Matthew pivoted in air and came down on J's back. He pushed J toward the bathroom wall, crumpling the man into the same corner that Matthew was just in. Within a split second, Matthew went from a shivering, watery-eyed ball to a confident and nimble warrior.

The growl disappeared as the laughter returned.

"J!" Matthew tried calling to his friend, but still nothing came out.

Matthew stepped forward, over J, and looked down at him. He reached over and lifted the top of toilet's tank over his head. In Matthew's peripheral vision, he saw himself in the mirror shards. Moments ago, he was mixed with the demon, half-and-half, but now, his human form was hardly visible in the broken mirror. The red-eyed demon held up the porcelain slab, ready to crush J's skull.

"No! In Jesus's name, Lord, help us!" Matthew called out, trying to pull back with all his strength. His body twitched, temporarily delaying the deadly blow as his muscles flickered. He felt himself losing the internal struggle. Matthew felt like his arms were a finger, feeling the trigger of a gun, softly squeezing it as it waited for the bang.

The momentary delay gave J time to move. He spun from his crumpled position, still holding both Bibles, and shot into

Matthew's stomach. The porcelain cover fell to the ground and shattered, cutting into the hardwood floor.

Matthew felt a horrible pain in his stomach, like his midsection was being ripped apart, as J drove him out of the bathroom and into the hallway wall.

J pressed the two Bibles down on Matthew's stomach, pinning him as Matthew's body squirmed and jerked to free itself.

Matthew felt his fist ball up, ready to strike the side of J's head, but he tried stopping it. The hesitation in Matthew's arms once again gave J all the time he needed. He kept one Bible pinned to Matthew's stomach and raised the other, moving it to Matthew's face.

Matthew's flesh crawled. He felt as if his body were being torn apart. Horrible pain twisted and pulled on every cell of his body.

The angry growls now became roars from the depths of his mind.

In his agony, Matthew had a memory. He remembered the first time his father gave him a piece of the Ark and the sting of pain that shot through his body. The feeling was a minor version of the tremendous pain that now shot through his body, the difference between a static shock and being struck by lightning.

"Get out of him!" J said as he moved the Bible toward Matthew's head.

From the backseat of his mind, Matthew felt the internal struggle continue. Once again, a memory surfaced. This time of Ignace reaching for Zech's Bible in the church office. How Ignace's hand distorted, as if the Ark repulsed his skin in such a way that it melted and reformed it halfway up his forearm.

Matthew feared he was watching his hand contort and warp just like Ignace's. After quickly swinging it, trying to smack the Bible away, his hand stopped. An invisible force field around the Ark held his hand back.

Matthew saw a flash of his hand separate from a black, shadowy hand.

J screamed, struggling to pin down Matthew as the demon within fought for freedom. Matthew had a third memory flash through his mind like a bright light. The loving feeling of warmth and welcome that came after the first pain of touching the Ark.

The memory of the feeling helped drown out the intense pain that shot through his body as he focused on his hand. At first, the demon inside him had raised Matthew's hand, trying to smack the good book away, but the force of God within the Ark stopped the hand cold. Now, Matthew held it there. Pain seemed to boil his flesh from the inside out. He felt the demon trying to pull away, but the balance of power within his body and soul was shifting. The memory of the feeling, the love of

God personified through the soft, warm glow, drove Matthew as he blocked out the pain and focused on moving his hand toward the Bible.

As Matthew focused on controlling his hand, the demon within was pushing J back.

J tried repositioning, but as he moved his feet, the demon raged and curled free. J gathered himself and expected Matthew to get up and bolt out the door. But Matthew's body twitched, remaining exactly where it was.

Then, J saw it. As the demon threw J back, Matthew grabbed hold of one of the Bibles. He held it to his stomach and pinned down the demon within.

From Matthew's point of view, as J flew off him, he redirected his efforts to the Bible resting on his stomach. He felt the demon tugging on his midsection, trying to roll away, just as it fought Matthew's hand from getting closer.

As Matthew overpowered the demon, his hand inching closer and closer to the Ark, he saw his one hand become two. The human version of his hand grasped the book, while the light of the Ark held back the opaque hand of the demon.

A sense of relief flooded J as he watched on in amazement at the exorcism in front of him. J didn't see the dark hand peel back from Matthew's but he saw a contorted form, Matthew's flesh twisted and melted in the heat of the struggle. Like a mirage, the deformed appendage finally regained its shape as Matthew took hold of the Bible.

As his hand grabbed the Bible, gripping the binding that held the Ark tightly, Matthew seized the opportunity and rolled into a ball around the book. To J's eyes, his entire body resembled silly putty that was being pounded and bent into various forms. To Matthew, a sharp pain ripped through his body, not a cell left untouched by the demon's grasp.

Then, the strange, yet welcome, sensation of love, peace, and safety washed over his body.

Above him, the dark cloud rose, roaring in anger at its lost host. Matthew looked up to see the red-eyed abomination stare back at him. The cloud held the loose form of a man, but even without a facial expression, he could read the hate in those horrific red eyes.

The shadow then bolted for J, ready to claim a new victim, but it froze as J held his Bible.

"Stay still," Matthew said. Then he stood up and moved next to J.

Both men held their Bibles at their chests. They created a stronghold against the enemy charging at their hearts. The light of the Ark within their Bibles glowed as it refuted the demon's advance.

The evil haze evaporated, conceding defeat.

Matthew collapsed, the Bible falling on his chest.

Chapter 36

Back on Your Feet

Matthew

"Hey, don't these things just pop out?" J called from the bathroom as he examined the medicine cabinet with the shattered mirror.

"There are screws on the inside. Two per side," Matthew called back. He sat on the floor, leaning against the couch, a fresh glass of water in his hand and an exhausted look on his face.

J stuck his head out from the hallway. "Where's your screwdriver?"

"You really don't have to do that now," Matthew said before taking a sip of the cool water.

"Yeah, yeah. So, where is it?" J replied.

"Pantry, middle drawer. I think you just saved my life, and likely my family's lives if that *thing* had stayed inside me."

J moved toward the pantry. "That's why I went to seminary!"

"You went to seminary to save me from being possessed?"

"Not exactly," J laughed. "But yeah, to save souls. So, yes!"

"Touché," Matthew said as he took another sip.

"Honestly," J said as he searched for the screwdriver, "all I did was hold you down and give you the Bible. You threw me off, and I outweigh you, so that's not an easy task. That final step of grabbing on to the book and the power inside, that was all you, brother."

Matthew nodded in agreement as J found the screwdriver and walked past Matthew on his way back to the bathroom.

"Regardless of how it ended, thank you for starting it. You came after me," Matthew said.

"You're welcome. Now, if you're feeling better, why don't you help me with this thing?"

Matthew heard J drop screws on to the bathroom countertop before pulling on the shattered mirror door.

Matthew slowly sat up and stretched. His body ached, but the feeling of love gave him hope. The spiritual revival helped him look past the physical pain.

As he turned the corner into the bathroom, he saw dozens of jagged white pieces swept into a pile. A dent in the hard wood from the toilet cover was right in the middle of the floor.

"Think Liz and the girls will notice all of this?" Matthew said.

"Only if they use the bathroom," J said with a mocking, hopeful expression.

"Speaking of the girls, have you heard from Ashley?"

"Not since lunch," J said.

Matthew walked back to the kitchen, where both of their phones rested in the corner of the granite countertop.

"Whoa," Matthew whispered as he saw all the missed calls from Liz. A text message caught his eye, a picture of a giant cloud engulfing an arena. Then he zoomed in on two people in front of the arena. Terrence and a woman.

"J!" Matthew shouted out. He tossed J his phone as he came around the corner. "Leave the mirror. Get your things."

J looked at him, confused, then he looked down at his phone. He quickly scrolled through to see missed calls and texts. Seconds later, both had their phones up to their ears and were heading out the door.

Hopping into Matthew's truck, they sped out of the neighborhood toward the interstate.

"I can't get ahold of Liz. Straight to voicemail," Matthew said.

"Same with Ashley. It was at the arena. You think they'd attack a women's conference?"

They met eyes and exchanged concerned looks.

J turned on the radio and scanned stations. Breaking news sections came on, but they learned nothing beyond the bits and pieces gathered from the texts and pictures sent by Liz and Ashley.

"Thousands are trapped inside as the smoke clears. Our report says special biological hazard units are preparing to enter the arena."

"They're trapped inside... They trapped my wife and daughters inside a ring of poisonous gas?" Matthew jammed his foot on the gas pedal and the truck lurched forward.

"Lord, be with those women, be with our women, Lord," J prayed and Matthew repeated alongside his friend.

"Still exhausted?" J looked at Matthew.

"What?"

"Earlier today you told me you were exhausted, that you didn't want to fight anymore. I'd say that's changed."

Matthew's jaw clenched, his vision straight ahead, focused on the road ahead as he swerved through traffic. "What was that verse about Jesus flipping tables? Now's the time for action."

J nodded in agreement as he observed his friend's newfound determination. He tried Ashley's cell again.

Moments later, Matthew's phone buzzed as he took the on-ramp toward I-95 South.

"It's Luke?" Matthew said, confused. "Hey, you see Orlando?"

"Yes. You get ahold of Liz?" Luke asked.

"No. Straight to voicemail."

"Millie called me from the hotel line. Apparently, cell phone towers are down," Luke said.

"Wait, hotel? As in, hotel outside the arena?" Matthew's voice rose.

"I did. They're out, brother," Luke confirmed.

"The girls, all of them?"

"All of them. They made it out just as the smoke went off."

Relief washed over Matthew as the tension in his body fell. He let up on the gas, still speeding, but now only ten miles per hour over the speed limit instead of twenty. "Thank the Lord."

He turned to J, "They're out!"

J let out a giant exhale of relief.

"What happened?" Matthew asked.

"They were playing with the girls, and they saw something..." Luke trailed off. Matthew heard Luke clear his throat. "Terrence. They saw Terrence planting the gas."

"Liz sent a picture. It's from outside the arena. She must have seen him and got away." Matthew shook his head.

"Yup, back at the hotel. Girls are good."

Matthew let out another breath of relief.

"I'll give mom and dad a call, keep them posted. Drive safe," Luke said.

"Love you, brother," Matthew said as he hung up the phone and sped through traffic.

An instant later, his phone rattled in the plastic cup holder.

"Unknown number," he said as he picked it up.

"Hotel line?" J suggested.

"Liz? That you?" Matthew answered.

"No, but she's here," Matthew's heart sank as he recognized the voice. "And so are your girls. It's nice to see everyone in person," Terrence's sinister voice hissed through the phone.

Matthew's face went pale.

"Who is it?" J asked, noticing his friend's expression. "What?"

Matthew brought down the phone and hit the speaker button.

"You know, running into these ladies is like an act of God. What a coincidence, don't you think?" Terrence said. "Don't you think, ladies? Go ahead, you can talk."

"Matt, we're here. We're safe," Liz said with a restrained voice.

"Terrence, let 'em go!" J screamed into the phone.

"I'm glad you're there, sidekick. You can show me the Houdini trick you pulled last time we spoke face-to-face."

"That wasn't me. It was—"

"You're right, it wasn't. The power of the Ark is wasted on you watered-down fools!"

"Hurting them won't help you," Matthew said.

"You know, I'd rather not. In fact, I'd rather just kill you two, take the Ark and be on my way," Terrence said.

"You can have the book. Let them be," J said.

"Bring the Ark. No police, no one else. I want you to walk right past the front desk and come up to the room. I'll have eyes on you two. No one else. If I see a maid's cart too close to the door, your family dies."

"Deal," Matthew said through gritted teeth. "I want to talk to them—" Terrence hung up.

Matthew and J looked at each other, then back at the road. He pressed his foot down, speeding up.

"You think we should call the cops, anyway?" J rolled his phone over in his hand.

"I don't know," Matthew responded. "I want to, and we probably should..."

"But it's different when your loved ones are on the line," J finished.

"Yeah."

They remained silent as Matthew's truck moved down I-95 South and merged on to I-4 West.

The two were quiet as the truck covered the miles to Orlando. A thought kept bubbling up in Matthew's mind from earlier when J helped him exorcise the demon.

"How did you know?" he said, glancing at J.

"What?"

"How did you know the demon was in me?"

"You told me last time what you saw after looking in the mirror. And your mood never changes as quick as it did when we were on the porch," J said.

"You're acting like it's nothing, ignoring attempted murder with the tank cover of a toilet."

"We're past that," J said.

"What?"

"Hey. I don't know what it's like to be possessed, but I know the healing of the Gadarene Demoniac. His life was a total one-eighty after Jesus sent the legion of demons into the swine. I knew you before that devil attacked your soul."

"Thank you for being there."

"You're welcome," J replied. "So, do you still see them?" J motioned out over the dozens of cars immediately around them.

"Yup. That van has none." Matthew pointed to a van next to them, with a man and woman in the front seat and four kids in the back. The couple laughed and talked together while the kids bounced in their car seats and seat belts.

"That van looks like chaos on wheels," J joked.

"It does, but look," Matthew pointed. "The couple is enjoying a conversation while the kids talk and play games."

As they watched, a deck of cards passed between two of the kids. Another two kids laughed.

"That peace isn't easy. I've yelled to the backseat countless times when the girls are misbehaving. Even them being too excited and getting loud drives me nuts. But they've found a balance in that van, and with it, peace. No demon pulling their strings."

"What about that one?" J asked as they passed a black Tesla SUV. The clean paint sparkled in the sunlight as they passed, and two people, a man and woman, sat quietly in the driver and passenger seats.

Matthew watched the car for a moment as they passed. Soon, he was watching it in the rear-view mirror. "They have 'em. One for each, but it sort of blends together. Like a giant haze over the entire roof of the car."

"They looked peaceful," J said.

"I'd bet they were ignoring each other."

J nodded, then asked the question on Matthew's mind.

"You think Terrence has one?"

"Without a doubt," Matthew said. "Maybe a better question is, how big and powerful is Terrence's demon?"

"You know, if only we had a Bible-toting hero who could see these evils, and then smack 'em with an artifact of God's presence..." J shook his head as he trailed off.

Chapter 37

Standoff

Matthew

The two men decided not to get the police involved. After taking a detour around the arena, and the chaos of the police and crowds, they parked at the hotel and walked straight past the front desk.

J had found a blueprint of the hotel's fire exits online. They went straight for the stairs. Both men had their Bibles, and the Ark within it, tucked into the back waistband of their pants.

Matthew and J ascended the dimly lit stairwell, each step echoing with a foreboding sense of urgency, like the bell tolling on an ancient clock. The weight of their mission pressed upon them, and before opening the door to the fourth-floor hallway, they stopped and said a prayer. Matthew's trembling hand steadied after the prayer, and both took a deep breath.

He inched open the door, peering down the hallway. A long stretch of dark blue carpet with decorative white swirls centered the white walls and white crown molding.

"Nothing," Matthew said. They crept out of the stairwell and down the hall.

The air grew thick with tension as they neared the door of the room where Terrence held their loved ones captive. A hushed silence enveloped them, broken only by the distant sounds of muffled voices and doors closing in the maze-like hotel structure. All the noises stopped as Matthew and J walked cautiously into the hallway. The corridor was still, as if the room held its breath, aware of the imminent clash between light and darkness.

With determined resolve etched upon their faces, Matthew and J reached the door. Matthew's hand, still steady, gripped the doorknob, knowing that the fate of his loved ones rested on the choices made within these walls. The door swung open, revealing a scene bathed in darkness, save for the faint glow of a television and single lamp in the corner. The blackout shutters blocked the light from the room as Liz held their daughters. They sat on the couch, engrossed in animated cartoons dancing on the television screen. Aunt Millie, with her fiery spirit undimmed by the ordeal, stood defiantly by their side. The two women book-ended the young girls.

Matthew wanted to run for Liz. She looked at him, and looked as if she might leap into his arms, but she paused. His lungs held still as his heart pounded in his chest. The enemy in the room was watching them both.

"Dad!" Beth called out, but Liz put her arm on the child and kept her in position.

"Welcome," Terrence sneered, his eyes glinting with malevolence from the back corner of the room. The glow of the television showing a gun resting on his lap.

"Please, come in."

As they entered the room, J's eyes searched the area while Matthew locked eyes with Terrence. The dimly lit room concealed the giant haze of darkness surrounding Terrence.

"Where's Ashley?" J craned his neck into the bedroom portion of the two-room suite.

"Not in there," Terrence said. "But she's safe, assuming all goes well."

J's displeasure was obvious, already feeling betrayed by the man who had once pretended to be a loving mentor.

"Come around," Terrence motioned with his gun, directing the two men to the tiny kitchen in the suite. "Put the books, and the Arks, in the case."

A black suitcase filled with padded foam rested on the counter in the kitchen's corner. Matthew moved toward the case, sliding the Bible from his lower back. The sensation he felt against his back now shifted to his hand and up his arm. It gave him a peace he couldn't understand in the dreadful situation.

"I don't see Revelation in this," J said. "Paris. New York. Your gruesome, misguided work on display for the world to see, but this?"

"Your New Testament mindset forgets how Joshua took the Promise Land. Entire cities, men, women, and children. All wiped out."

"There were over two-hundred worshippers in New York. You're killing the same side," J said.

"Watered-down messages that allow idol worship in the temple is NOT the same side. Have you read Ezekiel? The statues of their worship are in the temple," Terrence scoffed. "Besides, I wasn't in New York."

J tilted his head, brow furrowed in confusion.

"Dad!" Lyn interrupted, a scared tone in her voice as Liz wrapped an arm around her.

"It's alright, sweetheart. We'll be heading out soon," Matthew replied. "And you can tell me what's going on in that show."

"Yes, tell her it's alright. Keep enabling potential followers to not face the idols of the world. You cut off the tops of weeds but leave the root."

"She's a child," Matthew snapped.

"You're the child," Terrence said in an unnatural voice that reverberated through the room. The girls quivered in Liz and Millie's arms.

Matthew saw pieces of a dark giant above Terrence as he stood and moved around the room. He slid against the walls with his gun trained on Matthew and J. Millie's angry stare looked like she was ready to reach out and punch Terrence as he moved past, but she wrapped her arms around the girls and Liz.

"Put it in the case," Terrence directed, his voice back to his normal sneer.

J followed Matthew and placed his Bible in the oversized black case.

"Move," Terrence directed them to the back corner. Matthew and J slowly sidestepped, keeping their eyes on him as they rotated around the girls. Like satellites, the men orbited the women and children in the center of the room, swapping their original positions.

As Matthew and J reached the back corner, Liz released the girls. They jumped up and hugged their father. Liz and Millie darted next to Matthew and J.

The two men stepped in front of them to face Terrence.

Terrence kept his gun trained on the family as he glanced at the Bibles. The soft glow of the warm, amber light slipped out of the binding and fell on the padding of the case. He closed the case and snapped it shut.

Matthew noticed Terrence's hand cautiously take hold of the handle. He knew the villain remembered how it mangled Ignace's hand without a touch, and how he couldn't approach it during the gunfight at the Shipping Yard.

Terrence lifted the case. He smiled and backed toward the door.

"Where's Ashley?" J demanded.

"Oh, right," Terrence feigned surprise as he opened the door and slid into the dark hallway. "Room five-oh-nine."

He glanced at the black watch on his wrist. Matthew investigated the hallway around Terrence. It was bright when he and J came through, but now, around Terrence, it was pitch black.

"She might still have time, but yours is up." In one smooth motion, Terrence raised the gun and pulled the trigger.

Matthew looked down the barrel and saw the flash of the bullet leave the gun. Time seemed to slow as he watched the pop of light pointed at his face.

In the millisecond after the bullet was fired, he saw another flash. A streak of brilliant, yet nearly imperceptible, light shot from left to right across his vision. It moved exactly in line with the bullet's trajectory. He felt the bullet go past his ear.

Terrence aimed at J, but he never got a second shot off. Two men in full SWAT-like uniforms pounced, knocking Terrence, his gun, and the suitcase down before pulling his hands behind his back.

Terrence's painful surprise turned to confusion, then hatred, as he looked up at Matthew and J. His face was pushed against the blue carpet as officers hauled him off the ground.

Matthew and the others looked on, eyes wide and smiles forming.

But as they took Terrence into custody and a swarm of officers came into the room, Matthew saw why the hallway looked so dark. A towering demon stood above Terrence.

The girls all smiled as Matthew watched the men move Terrence out of view. He noticed a smile creep across Terrence's face.

J shot forward to the officers, who looked more like flexible robots in their full black uniforms and goggles. One officer raised a gun at him as he dashed forward.

J stopped and put his hands up. "There's someone else held captive. Room five zero nine, she's in trouble!"

The officer looked at his companion, as if contemplating his next action. Then, a third uniformed man stepped forward, commanding the group to act on J's information.

J ran behind the wave of officers that headed to the stairwells at each end of the hall, while the others remained with Terrence.

"I'm going with him." Matthew hugged Liz and gave her a kiss. As he did, he saw outside the window and into the parking lot below. Police cars and a SWAT van surrounded the building. He bent down and kissed his girls, then gave Millie a quick hug as well.

He bolted out of the room, following J.

Chapter 38

The Dragon

Matthew

"Stay back. We will clear the floor and enter the room first. Do NOT run forward or you will be put into custody," the leader of the small group told J as he noticed the two civilians following them to the fifth floor.

"Yes, sir," they both said. Matthew looked ahead at the group as they moved as one. His and J's shoes were making more noise on the concrete stairs than their entire group's. He thanked the Lord for trained soldiers.

J and Matthew stayed back in the hall as the second portion of the team came out of the opposite stairwell. The two groups converged on room 509. They stealthily examined other open doors and maid carts as they cleared their path.

The silent hallway held an eerie presence as the group inched closer.

An elderly man opened his door and stepped out, but after seeing the armed men, he darted back inside. Matthew heard the man bolt the extra lock of his door.

One soldier pulled out a hotel card and crept toward the electronic lock as two others took cover positions.

"Wow," Matthew whispered to J. "Master key."

With a smooth swipe, the soldier unlocked the door and threw it open. He stayed crouched as he entered, and the two in cover positions quickly dashed in with him. Two more men stayed in the hallway with eyes on the door.

Matthew and J stepped forward, trying to get a glimpse of the room. J whispered prayers of protection for Ashley.

As they inched forward, they passed a room with an open door. The maid cart held the door open, but the maid was long gone. The two men paused between the open door and a small alcove containing the ice dispenser and a vending machine.

"Do you hear that?" J said. "Sounds like splashing water?"

Before Matthew could reply, a woman spun around from behind the ice machine and swung a bat at Matthew, striking his shoulder. He fell into the open room and the attacking woman pulled a gun out and swung it at J as he turned back.

The pistol smashed against J's forehead, opening a gash over his eyebrow. The woman shoved him into the open room and followed behind them, kicking the maid cart into the room and letting the door close.

Once inside the room, Matthew and J, laying on the carpet, looked up at the woman. The tail of a dragon peeked out of her black shirt sleeve and a claw stretched out of her neckline, wrapping around her throat as if choking her.

"You?" J vaguely remembered the bartender from the prior year.

She didn't respond.

"I know you. And I met your mother, in France." J raised his hand to the blood pouring from his forehead.

"You passed me aside like trash," she said.

"I invited you to church," J replied.

"You scared my mother into addiction. She's lost in Europe because of your preaching."

"Your mother helped me, then tried to kill me before running—"

"Shut up!" she screamed, before lowering her voice.

"I'm done with this. I'm done with you, and your whole family, and your whole church," she said, shaking her head. "My whole life, I tried. Did you know I had a son? No, of course you didn't. Did you know who his father was?"

J and Matthew looked at each other, then back at the woman. Matthew noticed a black cloud flare around her.

"You killed him," she said. "First, you mangled his hand. Then, your murdering grandfather killed him."

"You're with Terrence," J said.

"I'm not *with* anyone. I'm finally pushing back on a world that chews up people like me, people like my mother, and my brother..." she turned away as a glint of a tear flashed in her eyes. "But I'm on the offensive now."

"You're not the same person we met at the sports bar," Matthew said.

"That seems to happen when religious zealots kill your loved ones," she said through clenched teeth.

"So, you kill in response? Where's Ashley?" J stood up as he asked.

"What's that saying you folks have, an eye for an eye?" She glanced toward the bathroom.

"What's your name?" Matthew rose to stand next to J.

"Selena," she said, raising the gun from her hip and pointing it at his face. She held a bat in one hand and the pistol in the other.

"Selena," Matthew said. "There's a SWAT team out there. They took Terrence and he'll go to jail to pay for his crimes. When they find out the room they're searching is empty, they'll come looking for us."

"Come here," Selena motioned with the gun.

Matthew stepped closer and Selena snapped the gun, the steel striking the side of his head. He fell to one knee as she looked down at him. Matthew felt a trickle of blood flow behind his ear.

"Let 'em come," she said.

The black cloud swelled around her.

Matthew shook off the blow and slowly stood next to J. He eyed the haunting figure that floated in and around her. It was like an up-lighting effect followed her every step, casting a giant shadow on the ceiling and walls behind her.

A bubbling noise rose from the bathroom.

"She's here," J stepped forward, trying to see through the cracked bathroom door.

As J stepped forward, Selena dropped the bat and, like a trained assassin, pulled out a switchblade and stabbed J's leg. She motioned the blade at Matthew as he moved towards J. Then she kicked J back and leaned over him with a mocking *shush* motion, a finger over her lip from the hand that held the bloody knife.

J clenched his teeth and looked at Selena, then found Matthew's eyes.

Their lifelong friendship of exchanging countless glances led to a split-second understanding. They couldn't wait for the police. Selena would slowly kill them and let Ashley die.

Selena backed up, and Matthew stepped forward, going down on his knees to J.

"She's got one. A demon," he said. "It's big, and it's growing."

"We have to get to Ashley," J whispered through the pain as blood soaked his jeans.

Matthew looked up at Selena, a fiendish smile across her face. He looked back at the wound in his friend's leg.

"She's the dragon."

J heard him and looked at his leg. The dream came back to him at once, remembering the fatal train ride. It ran past his parents, then the Light family, eventually coming to Ashley and Matthew. The worm in front of the train grew into a snake, then into a dragon before swallowing J, Matthew, and Ashley. In J's dream, he took a long fang straight through the leg. It hit the same spot as Selena's knife, and close to the spot the extremist in Paris had sliced his thigh.

J looked up at Matthew. He nodded in agreement.

"What happens after the teeth come down?" Matthew asked.

"It swallows us. We're in the... Sea of darkness," J said.

Horrifying memories came back to Matthew during his three days of unconsciousness. The red-eyed demon tried to pull his soul into the sea of darkness, but a strange light saved him. The light then brought him to a huge Bible where he watched his grandfather struggle against a demonic current. Rushing waters washed away the rest of the Light family, but Isaiah withstood the onslaught. He held his ground and turned a key that magnified the light and blasted away the darkness.

"I'm not going into that sea," Matthew said. "And neither are you two. Whatever happens, get to the bathroom. Get Ashley."

"The Ark," J said. "We don't have it."

"We can't pray and wait. It's time to pray and work," Matthew said.

J nodded.

Matthew stood up and faced Selena. Her petite frame magnified by the demon in their presence. Her shadow was shaped like an immense silverback gorilla. The darkness hung above and around her frame. It bobbed as if breathing deeply and preparing for another fight.

"Do you know why Terrence took my family?" Matthew asked, stepping toward her.

"Stop," she demanded.

"He tried to kill me before. He's tried to kill J before, too. But *every* time, he fails."

Matthew took another step forward.

"I said stop." She raised her gun.

"She's in there, isn't she?" Matthew glimpsed the bathtub through the cracked door. Ashley was underwater. He couldn't see her face but saw her hair flow in the water. Countless strips of gray duct tape covered from shoulder to knee and held her to the bottom of the tub. Her hands and legs held in the watery cocoon with a single straw coming up from her mouth, breaking the surface of the water. If she remained calm and breathed through the straw, she'd live, but if she lost it, her air was gone.

Selena raised the gun and moved to meet Matthew, putting the barrel straight to his forehead.

"Shut your—" Matthew didn't allow her to finish.

"No," Matthew demanded. "I'm here to tell you that Terrence failed once again, and so did you. But thankfully, failure is an event, not a person. Jesus bled for you. Died for you. And it's never too late. *Never.*" As Matthew spoke, he leaned in, pressing his forehead into the gun barrel and causing Selena to take a step back.

"Stop," Selena's voice wavered.

"I've seen the pit of darkness that pulls you. The monster that pulls at you now, it's pulled at me too. It would have won if the light didn't save me. It can save you, too. Refute the evil in you, accept the light. Accept Jesus," Matthew said.

The gun trembled in Selena's hand, centimeters from Matthew's head. He could see the black cloud around her pulse and rage like a storming sea.

"I'll kill you," Selena forced out. Matthew remembered the helpless feeling of being locked in his own mind and knew the internal struggle she must be going through.

"If I die, I know where I'm going," Matthew called her bluff. "Do you?"

With Matthew's question, Selena's gun twitched, pointing up to the ceiling, but the demon flared in response. The darkness twisted Selena's body and swung her hand with the switchblade at Matthew's side. But Matthew saw it. The world seemed to slow down, just like when Terrence shot at him moments earlier.

A light flashed at his side, delaying her deadly swing as he pushed her with one arm. She fell back, off balance, and the blade swung in front of Matthew, missing his chest by less than an inch.

As Selena fell back, J took off, crawling with his injured leg dragging behind him. A path of blood soaked into the blue carpet, leaving a purple line behind him that led into the bathroom.

Selena slammed into the door with a thud that echoed into the outside hall. As she fell, the gun in her hand went off and blasted a hole in the drywall. Dust fell from the hole and on to her.

J reached into the tub and ripped at the tape holding down Ashley. Water splashed across the white-tiled bathroom as he furiously pulled on the tape. In the commotion, she lost the straw and bubbles rose from her mouth as she silently screamed from the water. J turned to the drain but more tape clogged it. He went back to Ashley, pulling on more strips as she shook to free herself. Moments later up, she erupted from the water. She gasped as J took her in his arms and pulled her from the tub.

A split second later, the SWAT team barged in, the door swinging open and pinning Selena to the wall.

She screamed in pain.

Chapter 39

The Stuck-up Savior

Matthew

An hour later, Matthew and J sat in a police van. Matthew's daughters were in his lap and Liz at his side. Aunt Millie stood outside the open side door, near J and Ashley. J's arms wrapped a blanket around her as she leaned into him.

"Thank you for your time," the investigator said as he closed his notebook and moved away. He left the Bibles with them after inspecting Terrence's black case.

"Give us a few hours upstairs, but then you can have access to your things." He nodded and moved away.

Police and medical staff moved around them. Lab workers took blood draws to search for traces of the poisonous gas, but so far everyone was well.

Their guard finally down as Matthew took hold of his Bible and closed his eyes, his daughters finally resting instead of bouncing on his knees. Liz leaned on his shoulder and closed her eyes.

"They didn't notice the Ark glowing in it," he laughed.

"They didn't notice the butter knife tucked away in my sock either," Liz said. Her eyes remained closed, but a smirk formed on her face.

Matthew's eyes shot open. "What?"

"Yeah, if he got close enough, I was going to..." Liz smiled and made a stabbing motion with her hand.

Matthew shook his head. "I love you."

"It was Millie's idea," Liz shrugged.

He looked out at Aunt Millie, who overheard their conversation. "That's right, and I had chop sticks. He's lucky he didn't get them through his eyes," she said.

The family laughed and relaxed as best they could in the chaotic environment.

"I'm sorry about all this," J whispered into Ashley's ear. "You didn't deserve to be pulled into this war."

Ashley turned in J's arms. "I don't know how long I was in that water, but you know what I thought about?"

"What?"

"Losing you again." She reached her arms out of the blanket and wrapped them around him.

"I'm so glad you brought the cops," Liz said quietly into Matthew's shoulder.

"We didn't," Matthew said, but Liz was already drifting to sleep. He felt the tension in her body release as she relaxed.

Matthew allowed himself to keep his eyes closed, leaning his head against the headrest of the cloth-covered seats in the van. He thought about what would change with the New Christians now that their driving force was gone. Soon, he stopped thinking and breathed easier with his loved ones around him.

"The Light family takes a beating but survives once again," a female voice rang out as the clicking of high heels approached.

Matthew's eyes shot open and quickly focused. He recognized that voice.

Standing in front of them, Nancy Pawly, with two secret service men at her side.

"No need to talk," she said, raising one hand in a stopping motion. "I'm just here to say that I'm glad you all are okay and that we could save you in time. Our manhunt for the Christian Terror is thankfully over."

"Christian Terror?" J said as Ashley turned to the woman.

"The media runs with these things, you know?" She shrugged.

"I remember you running with a false storyline about our church, costing us millions. What do you want?" Aunt Millie stepped closer to the woman, refuting Nancy's friendly manner.

"I did my job, and we carried out justice." She stared back into Millie's eye, her face tightening at Millie's challenge.

A moment later, she snapped back to playing the friendly politician. "How about that, though? We were at odds earlier this year, but now, because of me pushing for religious protections to find and bring the Christian Terror to justice, we're on the same side."

No one commented as Nancy stood smiling like she was posing on the red carpet.

"Well, glad you are all okay and that we could help. We've been tracking Terrence Shade, Junior for days now, ever since his flight to the US under a fake passport. I'm just sorry we couldn't get here sooner. We might have saved all the trouble in the arena. Thankful, there were no casualties today. It could have been a lot, and I mean a *lot*, worse."

Still, no one responded to her as they stared in distrust.

"One more thing, he's asking to speak with you two," she pointed to Matthew and J. "He doesn't want a phone call, nothing. Just wants to talk with you two."

Matthew slowly opened his mouth as he glanced toward J.

"Don't worry, we're not allowing it. Terrorists don't exactly get phone calls. But I'll be doing a network exclusive from the jail in a couple of weeks. The American people need to confront this monster to help us heal. Let's save your conversation for when the cameras are rolling. I'll tell my people."

She spun and walked toward a black sedan. One of the secret service men opened the door and let her in.

"*She* brought the cops. And a lot more." Matthew watched as the massive, red-eyed demon floated over Nancy and stared at him.

Chapter 40

Government Lockdown

Zechariah

"They've done it," Zech said to Mary. He shook his head and pointed at the television.

"Keep it low. They're all sleeping," Mary whispered.

"How are Grace and the kids?" Jimmy's soft voice rang out from Zech's phone on the coffee table.

"I should have known it wasn't the TV making all that noise. Where's Paul?" Mary asked.

"It's unconstitutional!" Paul shouted through the phone along with the sounds of him beating his hand against a table.

"Quiet down, Paul!" Mary said in a raised whisper.

"No! We can't stay quiet about this! It's unconstitutional!"

"So was Roe vs Wade. That didn't stop it from being on the books for fifty years," Jimmy responded.

"I have a daughter-in-law and two grandbabies fresh off a hellish ordeal and thirty-six hours of travel. If you want to scream, do it away from the phone."

Paul grunted through the phone. "Yes, ma'am."

"Yes, ma'am," Jimmy whispered.

Their eyes all went to the screen, where the special telecast interrupted the nightly news. Nancy, alongside the Vice President and Speaker of the House announced special restrictions to *protect* church goers.

"But if Terrence is in custody, why do they need all this?" Mary asked.

Zech opened his mouth, but Paul's voice rang through the phone first. "Cause it ain't about saving people."

Zech looked at his wife and nodded. "Fear is taking over."

"And we've lost all common sense and logic," Paul quipped.

"I'm afraid the damage is done. Terrence is behind bars, but the body count, and images of the attacks," Jimmy paused. "They're still on everyone's mind."

"It's a political slam dunk. Nancy rides the wave of popularity with her manhunt and now the public hangs on her every word. I can't believe this," Paul scoffed. "Years ago, you'd have a civil war if the government told folks they couldn't go to church. But now, how many Christians will happily accept the government recommending they stay home?"

"You noticed what they called the attacks, didn't you, the *Christian Terrors*?" Jimmy said.

"A quickly rising politician, whose extreme views segregate one culture and religion. Now, let me think, where has this happened before?" Paul asked sarcastically.

"Paul, you think everything is Hitler." Zech came back into the conversation.

"Tell me I'm wrong!" Paul retorted.

"In this case, unfortunately, I see the parallel all too well," Zech said.

"Hush up and listen," Mary said as she leaned in.

"And that is why I'm recommending no in-person church services for the American public. While we all rejoice at the capture of a global terrorist, there is still an extreme group out there that may retaliate. Let's not give them the chance to take more lives. We'll use technology to keep the religious freedoms that we founded our country on. I implore all Preachers, Pastors, and Priests, all the Rabbis and religious leaders from Judeo-Christian organizations across the country: it's time to go virtual. Lead your people in a new way," Nancy paused, taking a deep breath. "Now, we know many of you don't like this option. You'd rather meet in person—"

"The first honest thing she's said," Paul quipped.

"We know some leaders will ignore the warning, regardless of the obvious threat to your people."

"Oh, please," Paul said.

"She knows how to choose her words," Jimmy said.

"We also know that freedom is your choice and a bedrock for all Americans," Nancy continued.

"Why do I feel like there's a–"

"But," Nancy said.

"There it is," Paul added.

"As public servants, it is our duty to protect the American people. All our choices have externalities, outcomes that hurt the life and liberty of other Americans. If you are causing harm to the American people, then those of us who took the oath of office must step in."

"She's a lawyer. She didn't take any oath of office!" Paul said.

"If these respective organizations and their leaders choose not to follow our guidelines to protect Americans and religious followers, then they are choosing to ignore their five-oh-one C-three tax-exempt status with the Internal Revenue Service."

Zech's jaw dropped.

"She just wiped out tithes," Paul said.

"No, she's forcing a choice, money or in-person," Jimmy added.

"That's what I said. She wiped out tithes," Paul said.

"She's forcing virtual. Millions will be impacted... isolated," Zech said as the conversation with T flashed in his mind. "Evil is trying to divide us. We're easier targets in isolation."

Mary leaned back from the broadcast, her face contemplating the statements. She turned to her husband. "Our church already went one-hundred percent online. What happened to attendance and tithes?"

"Attendance dropped eighty percent, then rebounded," Zech said.

"What was it, thirty percent of tithes now versus back then?" Paul asked.

"Yes. Thirty-five to forty," Zech continued. "Thankfully, the folks who stuck around were the biggest givers. But we've seen a lot of challenges. Not only in the church, but in our members. One look at social media and you'll find out what isolation is doing."

"Zech, you remember your message a couple of years ago? The one on the decrease in church attendance and the rise of mental health issues, crime, divorce, fatherless kids?" Jimmy asked.

"I do," Zech said.

"What happens to the country when we lose four out of every five Christians?"

Zech didn't immediately answer as he looked at Mary and shook his head. Sadness etched across his weathered face. "The country will see an exponential rise in mental health issues, crime, divorce, and fatherless children."

"Terrence is finally behind bars. Why do I feel like we won the battle but lost the war?" Paul said.

A long silence followed.

"Let's pray," Zech said.

Chapter 41

The Stars Aren't Shinning

Jeremiah

"Our Sunday service views are up tenfold," J said.

"That'd normally be a miracle, but..." Zech added as he sat at his wooden desk, making notes to an upcoming sermon.

"Exactly. *But* all our sister churches are at less than ten percent of normal in-person attendance," J stood across the room, double checking connections and testing the cameras.

"What?"

"Yeah," J nodded. "At first, I thought maybe social media feeds weren't counting right. But I've triple checked it. Church attendance has fallen considerably. Far less than even our conservative estimates."

"Please tell me giving hasn't been hit so hard," Zech looked up and asked.

J's shoulders sank as he shook his head.

"How bad?" Zech asked.

"Less than five percent," J rubbed his eyes. "I spent hours on the phone with our church leaders. The numbers are right."

Zech looked out of his window. "Others are down, but if our views are up ten times normal, what about our tithes? Maybe we can redistribute until the rest get back on their feet."

"Nothing. They're flat."

"What do you mean, nothing?"

"Our tithes aren't up, only our views," J said. "Have you noticed the sentiment on social media and in the news? I've seen countless memes of some celebrity washing their hands and the text says: Not going, not giving."

"Pontius Pilot over all again..."

"It's my dream all over again. Every star in the sky is being suffocated out as darkness reaches across the Heavens. We come together to fight it."

"But my son dies," Zech looked at him.

"My dragon dream eventually came true, but we survived. I'm going to have a limp for months," he looked down at the wound in his leg. "I don't like it any more than you, but we have to figure this out."

"And what exactly are we figuring out?" Zech said in a frustrated tone. "How do we revive a nation's commitment to church?"

"Get all the pieces together, for starters. Then we confront Terrence. We go on the offensive," J said.

"And then what, wave the Ark in front of his face? Try to melt him like his sidekick's hand?" Zech threw his pencil. "I'm sorry. It feels like this is over. We got him, but the country is only getting worse. I saw on the news this morning, a church out in Oregon went up in flames. Some kids, kids! Set fire to it in the middle of the night. And you know what the so-called *objective* reporter said?"

J shook his head.

"Now the town can rezone that property." A look of disgust came upon Zech's face. "I can't believe it, and I should have known."

"How so?" J asked.

"You were in France when I showed the Ark to the world," Zech held up his Bible, pointing to the binding that hid the Ark. "I showed the world, and we promoted the video all over the web. But ninety-nine percent of YouTube comments called me crazy, or worse. Much worse..."

He shook his head.

"Since when have you let the world judge what you do on the pulpit?" J smiled.

A smile flashed across Zech's face.

"Well, we want all the pieces together and we'll get your wish. With Lucas found, Mark is going to fly in to be with Grace and the kids. He's bringing Lucas, who is walking again."

"Praise the Lord."

"Once Lucas can travel, Mark is putting him on a plane," Zech said.

"That's great, but we're still missing one," J said.

"Nope. Luke is coming down in a couple of days. He wants to be nearby for the Terrence interview," Zech said.

"Matt and I are going. You really going to miss it?" J replied.

"I guess not," Zech leaned back in his chair. "Why are we glorifying this evil?"

"*We* are not. We'll be behind the cameras and only there to see why Terrence wants to see us."

Zech grunted. "You're right."

He stood up and smiled at J. "Why did I ever bring you into this family?".

"Because you loved my father and you're a good man." J picked up the pencil and handed it back to his mentor.

"If you say so," Zech smiled.

J looked into a camera set on a tripod and focused it on Zech.

"Now, let's record this sermon," J said.

Chapter 42

The Dirty Mirror

Zechariah

"There are three types of people in the world," Zech said into the camera. J stood behind the device watching the feed on a nearby TV with headphones on.

"People that think this world is all about matter, the physical state of things. These are the extremists of science who won't believe a thing unless it's tested in a lab and peer reviewed. To them, our entire existence is an anomaly. Life is a random, once-in-a-billion-trillion chance. The big bang popped us into life, and eventually all the heat in the universe will dissipate. We'll all die and that's that.

"Then, there is the other side, people who think it's all spiritual. To them, our physical world is a mere cover of the ideal. They believe there's a way to get to pure nirvana—if we all conform to some *great knowledge* or understanding of enlightenment.

Once we learn it, we're *enlightened*." Zech raised his hands and wiggled his fingers.

"Finally, there's a third that is somewhere in between those two opposing views. It believes that there is *both* a spiritual and a physical realm, and that they are two distinct things that together make up our reality. Most of us are here, in the third bucket. For example, we believe God created the universe, a physical universe that is distinctly different from himself, a spiritual being.

"Our country is going through one of the darkest times in its history. During the time of America's founding, other governments, typically a monarch, believed that the government gave rights to individuals. For example, in their worldview, their government said what civilians could lawfully do. If the government didn't say you could do it, then they could come after you for it. However, when Benjamin Franklin edited Thomas Jefferson's first draft of the Declaration of Independence, he ensured it read *life, liberty, and the pursuit of happiness*. Liberty. The founders wanted our structure of government to only give a framework of what was *not* allowed. They wanted it to inherently grant the individual with all inalienable rights. Said another way, each person, just by the sheer fact of being alive, had their own religious freedoms and individual rights."

Zech shook his head and turned to face another camera as J hit a button to switch the feed.

"Now, I understand we must be safe, but we also need to live. Encouraging one another is mostly an in-person sport, like giving a hug to a brother or sister in Christ when they need it most, or just to say hi, or to say thank you. In fact, social interactions are the most correlated factor to one's happiness. Go look it up. A book called *The Good Life* tells the entire story over decades of research. But now, believers are now being forced to stay home, to put at risk the relationships that bind our community–the body of Christ–together.

"You want to know what I think will happen? We're going to make the mirror dirtier."

Zech paused and stared into the camera for effect, then straightened his papers.

"You see, those of us in that third bucket of believers, we believe in the balance between the physical and spiritual. We believe God made this world and since he is unchanging, there are unchanging laws that govern it and an unchanging moral truth. But God is the original, we're only a copy of him. *Made in his image.* And what is an image, but a reflection of the original?"

Zech cleared his throat and took a sip of water.

"Have you noticed that on the fourth day, God created light–the sun and moon? The sun is a giant ball of fire, too powerful and bright to look straight at it, but the moon is a beaten-up rock just trying to hang on to its orbit. All day and night, the moon reflects the sun. Let me say it this way: the *imperfect* moon reflects the sun's blinding light.

"Now let's jump a couple of days. On the sixth day, God creates humans, and he does it *in His image*. We're the beaten-up rock trying to reflect God's glory, a glory so awesome and bright that we can't look straight at it–think of the Holy of Holies in the innermost part of the Old Testament Temple. If you had any crumb of uncleanliness, you couldn't approach it."

Zech took another sip of water and smiled.

"Let's move from the moon example to a mirror. In mirrors, we see reflections, and an image is a reflection. We all look at mirrors every day, some more than others," Zech flashed a smile at J. "Think of our life as the mirror that reflects the imagine of God."

He paused and nodded.

"The longer we go without our Sunday service, our small groups, and our coffee and whatnot meet-ups, the dirtier the mirror gets. The dirtier the mirror gets, the more the reflection doesn't show the original.

"Now, if I'm stuck in my head, it's easy for my thoughts to lead away from the truth. I can convince myself of things that aren't true. It's easy for Pastor J to think all his thoughts are just random, evolutionary electrical bursts in a wet ball of matter we call the brain." Zech winked at J. "The Bible says iron sharpens iron, and for that to be true, the iron must engage, it must touch! You can see me through this technology, but it's a lot harder to sharpen a blade, to engage with you brothers and sisters in Christ through a TV screen."

J motioned for Zech to turn back to the original camera.

"To get through this dark time, we're going to have to face the dirty mirror that we each have. But thankfully, there's hope. Jesus reminded Nicodemus about the Israelites in the time of Moses, how they had to look at the serpent of bronze to be saved from venomous snake bites. They had to look towards an object, an image of what was literally killing them to be saved. They faced a small version of death every time someone had the faith to look at that image. Them, there's Jesus, who took the example God laid out centuries before and made it more real. He faced His own death in order to have life.

"We're all living in this world more *alone* than ever. We're walking around with the cause of our own death, our sinful hearts, and it's slowly killing us. But remember, the largest dragon protects the most valuable treasure–our deepest fears are often our salvation. Jesus proved it with His life on Earth. He faced death to give us life.

"I ask you, keep your faith, keep reading your Bible and meeting in small groups. Help each other by helping to keep our mirrors clean, because ultimately, all we're here for is to *accept* and *reflect* God's love."

Chapter 43

Broadcasting Live from Prison

Matthew

"How in the world is this going to go?" J whispered to Matthew. The two of them were standing behind Zech as the huge sliding bars slammed behind them.

They were now through security and into the prison.

"I don't love the idea of Nancy and Terrence in the same location," Matthew kept his voice low, for only the three of them to hear.

"Like a black hole of evil. I'm glad you insisted on bringing our Bibles," J replied.

"You can never let them take that away, prison or not," Zech said as they waited for the guard to clear the next space and open another massive sliding door of thick bars.

"Yeah, unlike Matt's pocketknife," J joked. "I can't believe you tried walking into a prison with a knife."

Matthew rolled his eyes. "I've had one in my pocket ever since Isaiah gave me one as a kid. I don't think of that as a weapon. It's a tool!"

"So, is a screwdriver okay to bring into a maximum-security prison?" J smiled.

"Yeah, yeah, you made your point. I forgot," Matthew said. "But hey, Beth knows how to use a pocketknife. I'm just saying it's a valuable *tool*, not always a weapon."

"Don't let that slip when the cameras are rolling," Zech said. "I can see the headline now. Christian children play with knives.""Great job, brother. Making a bad name for us all," J said.

Matthew rolled his eyes.

The guard led the three men into the last room. An open room filled with chairs and tables, all of which were bolted to the floor. A production crew transformed the visiting room into a television interview studio. Two huge cameras, microphones, and wires weaved a web across the room as guards stood blocking the entrance and exit."No Swiss Army knives allowed, but all this is, huh?" Matthew quipped as they took in the room.

Nancy sat in a corner. She waved aside the makeup artist and walked over to the three men. She moved with the confident stride Matthew remembered from the courtroom. Once again, she dressed to impress with a sleek business suit, dark blue with a black blouse, and her hair up in a tight bun. Even in the middle of a maximum-security prison, she could have passed for a CEO, or today, an investigative reporter.

But Matthew now knew the source of her inflated confidence. As she walked over, only he saw the towering mass of black hovering around her. Matthew stood firm, holding the stare of the red-eyed demon that had haunted his life and loved ones for the past year.

"My former legal adversaries turned allies. Welcome," Nancy said.

Zech frowned at her.

"I'm glad you could be here, even if a mass murderer extended your invite. Tell me, how comfortable is your community now that our safety policies are in place?" Nancy eyed Zech.

"Our church is doing great. It's been tougher since someone falsely accused my father of being a murderer and sued us for everything we had. But it gave us a head-start in this virtual-only world," Zech replied.

"A success story, wonderful. Maybe I'll work that in during the conversation,." She said brightly. Her positive attitude in the face of closing America's churches wrenched Matthew's heart.

Zech cocked his head to the side as if he was gauging her comment as serious or sarcastic.

"I'll be clear with my opinion of your safety policies. They are anything *but* safe. You're damaging more than one generation and the underlying religious freedoms that made, and still make, this country great."

Nancy raised her eyebrows, then rolled her eyes as she turned to see the makeup artist waving her back. She put up a finger and motioned for the artist to wait.

"So, you'd have all the Christians go unprotected, Mr. Light."

"You're building a straw man and using it as an excuse for authoritarian power. The policies won't last. And if I've learned anything from evil in history, is that evil eventually eats itself," he replied.

Matthew noticed his father look above Nancy's head. The demon's red eyes hovered above Nancy, as if taunting the three Christian men with its presence.

"Your father killed twelve men, and the justice system held your church accountable for the horrific act. Now, you tell me *evil eats itself?*" she feigned a laugh. "You're quite right, and the *fruits* of your life are the evidence. Now, please excuse me. I have an interview to conduct."

She turned, two long strands of her blonde and gray hair swinging from the sides of her face as the tight bun held the rest in place. The black evil surrounding her glided smoothly, keeping her in its midst as her high heels clicked on the concrete floor.

"Nice rebuttals," J said.

A guard came over and motioned the three towards a set of tables on the far end of the room.

"Let's take our seats," Zech said, his eyes still locked on Nancy.

J and Matthew walked with him behind the guard and took their seats on one side of the table. The uncomfortable chairs felt like he was sitting on rocks.

"Dad, can you see it? You looked right into the demon's eyes." Matthew whispered.

J overheard and turned to look at Nancy.

"No," Zech shook his head.

"But I can feel it. It's cold, and not cold like a snowy day, cold like an absence of life. A cold..." he watched Nancy as he searched for the word. "A cold *isolation*."

"That's exactly what it feels like," Matthew said.

They watched the production crew finish setting up as another man came in through the visitors' entrance. His tan skin made Matthew think he was Indian or Middle Eastern, and his short beard was too black for the man's age, which Matthew guessed was in his sixties.

"Who's black beard?" he whispered.

"Nasir Kingsley. One of Nancy's party's biggest donors. Saudi Arabian billionaire. Family oil wealth, which he turned into much, *much* more," Zech replied.

"He certainly doesn't mind showing it. That watch is worth more than my house," J said.

The man's thin-cut black suit, black dress shirt and vest, and neatly cut hairstyle were hardly noticeable given the flashy watch and polished white shoes. The diamonds on the watch and white accents popped like a lighthouse on a dark night.

J starred at the man intently. "I know him. And not from political donations."

He pulled out his phone, quickly snapped a quick picture, and sent off a text.

"You got your phone in here?" Matthew whispered in surprise.

"Yeah."

"What?" Matthew replied. "You ride me for the pocketknife, yet you snuck in your phone?"

"Yeah," J said. "I'm recording this whole thing. We'll want the raw footage. Who knows what these people will release?"

"How'd you smuggled that thing in?"

"Hid it in my underwear," J said.

Matthew looked at J in surprise.

"It was your dad's idea," J said, motioning to Zech. Matthew's dad gave a sly smile and continued looking forward.

J glanced down before hiding his phone. He nodded and tapped Zech's side.

"That's Solomon," J whispered into Zech's ear so softly that Matthew hardly heard him. Zech's eyes shot wide open as he slowly turned to face J, giving a questioning look.

"Mark confirmed." J nodded.

"Who's–"

Zech raised a hand, stopping Matthew before his question came out.

J whispered to Matthew. "The head of the New Christians. His identity is a secret, but he calls himself Solomon."

Matthew's eyes widened just as his father's did.

"Mark and Lucas have been researching the group since T shot them both."

Matthew eyed Solomon as the billionaire took his seat on the far end of the room, opposite of them. He came in with two bodyguards who looked like they could pass for Secret Service.

"He has a shadow, but not exactly like Nancy's." Matthew squinted while trying not to stare at the man. As the guards prepared for Terrence's entrance, the room focused on the incoming prisoner. Matthew managed to get a good look at Solomon's demon. "It's tighter, darker than the others. It's not a fog, it's like a dense, black soup wrapped around him. Strong, yet hidden."

"Sounds exactly like a billionaire that hides his terrorist activity," Zech said.

With cuffs on his hands and feet, and a chain connecting the four cuffs, Terrence came in wearing an orange jumpsuit. Five guards walked him into the room and sat him in the designated chair. Two of them secured Terrence to the chair.

He looked around the room, smiling at Nancy and the television crew. Then he looked at Solomon and flashed a broad smile.

"Why is Terrence acting like a Wal-Mart greeter? Does he know that's his boss?" J leaned in to ask Matthew.

"And what is Solomon's game here?" Zech asked as he eyed the billionaire.

"Quiet in the room," a crew member called out as he pointed to Nancy.

"We're live in three... two..." he mouthed 'one' as a green light came on above the camera centered on Nancy. Zech, Matthew, and J watched a large monitor that the production chief stood at.

A news anchor came on the screen. She was younger than Nancy, but her style matched the older woman. From the glasses to the tight hair and the business suit, the anchor's look imitated Nancy.

"Recent terrorist attacks on religious locations were truly horrific and shook the nation. As we heal and move forward, we have a special, one-of-a-kind exclusive for our Daily Live attendance."

The monitor went to a split screen. Nancy and the young woman were now side-by-side, both smiling.

"Tonight, we welcome the woman who is being heralded as not only America's champion for freedom but the leader who spearheaded the manhunt and capture of the so-called 'Christian Terror', Ms. Nancy Pawly. Welcome to the show, Nancy."

Nancy nodded and calmly raised her hand to check her earpiece. Meanwhile, Paul's voice echoed in the back of Zech's mind, calling out rebukes to the 'champion of freedom' comment.

"Thank you, Lisa-Michelle."

"So, before we get started with this amazing, one-of-a-kind glimpse into evil, I must ask, you're a distinguished and highly respected lawyer. You recently gave an unforgettable speech to congress that went viral and, I must admit, made me cry and pump my fists at the same time. Then, you lead a manhunt that a Navy SEAL would be proud of, and now, you're interviewing the most infamous man on Earth, like you're Barbara Walters in her prime." Lisa-Michelle raised her hands, a look of wonder on her face.

"Yes," Nancy smiled. "I didn't catch your question."

"Is there anything you can't do?" Lisa-Michelle slapped her hands on the black desk in front of her and a broad smile stretched across her face.

"That's very kind of you," Nancy raised her hand to her mouth as if she was blushing, but then she swiftly took over the conversation. "But you know, Lisa-Michelle, I'm just a woman out there in the world like so many others. If you work hard, are kind to others, and don't pin yourself down to ancient ways of thinking–the dogmas that drive fear in each of us–then any woman can do what I do."

The news anchor blushed, her cheeks flashing pink. "You are my hero, Nancy. And next time you're on my show, let's talk about which office you're running for next year."

"Oh, no, you don't Lisa-Michelle. I know your special gift of getting your guests to break news on your show." Nancy played along.

"This is like a tea party. Where's the infamous interview?" J said.

"It's all a show," Zech shook his head.

"What are you seeing, Matthew?"

"I'm not sure yet." He watched Terrence and the surrounding shadow. The demonic haze hardly moved, whereas Nancy's and Solomon's seemed to ripple at the edges; the flat surface of a still pond versus a river.

"I'm just saying," Lisa-Michelle threw up her hands like she was chatting with a dear friend. "I've heard rumors from trustworthy sources that your party is asking you to run. And for not just any office, but the highest office in the land."

Lisa-Michelle raised her eyebrows and leaned into the camera.

"I can neither confirm nor deny those allegations," Nancy said with a tight-lipped smile.

"Ah! Haha!" Lisa-Michelle pointed at the camera. "You're coming back, in studio, next week. Now, why don't you show the world the face of a monster? You're my hero, Nancy! Take it away!"

"Thank you," Nancy waved as the split screen faded away and she took over.

"America, tonight we heal. The lives lost from terrorist attacks impact countless families and cost our country precious resources that could be spent on education and help for the lower- and middle-classes."

"My goodness, this is a political campaign." Zech looked disgusted. "Forget about why Solomon is here. We were supposed to speak with Terrence, but if we're not, why are we here?"

Nancy continued. "Thanks to a generous donation from Nasir Kingsley, the CEO of the magnificent East Alliance Corporation, we're able to come to you live from a maximum-security prison. Through Nasir's leadership, East Alliance is helping to resolve thousand-year disputes across the Middle East and

Asia. As we constantly strive for equality in our own country, we can learn from the ideals of Nasir's work in action."

"We've had fake banter between the hosts and now a commercial for a hypocritical leader. You think they'll have a bear riding a unicycle in the next segment?" J said.

"Today, we take a step towards mending the broken bonds of society. Some have called me a hypocrite for leading religious policies that promote isolation. Those critics point to my legal career and the many cases I've debated. Chiefly, a recent case against the Light family on behalf of thirteen plaintiffs. Regardless of the clients and outcome, I brought the Light family here today to show we all must abide by the law, but as individuals, we all share responsibility for the world we live in. Thank you to all the religious leaders who are helping keep their flocks safe."

"That's why we're here," Zech whispered. "We're a political prop."

"Didn't Terrence invite us?" J eyed Terrence. "He seems too comfortable with all this."

"She's spinning it all for herself. Even my comments on isolation. Lord, let the American people see through this," Zech said.

Matthew and J watched Terrence. The prisoner turned and met their eyes. He smiled at them, a content smile, like he wasn't wrapped in chains, locked in a building of concrete and iron.

"He's enjoying this," Matthew said.

"Doing his best impression of Paul the Apostle in prison?" J said. "I saw him in a vision before the Lord freed me from Terrence last year. Now it's like Terrence knows he'll be freed instead of locked away for life."

The three men watched intently. Matthew made sure his Bible was on his lap.

"Now, on to the main event," Nancy turned in her chair and faced Terrence. She gave a practiced smile. Matthew recognized it as the same warm, yet professional smile she gave to judges in her courtroom statements.

"Mr. Terrence Shade, you are a–"

"Junior. I'm named after my Earthly father, Terrence Shade, Senior, which makes me Junior. However, I'm following in my heavenly father's footsteps, not my Earthy one," Terrence said plainly, as if having coffee with a friend.

Nancy looked up, a perturbed looked flashing on her face, but she cleared it quickly and rolled with the interruption.

"I'm glad you bring up a distinction between heaven and earth. Many would call your *organization* a terrorist group, wreaking havoc here on Earth. However, as a member of the New Christians, how would you describe the group and its purpose?"

"How would you describe it, Nancy Pawly?" Terrence asked back.

Nancy's head moved back. Her eyes burned at him as she mouthed something inaudible.

Zech read her lips. "He's going off script in a live interview."

"He's not playing along," J said.

Matthew looked over at Solomon. He still appeared confident, not flinching at Terrence's antics.

"Well, I'd describe it as a horribly misguided religion that uses its money and influence to kill innocent people," Nancy replied.

"That's close," Terrence said.

"You're admitting to killing innocent people?"

"Tell me," Terrence took a breath, keeping the conversation at a slow pace. "Were the Canaanites innocent when the Israelites entered the Promised Land? Centuries later, were the Israelites innocent when the Babylonians came knocking?"

"Are you justifying mass murder with thousand-year-old stories?" Nancy asked.

"Certainly no more than you are," Terrence said.

Matthew continued to look from Terrence to Solomon and back at Nancy.

"Something is happening," he said.

Like a brewing hurricane, Terrence's once calm shadow now slowly spun above him. Terrence sat in the storm's eye as all the blackness in the room started slowly moving toward him. The haze around the guards was the first to join him. Yet, like a puppeteer, the growing cloud held a thin connection to the source, a black string stretching out to all the guards in the room.

"If you're referring to European settlers and the displacement of Native Americans, then no. That is not justified. It's a horrible black eye and an example of the deep systemic oppression from history and in our society," Nancy said.

"No," Terrence gazed at her, calmly. "I'm referring to New York. I'm referring to Atlanta. We both take extreme measures to progress towards the ideal state. The only difference is, I'm right."

"The atrocious attacks in the US mirror attacks in Europe and other parts of the world. Attacks that *you* and *your organization* have taken credit for. Are you now denying your involvement?" Nancy looked at him skeptically.

"That is a *curious* question coming from you," Terrence replied.

Matthew watched as the red-eyed demon above Nancy appeared to resist the pull from Terrence. Matthew's eyes shot to Solomon, and like Nancy's dark cloud, his demonic cloud seemed to flicker in resistance.

All the lighter, smaller demons from the guards and television crew went to Terrence immediately. But like a heavy bolt shaking to an approaching magnet, Solomon and Nancy's hovering evil resisted.

"Terrence is growing stronger," Matthew said aloud.

Back in the interview, Terrence looked smugly at Nancy. Originally, she was a picture of confidence. A powerful figure on top of the world, interviewing someone in chains far below her in the pecking order. But now the body language shifted. Terrence oozed confidence, regardless of his chains, and Nancy's perfect persona was cracking.

"A matter of time until what?" J asked.

"I don't..." Matthew felt the Bible on his lap. He gripped it tight. "Put your Bibles on you. Somewhere in between you and Terrence."

Zech and J looked at each other, then secured their Bibles and the Ark on their laps.

"Why is a question about your involvement a *funny* question?" Nancy prodded.

"Because I could ask you the same thing."

"Let's stick to the agreed upon format, Mr. Shade. I'll be asking the questions, and you get your chance to share with the America people," Nancy said.

From Matthew's point of view, he saw the black storm cloud above Terrence pull apart the red-eyed demon around Nancy.

"Terrence's shadow, his demon. It's raising up, pulling in the others," Matthew said. At first, he enjoyed seeing the tables turn on his tormentor. The red-eyed demon that had haunted him was now reaping what it sowed. But the slow torture, like watching flesh peeled off a hated enemy, was too gruesome. Matthew quickly pitied the demon that had tried to pull him into the sea of darkness. The red-eyed shadow resisted the greater evil, but it was like fighting gravity. A string of dark mist left the demon that once empowered Nancy, its strength sapped as it quivered. It shook and Matthew could hear the once terrible voice that laughed in the back of his mind. He heard it screaming in pain from another plane of existence, not perceptible to human ears.

As the cloud surrounding her shook and slowly lost to Terrence's greater evil, Nancy's posture broke down.

"You are quite good at what you do," Terrence said smugly. "I bet there isn't a single piece of evidence linking back to you."

Terrence's eyes locked on Nancy.

"I didn't expect you to play the insanity card so soon before trial," Nancy said, her voice weakened.

"How did you know I was in Orlando? You arrived rather fast, within hours of the attack. Nearly the same time as the Lights," Terrence shot a look at Matthew and J, "and I told them where I was at. I wanted them there because it drew *you* there."

"You left a trail. We followed it," Nancy's eyes now wavering and not staring at Terrence as they once did. The demon above her was nearly all gone.

"You know, I left too much behind, or maybe a better way to say it is unresolved. My *fearless* leader, King Solomon of the New Christians. The trip to Orlando was his idea, or so he thinks. He called me directly and told me about the importance of the mission."

Nancy didn't respond verbally, but shot her left arm down her side, signaling to the television crew. She stuck out her fingers and palm, shaking her hand back and forth as her eyes darted at the production manager behind the monitor. The man didn't budge. He was a statue with its eyes fixed on Terrence, just like the thread of darkness that connected his spirit to the black hurricane above Terrence.

"Thankfully, you brought Solomon here, so I can cut the loose ends myself," Terrence said.

"What is he–" Zech began.

Solomon, also known as Nasir Kingsley, the international businessman, abruptly stood up and went for the door, his bodyguards at his side.

Terrence didn't move, except for a slight smile that crept across his face. To the camera and all others in the room, Terrence sat quietly, waiting for the next question.

However, to Matthew, he saw the black cloud above shoot out like a tethered spear. It didn't bother to torture Solomon's demon, as it did Nancy's. Solomon's demon suffered a quick execution.

The spear-like shot from Terrence stopped Solomon dead in his tracks, while two more shots hit his security detail. Once harpooned, the two personal guards turned calmly and went back to their prior stances, as if Solomon had never stood up. However, the line of darkness dragged the leader of the New Christians across the room.

Like a fish being reeled in, Solomon came closer to Terrence, who continued to lock eyes with Nancy. She finally broke Terrence's piercing stare and watched Solomon's writhing and screaming body slide across the floor. Her eyes widened as her face went pale. All the guards and production crew stood silently, watching the horrible turn of events as if it was all a part of the show.

"How is that happening?" J whispered to Matthew.

"It's Terrence, and a demon around him. It's stronger than all the others, pulling them in and absorbing them somehow."

"He's showing off," Zech said. "This is revenge, a display of power from one evil over another."

"I'd like to bring you two together formally for the world to see," Terrence said as the black power around him slammed Solomon into Nancy, both now filling the monitor.

"While I was in Europe, what were you doing?" Terrence asked.

Nancy's demon, the red-eyed demon that failed to capture Matthew, was just a wisp of black dust. His punishment at the hands of a superior evil was nearly complete.

"Organizing our efforts," Solomon said, his deep voice in a trance-like state.

Terrence shifted his eyes to Nancy.

"Our efforts to silence oppressive Christianity," Nancy said, her once confident voice now a weakened shell of its former self.

"And what were those efforts?" Terrence asked.

"Eliminating watered-down believers, enabling us to take control, and set you up to take the fall," Nancy said from her hypnotic-like trance.

"Are you now claiming involvement?" Terrence mocked Nancy's earlier questions.

"Yes," they said in unison.

As the puppet show went on, Matthew noticed more lines of darkness shooting out from Terrence. They went through walls and barred doors like evil strings of mist building a web around its center.

"You, the proclaimed *champion of freedom,* are a hypocrite and a mass murderer?" Terrence mused at Nancy.

"Yes," Nancy said. Her voice was a robot-like trance, but her expression showed horror. The more powerful demon controlled her voice, but the women inside saw her life coming to an end

Matthew knew what it felt like, and without J's fight to save him, he would still be locked away, a prisoner in his own mind. He knew what Nancy saw. He'd seen it when the red-eyed demon knocked him unconscious.

Matthew remembered J saving him. He also thought back to his experience in the hospital, when brilliant flashes of light saved him from the sea of darkness. Both times, others saved him.

Matthew knew her soul looked on the sea of darkness, an endless void of anguish and tortured souls. As if countless swimmers were thrown into black quicksand, their hands clawing at others as each soul grasped for a shred of life within the inescapable black hole of despair. Matthew shuddered as he remembered the hopeless cold he'd felt when he'd looked upon that hell. It was more than a coldness deep in his bones; it was as if his soul lost all love.

Nancy and Solomon both looked ahead, focusing on something the rest of the room could not see. Their terrified expressions didn't last long. A moment later, their bodies fell lifelessly to the side of the chair, their souls removed and now in the sea of darkness.

Chapter 44

A Higher Order Evil

Terrence looked away from the lifeless bodies on the ground and raised his head toward Zech, J, and Matthew. The guards and production crew all turned to face the three men as well. Their blank expressions watched the three, as Matthew saw the puppet string-like black lines going from each person back to Terrence.

"That was fun," Terrence said. He stood and the half dozen chains that held him down melted away, falling to the floor like hot wax.

"I can do that trick, too," Terrence referenced J's supernatural escape from Terrence's chains. The man wiggled his arms and rolled his shoulders.

"Ah," he sighed, as he rolled his neck. "Independence. It feels good, doesn't it?"

The chains sat at his feet, but Matthew knew the demon controlling Terrence wasn't speaking of the steel chains.

The sound of opening doors rang out from the hallways behind Terrence. A moment later, prisoners and guards alike filled the barred door and bulletproof glass behind him. They stood shoulder-to-shoulder, all with blank expressions that matched the guards and television crew as they patiently waited for the door to open. All of their eyes set on Zech, J, and Matthew as dark lines connected them to Terrence.

"We should go..." J said as the three stood up.

Zech took a step toward Terrence, his firm posture holding strong.

"Dad?" Matthew said.

"Let them go!" Zech demanded.

Terrence laughed. "What authority do *you* have over me?"

"I have none, but Jesus has everything. And in His name, the name of Jesus, I command you to let them go!" Zech held up his Bible toward Terrence.

Matthew noticed the cloud flinch, but Terrence's body was far enough away from the Ark.

"Is that it? A piece of gold?" He casually walked around the small tables and chairs bolted to the floor. He dragged his fingers on the table, picking them up to see the grime it picked up.

"It must be a wonderful magic trick for people like you. Your *magical* piece of gold a weapon against those who disagree."

"I rebuke you, evil one. In Jesus's name, let them go!" Zech demanded as he stepped forward.

The expressionless guards and prisoners also stepped forward, like a frontline of troops. Terrence stood, watching Zech.

"Evil one? It's always so black and white with you all. I mean, look at this one," Terrence motioned to Nancy's body. "She was all hope and justice when she started out. She was going to change the world! Hooray!"

He raised his hands in mock celebration.

"Did you know her dad left her mother when she started law school?" A grin came across Terrence's face. "It's true. I was there. He left after finding out that she was unfaithful, and she was unfaithful after finding out his love was the law and not her. So sad... She poured her heart out to him and wanted to work it out, but he refused. He ran off with another woman weeks later."

Terrence walked by the television production manager. The man stood by the now blank monitor as static flashed on the screen. Terrence leaned in, eyeing the man closely and waving his hand in front of his face. The possessed man didn't flinch.

"Amazing, isn't it?" Terrence nodded. Then he flicked his hand toward one guard. The man responded and opened the sliding bars. The room flooded with orange jumpsuits as prisoners and guards walked into the room. Like robots, they filled the space and waited patiently for their next order.

"She was fresh out of law school, top of her class, when she finally found out the reason behind her parents' divorce. She blamed her mom, screaming at her in tears. Her mom committed suicide the following year. Guilt is easy for us to sow, especially over a lifetime. When Ms. Nancy here saw her dad at the funeral, she confronted him! And you know what? She found out her dad was attending church. He wanted a religious ceremony for his former wife, and for his new wife to attend."

Terrence raised his eyebrows in mocking surprise. "You call me evil, but you act like my lord shoved the apple down Eve's throat. She chose and bit willingly. Just like ol' Nancy here, who has hated religion ever since. Oh, and for the record, now she blames her dad for the divorce."

Terrence walked through more of the motionless men, then looked at the Bibles.

"You stopped me from ridding the world of that pesky relic once, and I've enjoyed this little game of cat and mouse we've played since. It was good training for the less experienced of my kind. But, ugh, the failure in the ranks."

Terrence shrugged and looked at Matthew. "You're the one with the eyes now, huh?"

Zech side-stepped and got in between Terrence's gaze and his son. Terrence smiled, and the huge black cloud around him seemed as relaxed as the morning fog. The haze spread over all the possessed men in the room.

Matthew locked eyes with Terrence. The man's eyes were darker than the last time Matthew saw him. Cold, endless black pits watched Matthew. The black pits pulled him in, as if in a trance, but then he felt a tug on his arm, then his other arm. The distraction broke his trance with Terrence's stare, causing him to look down as Terrence sneered at the loss. Tiny flecks of light were pulling and pushing on him. The mini pops of light moving him backwards.

"It's time to go," Matthew looked at J, who nodded in agreement and took a step back.

"Dad, let's go." But Zech wasn't moving.

Terrence, and the evil within him, now locked eyes with Zech.

"I remember how you felt, Zechariah," Terrence said as he stepped closer.

"If you hadn't fought back, he would have killed you. He would have beaten you down and taken your Bible, including the piece of gold in it."

Matthew looked at his father's back and saw the once firm posture sag.

"I should know. I was there," Terrence opened his arms like he was approaching Zech to hug him. "One little push."

Terrence stopped walking and held Zech's eyes. "One little push, that's all *you* needed. I whispered anger in your ear, your righteous ear, and you killed your best friend. Call me the evil one? You killed your best friend over a book!"

Matthew could see black lines coming from Terrence towards Zech. The hurtful words were a distraction, like enemy soldiers throwing ladders against the city walls as the real threat rammed down the door. Matthew saw darkness hovering around Zech's head.

Zech's shoulders dropped. A second later, he fell to one knee. As he went down, the Bible fell from his hand and struck the smooth concrete floor.

Terrence nodded, and two men shot forward, pouncing on Zech.

"No!" Matthew called out. He jumped in front of his father and held up his Bible as the two men lunged. Like an electric fence, the Bible glowed and held off the two attackers.

J shot forward and picked up Zech's Bible, pushing it back into his hands and helping his elder back up to his feet.

Zech shook his head like a boxer regaining his composure after being caught by a haymaker.

The two attacking men stood up, their faces and arms disfigured from the Ark's repulsion, but they didn't scream in pain or even seem to care. They stood patiently waiting for their next command.

"Nice moves," Terrence mocked. "Hey Jeremiah, how about a high-five? Oh sorry, maybe a high-three?" He motioned to J's hand, where he was missing two fingers.

J looked back at Terrence with an icy stare.

"What?" Terrence shrugged. "You took my follower's hand, so I took yours. Eye for an eye, am I right?"

Matthew once again felt the bits of light nudging him toward the exit.

"Let's go," he whispered and backed up into Zech. Matthew's father now moved back with him as the three of them inched back toward the door.

Terrence laughed. "And where are you going to go? Hey! Let's go back to the Storage Yard. You know, finish what we started?"

Terrence raised his eyebrows, but the three didn't respond as they took another step away.

"Oh wait, I almost forgot! I want to show you something." Terrence motioned to the monitor and a security camera's view of Paul's Storage Yard replaced the blank screen.

"What's that?" Terrence questioned. "Oh, yeah. I'm afraid we can't meet there."

On the screen, Matthew saw his father-in-law, Paul Stollard, get out of his car and walk towards the entrance. He stopped and turned as another car came into the parking lot. Paul moved toward the car as the driver came out. Jimmy stepped out of the second car. The two men hugged as they greeted each other, then pivoted to go inside.

"That's nice," Terrence said. "But I think something is going on inside..."

The screen changed and now footage from a camera inside the Storage Yard displayed. A group of men in combat uniforms, covered in black from head to toe, were leaving rooms and entering a hallway.

"That's our vault," Zech whispered. "The crate."

"You're right!" Terrence said smugly, hearing the inaudible whisper from across the room. "This is interesting. Let's see how it plays out."

The group of men looked like a commando unit raiding a compound. Except they weren't going in, they were swiftly and silently exiting the building. They covered each other around every corner, one raising a gun as others moved forward, then swapping positions.

"No..." Zech whispered.

"Oh, don't spoil it!" Terrence let out.

As the camera angles changed, following the soldiers, soon a view of the lobby came on screen.

"Watch, watch," Terrence pointed at the screen.

Meanwhile, all the possessed men around him still stared at the three with blank expressions.

"This is where *we* had our gunfight. What a fitting place for—"

The loud pop of automatic weapons cut him off as Paul and Jimmy entered the lobby. They were met with an ambush. A wave of gunfire tore through them. The two men dropped, their bodies motionless.

"No!" Zech yelled.

Matthew and J watched the dark pools of blood grow under the bodies on the screen.

Terrence shook his head, taunting them.

The camera panned back to a view from the guard gate as the masked men fled. The dark parking lot took up a third of the screen while the front lobby and main building filled the rest of the monitor.

"Three, two," Terrence pointed to the TV and mouthed the word one, just like the production manager did with Nancy, as if he was directing the horror scene playing out.

On cue, the Storage Yard exploded in a ball of fire. The monitor went black.

Zech dropped to his knees and closed his eyes. He mouthed a prayer after watching the murder of his two best friends.

Terrence still watched the blank monitor, raising his hands like he was celebrating a soccer goal.

Then he turned to face them in mock sorrow. "Guess we can't go there. Sorry."

Matthew could feel his father's deep breaths behind him, but for a third time, the tiny blasts of light pushed on him. He opened his arms and looked down, examining them but not moving with their gentle nudges.

Terrence watched him and smiled, then the villain's gaze went over them, to the door behind their escape.

Matthew glanced back, and his eyes widened. The barred doors behind them were open, but the once empty passageway was now packed with prisoners and guards. They stared blankly at the three men.

Surrounded and outnumbered, Matthew turned back to Terrence.

Terrence shrugged, then his causal expression disappeared. His face now a hateful stare as his eyebrows dropped, his eyes thin black slits, and a fiendish smile came across his face.

"Kill them."

Chapter 45

The Inevitable

The three men stood in the middle of the prison like a fallen baby bird, unable to fly and predators all around.

The first wave of attackers hit Matthew first. He swung his Bible and repelled three men as they shot away from his Bible like they were fired from a cannon.

Now the three all back-to-back. Zech and J swung their Bibles, repelling more possessed men back.

The waves of prisoners kept coming.

The three men swung, pushing back attackers, and pivoted back to protect each other's blindside. Yet for every few they pushed away, another five closed in as the onslaught continued. A shrinking circle gradually constricted around them, like a snake squeezing its prey.

Matthew saw above the crowd and caught Terrence's eye, an unhappy expression on the evil leader's face. Terrence stepped forward and his army parted, yet on other parts of the deadly circle, men in orange jumpsuits still came at the three. The possessed men sprinted, leaped, and even clawed to get hold of a leg or foot.

One prisoner grabbed J's ankle, pulling it out as he lost his balance, but Zech swung a backhand with his Bible. The repulsive force acted on the possessed man and separated his arm from his body at the shoulder. J kicked away the severed limb, but in horror saw the man stand back up, unphased. He charged again and J swung the glowing Bible, permanently disfiguring the man's face. The one armed man finally fell back into the crowd, swallowed by more prisoners.

Terrence moved through his troops, making a beeline to Matthew.

Matthew saw him, but also felt the tiny bursts of light. They moved past him, toward the tunnel where they'd entered the visitor's room.

"We have to go!" Matthew motioned to the light.

"Go where?" J screamed as he fought off another attacker.

"Back!" Matthew pointed to the tunnel. "Use the Bible, clear a path!"

Zech and J pushed forward together, clearing a path. But Zech's movement left his back exposed. A hand shot under his left leg and swept him to the ground. He grunted as he landed on his shoulder.

In a flash, three men were on him, clawing at his eyes and pummeling him. One prisoner pinned him down with his hands on his shoulder blades, then lifted his lower body and brought a knee crashing down on Zech's spine.

Zech screamed as he felt a rib painfully pop.

Matthew spun, kicking the bodies off his father, and swinging his Bible like a baseball bat. He helped his dad up as they both held up their Bibles, keeping the mob at bay.

"Come on!" J screamed as he made a path.

The three stayed close together, tied at the hip. Zech regained his footing and fought on but hunched over and cringed with every big movement.

"It's locked!" J called out as they approached the exit. He jerked on the door, but it wouldn't budge.

Terrence and his empty, dark eyes were getting closer.

Matthew turned back to see the closed bars; he saw a sparkle of light go into the lock. "Try it again!"

J looked confused, but as he pushed back another hand reaching to claw at him, he grabbed the door and pulled with all his strength. To his surprise, it shot open. They ran into the lobby area, the outside light a beacon of hope. The mob rushed behind them.

Only Matthew saw the dark cloud close around them, blotting out the incoming sunlight.

In the middle of the lobby, an invisible force stopped the three men as if they ran into a wall. J hit it first. He kept his balance, bewildered by the invisible force that stopped him, but Matthew and Zech slammed into him, tumbling them all to the ground.

Their Bibles fall from their hands and the protective bindings snapped open. Matthew scrambled to reach his. He grabbed the book just as Terrence reached down and picked him up by his shirt. He lifted him up with supernatural strength, choking him as his cold, dead eyes stared into Matthew's.

Matthew squirmed and raised the Bible, swinging it toward Terrence's head. He prepared himself to be free, expecting the holy force of the Ark within the book to repel Terrence. But to his surprise, Terrence grabbed the incoming Bible with his free hand. His dark eyes never left Matthew's. He ripped the Bible out of Matthew's hands and held it up next to the two-hundred-pound man as if both were as weightless as a beach ball.

Matthew choked, gasping for air as his eyes darted between the Bible next to him and Terrence's hypnotizing stare.

"Missing something?" Terrence sneered.

Fear shot through Matthew as his one weapon against this evil now seemed powerless. From the corner of his eye, he saw a glow. The golden piece of the Ark of the Covenant was on the ground, six feet away, and not inside the Bible.

With a flick of his wrist, Matthew's Bible went up in flames in Terrence's hand. The villain smiled at Matthew and then let him drop to the ground.

He walked over to Zech and stood over him. Matthew's heart dropped as he saw his father's Bible separated from the Ark as well. The gray duct tape holding Zech's Bible together, the same tape that repaired a shotgun blast from Terrence, now laid ripped and peeling from the fight. Like Matthew's piece, Zech's Ark fell out of reach, away from the broken spine of his Bible.

Zech tried getting to his feet, but he grimaced in pain as he tried to raise up. His broken ribs mimicked the broken spine of the Bible near his feet.

"You will be first," Terrence bent down and picked Zech up by the neck, squeezing the life out of him as the patriarch of the Light family's eyes bulged.

"No!" Matthew rolled toward his father, trying to grab the Ark. Terrence didn't turn his head from Zech's dying eyes. With a wave of his hand, a dark cloud shot out of Terrence and sent Matthew flying back. The impact of the strike was like an invisible brick slamming against his face. A searing heat followed the collision, like the brick just came out of a kiln, the stone a fiery red. The heat burned up the paper in the other two Bibles laying on the ground. As Matthew landed, he saw his father's eyes close.

He struck the ground, and hopelessness filled his body. The Ark rested out of reach and Matthew felt alone, away from the presence of God. His body was screaming in pain and his father was dying before his eyes. He watched Terrence strangle his father, the possessed mob watching like robots all around them.

Then, like a rising sun in the darkness, a beam of light shot through the room. It swung like a sword, cutting through Terrence and sending him back into the mob of his followers.

"No!" Terrence echoed demonically.

Matthew looked up, expecting to see an angel, but he'd forgotten about J, and so did the devil inside Terrence.

As Terrence tormented Matthew and choked Zech, J inched closer to his piece of the Ark. Remaining silent, and a split second before Zech's last breath, J exploded, grabbing the Ark and swinging it at Terrence, knocking him back. As Zech fell, J reached out with his three-fingered hand and grabbed his mentor.

He pressed part of the Ark to his mentor's chest and tossed Matthew the other piece.

"We're leaving," J said as he helped Zech up.

Zech coughed and gingerly rubbed his raw throat.

With renewed life, Matthew got to his feet and, holding his piece of the Ark, he punched through the black cloud like J before him.

He glanced back at Terrence while running for the exit and saw him back on his feet. The expressionless faces of the prison mob surrounded their leader.

The dark eyes watched Matthew as he ran.

Matthew heard, not through his ears but somewhere deep in his being, the demonic voice call out to him, like a professor correcting a student.

"Inevitable."

Chapter 46

A Spiritual Location

J's red Jeep sped down the interstate. The roads were emptier than normal, and they quickly put miles in between them and the prison.

"That was brilliant!" Matthew said to J.

Zech nodded in agreement, but then curled over in the shotgun seat of the Jeep. His arm reaching behind him to feel his back. As he bent over and tilted his head, Matthew saw his father's neck. Terrence's hand had seared the skin, causing painful looking blisters and burn marks.

"You okay, Dad?"

"No," Zech grunted. "I'll be okay, but Paul, Jimmy…"

"We're close to the Storage Yard," J said as he shifted gears and sped up. "The river is just south of us. An explosion that big…"

"Wait, you're right. A fire would still burn, but I don't see any smoke from here," Matthew added.

The three scanned the horizon for smoke clouds in the distance. Zech pulled out his phone and dialed Jimmy.

"Hey, young man," the elderly man's voice came into the phone.

Zech's eyes seemed to explode with joy and surprise.

"Zech? You there?"

"Jimmy, is this really you?" Zech asked.

"About as real as the switch your daddy used when you questioned him."

"Fair enough," Zech laughed and turned to Matthew and J. "He's okay."

"Of course, I'm okay."

"Jimmy, I'll explain when I see you, but we're under attack," Zech said.

Jimmy hesitated. "What kind of attack?"

"The worst kind, and no one who knows about the Ark should be alone."

"The Storage Yard?" Jimmy asked.

"No," Zech shook his head as he thought.

"It's the best defensive location I can think of, but I just saw a vision of you and Paul dying there."

"Okay, okay... Well, if this is the *worst* kind of attack, physical defense won't do us much good," Jimmy said.

"The church," Zech said.

"Agreed. On my way."

Zech began making another call.

"The church? Dad, we don't own it anymore," Matthew said.

"Isn't it scheduled to be demolished?" J added.

"Yup. But it ain't down yet," Zech said.

"Take us there. And call your families. No one alone today."

Matthew pulled out his own phone to call Liz as J dialed Ashley.

"Paul?" Zech shouted into the phone. Once again, a look of joy came across his face before he steeled himself.

"Yeah?" Paul crackled into the phone.

"We're under attack, Paul."

"Don't joke like that, Pastor?"

"I'm serious."

"Threat-level?"

"I don't know what your threat levels are, Paul, but it's demonic, and it's big. It's taking people over. Get your butt to the church and bring your gear! I don't know if it'll help against this one, but we need all the firepower we can get."

"Yes, sir. Threat-level five: Rifles, shotguns, pistols, grenades, smoke..." Paul rattled off a list of weaponry that would make any five-star general proud.

"Bring it all, Paul. Bring it all. And Paul, no one alone. Get there as soon as you can," Zech said as he hung up the phone and leaned on the door. Matthew hung up with Liz and watched his father from his view in the back seat. Zech's hand squeezed the piece of Ark in his lap. His hand white as he gripped it with all his strength and his lungs struggled for breath.

"Ashley's on her way," J said as he set his phone in the cup holder.

"Liz too," Matthew added.

"Your mom? Brothers?" Zech added.

"On it," J said. "I'll get Mark and Lucas."

"I'm on Luke," Matthew pulled up his contacts.

"Good. I'll call my wife," Zech started dialing.

"Is it really this urgent to get everyone there *now*?" J asked as he put his phone to his ear.

Their Jeep passed by a cop car and a pulled over Corvette on the side of the road. Both the cop and driver stood motionless, their dead eyes following the Jeep just as all the possessed guards and prisoners had moments earlier.

"Yes," Matthew said. He saw a faint trace of black haze around the two men. "Yes, it is that urgent."

***

Twenty minutes later, the Light family and their closest friends huddled around their cars in the parking lot. The magnificent building lay dormant, a sleeping giant accumulating cobwebs.

Commercial real estate agents were the only consistent visitors since the family had sold the church to pay off the legal debts. Zech took plenty of walks around the church, taking up his father's habit. To Jimmy's pleasant surprise, Zech asked him to join the walks. Occasionally, Paul would join as well.

But they never tried to get inside. They'd speculate on the state of the nation, stocks, culture, religious trends, their families, and everything in between. The weekly walks brought noticeable life back to Zech after the heartbreaking ruling from the courts. The view of Nancy high-fiving her backers singed into Zech's mind, but over time, he'd gradually shifted to the next chapter in his life's work.

Now, as the family stood outside the church, they were hoping Zech's or J's keys still worked.

"You know I almost bought this place," Jimmy said from beside Matthew.

"What?" Matthew turned.

"Really?"

Jimmy nodded. "Seeing how we might not make it back out of this building, it's worth telling someone the story. My businesses own ten commercial buildings, one hundred and fifty single-family homes, three multi-family complexes, an oil rig, a silver mine, a self-storage business, and three golf courses."

He laughed as he rattled off all his assets.

"The bank didn't blink when I asked for financing."

"I forget you've been in the real estate game for so long," Matthew smiled. "So, what stopped you?"

"Your father. He said it was all a part of God's plan."

"It's hard to accept *God's plan* when it happens to you," Matthew said as he set Lyn down. She began playing with her sister.

"You know something, son?" Jimmy looked Matthew in the eyes. "It is. But that's a test to know if you really trust in God. No matter how joyful or painful it can be, you just gotta let some things go."

Jimmy and Matthew watched Zech and J fiddling with the giant real estate agent's lock on the door. Their key worked on the main door, but the agent's padlock still looped around the two handles.

"But other times you gotta fight back," Jimmy said.

Then he turned and hollered at Zech. "It's four-eight-six-eight!"

Matthew eyed Jimmy curiously.

"Oh, did I mention once it didn't sell that I bought it? Why do you think no one has developed it yet? I been holding it!"

Jimmy smiled then moved to help Zech.

Liz came to Matthew's side.

"My dad's almost here. Is all this necessary? We're going to hole-up in our abandoned church with dozens of my dad's guns?" Liz looked at her husband skeptically.

"I hope it's not. But hun, I didn't think we were getting out of that prison," Matthew grabbed her hand.

"I saw the live feed. He looked... so content yet so evil."

"It's not him anymore. The terrorist that kidnapped you has been kidnapped himself. There's a giant demon in him. The strongest I've ever seen."

"I don't want to think about it," Liz put her head onto his chest as Matthew put his arm around her. "I just want to grab a sword and cut his head off!"

Matthew leaned back and smiled at his wife. "I love you.

He watched his young daughters play with their cousins. They were so innocent, unaware of the evil coming for their family.

"Hun, I'll take them to the car. We'll drive away, and just keep driving," Liz offered.

"It won't matter," Matthew said with a frown.

"We make our stand here. And being close to these Arks is the safest place in the world right now."

He touched the golden piece inside his pocket.

"Ha! Got it!" J shouted as he popped open the door lock.

Jimmy shook his head as the group clapped. Ashley followed J inside. Zech labored behind them, with Mary supporting his steps. From the side of the group, Mark and Lucas approached. Mark put his hand on Matthew's shoulder, squeezing and nodding to his brother, then went inside. Lucas smiled and patted him on the back, then followed Mark. Liz kissed her husband, then helped Grace get the kids inside.

"Who wants to see the Sunday School rooms?" Liz called out. The kids agreed and the two women went in side-by-side.

Matthew turned to look at the horizon over the parking lot entrance as Luke stepped next to him. "Tell me what you see, brother," Luke said.

"Nothing yet. But he's coming. *It's* coming," Matthew said.

"Helen is standing by. If we need anything she can help with, call authorities, or whatever."

Matthew nodded. "Thank you. But I suspect we're on our own today."

Luke patted his little brother on the back and went into the church.

Matthew stood outside alone, watching the sun sink lower. He dropped his head.

"Lord, be with us," he said. Taking deep breaths, he stood alone a moment. The sound of squealing tires came from the parking lot entrance. Matthew looked up to see his father-in-law's four-door, heavy duty truck whip around the corner and speed into the lot.

Paul pulled up to the side of the entrance and hopped out. He grabbed two duffle bags and handed them to Matthew. He nearly dropped the bags, their heavy weight surprising him.

"What's in here?"

"Everything," Paul said.

"Everything?"

Paul nodded as he slung a backpack around his arm and picked up two more duffle bags. Handles of shotguns and rifles poked out of the backpack and ends of the bags.

"Let's do this," Paul said.

Chapter 47

Calm Before the Storm

B eth was the first to notice someone approach the church. She walked by the window as Luke and Mark moved tables out of a Sunday School room.

"Runner lady," she called out.

Liz came in from the hallway, stepping around her brothers-in-law, and moved to Beth's side.

The woman stood in a trancelike state at the edge of the parking lot.

"Mom, why's she just standing there? She's always running."

"I don't know, sweetheart. She doesn't look well."

"Hun!" Liz caught Matthew walking by and pointed out the window towards the woman.

From their distance, he couldn't make out her facial features, but he saw the black haze around her, like her edges were out of focus. He motioned to Liz, and she guided Beth away from the window.

"Must not be feeling well," Matthew whispered to himself as he double-checked the window locks and closed the blinds.

"But every time we see her, she's running. She comes from the apartments right over there." Beth stood in the doorway and looked back at her dad. "And she runs up through our drop-off area and back out. She only walks when she's on the phone."

"Something bad has been going around, sweetheart. We might see more people like her. Now let's stay away from the windows. It's not polite to stare," Matthew said.

Beth accepted the explanation and ran off to find her sister and cousins.

"Not polite to stare?" Liz whispered to Matthew with a smile. "My dad is arming every weapon that doesn't require nuclear codes and you say, 'it's not polite to stare'?"

Matthew shrugged and pointed back at the window. "There's going to be more, a lot more. The runner lady out there means he knows we're here. It won't be long."

"I'll get the kids. We'll start the storm drill," she hugged Matthew and went off down the hallway after Beth.

Matthew moved back toward the entrance, where the hallway of classrooms and offices opened into the large rotunda and coffee shop.

"He's coming. The first one is outside," Matthew said, catching his father's and J's eyes. They nodded, each with his own solemn expression.

Zech motioned to Paul. With a rifle on his back, the black strap slung across Paul's chest. He holstered multiple firearms around his waist. With Zech's nod, Paul trotted to the front of the rotunda and took a lookout position.

The family divided into three groups. Zech, J, and Paul were near the front of the rotunda, with Paul at the glass of the main doors looking out to the parking lot.

Luke, Mark, and Lucas raided all the offices and classrooms to bring out furniture. They used it to create a barricade-like system as the large rotunda funneled down to hallways. If the fight came inside, they could make a last stand by forcing the enemy to bottleneck.

Mary, Liz, Ashley, and Grace kept the kids in a hidden storage room. The tornado-safe spot turned into a play area where they cycled through crafts, board games, and coloring books. The spot was tight for four grown women and four kids, but to Matthew's surprise, everyone was smiling and chatting. He took solace in the tiny sanctuary that shielded his children from having to see the evil brewing.

Matthew floated in between the three groups, helping where he could and frequently peeking out the windows. There were now five people at the edge of the parking lot. Their cold, lifeless stares shot across the parking lot and at the church like emotionless snipers preparing for target practice.

"Someone's coming!" Paul shouted as he looked through his rifle's scope.

A light blue SUV swerved around the group of five at the edge of the property and sped into the parking lot.

Paul set his feet and steadied his posture. He looked like he was preparing to take down a charging bear as he looked through his scope at the oncoming car, but a moment later, he lifted his head up.

"A friendly!" he called out.

Moments later, Paul was opening the door as Aunt Millie ran in.

"Zechariah Joseph Light, how dare you!" the elderly woman snapped at Zech.

"Millie, you don't need to be in this fight. It's coming for *our* family. The ones who hold the Ark," Zech motioned to his three sons.

"Like all heck I don't! I've been working for and volunteering with you and your dad for decades."

Millie was truly upset. He'd seen the woman shout like an erupting firecracker countless times, but he'd never seen her angry.

"All the years we've been together, and you dare say I'm not in *your* family. We are all family," she waved to everyone in view. "I'm yours and your mine!"

A tear ran down the side of her cheek.

Zech's expression softened as he saw the hurt in her eyes.

"You are. I'm sorry," he hugged her.

Mary came out from the back room and ran to Aunt Millie. "Thank you for coming."

Millie nodded and slapped Zech on the arm. "Let's go teach these kids to pray."

"Y'all are doing prayer back there?" Zech said.

"You bet. In between every game," Mary smiled.

"What your wife means to say is she doesn't think all these pea shooters are going to do diddly," Aunt Millie said.

Zech's eyes shot to Paul, then back to his wife. "Oh, really?"

Mary shrugged. "My men are going to need prayer cover."

Zech smiled as the two women walked back through the barricaded area. Mary hugged her boys, including J and Lucas.

Before Mary and Millie were out of the hallway, Paul took everyone's attention.

"Enemy's here!" he shouted.

A wave of people walked into the parking lot. They filled all visible directions, flooding the parking lot and surrounding the building.

Matthew could see the dark cloud above and around them. The thick black fog overtook the horizon like a storm cloud.

Darkness surrounded the church.

Chapter 48

The Battle

The horde of possessed people flooded the parking lot. In unison, they stepped forward, shoulder-to-shoulder, hundreds of people. They expanded as more came in, filling all the parking spaces in the blacktop area and the grassy areas in between. All with the same hollow stare and, to only Matthew's eyes, all with a darkness above them. The evil puppet master marched his toys to the battlefield as the group surrounded the church.

"All other doors barricaded?" Zech asked.

"Yup," J replied.

An uneasy feeling hit Matthew. He remembered how, at the prison, Terrence's body comfortably sat in the chair, but the black cloud extended behind him, reaching through the prison. It found others and used them to open locked doors.

"Change of plans," Matthew said as he dashed to the hallway. "We can't rely on locks!"

He lept over the make-shift barricade of furniture and ran into the Sunday School hallways.

He approached a T in the hallway. To the right was a locked exit that his brothers had reinforced. To his left was the storage room where the women and children played.

A thin black cloud stretched across the floor. Like heavy fog coming through an open window, it slithered across the floor.

Matthew pulled the Ark piece out of his pocket and ran into the growing darkness. He swung the golden piece like a sword. Like a lamp flipped on in a dark room, the Ark chased the shadow away. He turned and ran to the storage room.

He burst in, surprising the girls. The four kids were in the middle of a game of Monopoly, while the others sat in a corner talking.

"What's going on?" Liz asked sharply.

Matthew didn't answer but focused on finding any hints of the shadow. He looked around, focusing on the dark corners of the room, and then he saw it. From an air vent in the ceiling, the thick black shadow crept in. He ran across the Monopoly board and jumped at the vent, swinging the glowing Ark. The darkness retreated into the vent and, as the females watched him curiously, he looked around the room. There was another vent above their heads.

"Come on, we're out of here," Matthew urged.

"Mom, get everyone to Dad. Stay close to him. No one wanders, no one far from the Ark. No one alone!"

The five adult women, Mary, Millie, Ashley, Grace, and Liz, shepherded the kids out of the room. Grace and Ashley made it a game as Mary and Millie led the way.

"Only step on light colors!" Grace said as Joy and Noah followed behind. With the older cousins happily bouncing through the hallway, Beth and Lyn were laughing close behind.

Liz held back, raising her hands to her husband. "We had it all set up, that room was our safe house. What's up?"

"There's an army outside, Liz," Matthew looked her in the eyes. "The shadow's over all of them. Hundreds, probably thousands, that are the demon's puppets."

"So why are we bringing our children closer? Why are you swinging at the air conditioner?" she tried keeping her voice down.

"Because those people are only the second part of his plan. He's coming in through the cracks in the walls, the air vents."

"The red-eyed shadow? The one after you?"

"This one is more powerful. The one in Terrence sucked up the red-eyed demon and all the surrounding darkness. All the shadows I saw in others, they're all joining this one. This *thing*, it's growing off the lesser evils. Like it's feeding on them."

Matthew took a deep breath and put his arms on his wife's shoulders.

"The only reason we're alive is because of these pieces." He held up his piece. "It keeps the evil at bay. That's our number one goal right now. There are five out there. J, my dad, Luke, Mark, and me, we each have one."

Matthew and Liz began walking back through the hallway to the opening in the rotunda.

"But we're sitting ducks in here. What happens when all those people charge? We have kids here, Matt, *our* kids," Liz said.

Matthew's jaw clenched, and he swallowed. With his hand that held the Ark, he brushed up against Liz's hand. She grabbed his hand, now both their hands holding the Ark and each other. "Our kids. What better reason to fight?" Matthew said.

Mary and Aunt Millie approached Paul and Zech. The two men were handing out weapons and paused, surprised, as the women and children came into the rotunda.

"Alright, Rambo. Load us up. If we're out here, we're going to show these demons our version of hell," Aunt Millie said.

"Uh..." Paul hesitated.

"Come on, Paul," Mary said. "I've taken down my share of ten-pointers. I can defend my clan."

"Oh really, Mom?" Luke said, smiling as he lowered his shotgun.

Mary flashed a glance at her oldest son, raising her eyebrows with a stern stare. Luke put his hands up in surrender. Zech gave a soft laugh and shook his head.

"Zech?" Paul looked at his friend.

"You heard 'em, buddy," Zech replied. "She holds the family record."

"Welcome to the front line, ladies. Happy to have you aboard," Paul opened up another duffle bag.

"Whoa…" Noah noticed the crowd surrounding the building. A silent ring of expressionless faces packed rows deep, shoulder-to-shoulder.

"Noah. Joy. What are you–" Mark started, but Grace put her arm on his shoulder. She looked towards Matthew. Mark's eyes went to his brother.

"It's coming in through the cracks and the vents. We need to stay together, around the Arks," Matthew said. He looked to J, who reached out to take Ashley's hand.

"Paul, you're going to need to load us up too," Ashley said.

Liz squeezed Matthew's shoulder and then went with Ashley and Grace to get loaded up with weapons and ammunition.

Beth and Lyn looked at their dad, confused and scared looks on their faces.

Matthew knelt and winked with a smile. They hugged him and buried their faces in his chest.

Glancing over the girls' heads, Matthew saw a dark shadow seep in through the hallway and offices. It crept to the edge of the rotunda.

"You girls remember those nature shows we watched? What the buffalos did when wolves surrounded them?"

The girls nodded.

"You mean the muskoxen?" Beth corrected.

"Yes, the muskoxen. What'd they do when their young were under attack?"

Lyn held up her hands, making a circle.

"Yes!" Matthew grinned with excitement at the young child.

"They got in a circle," Beth said. "They surrounded their young so the wolves couldn't get to them."

"That's right! There are some bad things about to come at us all, like a hungry wolf. Some you can't see." Matthew glanced at the shadow. It was getting closer, making the white and gray marbled floor appear black.

"And there's people out there who are confused. They think they're like a hungry wolf or lion. They're so starved that they think *terrible* things are *good* things. But they're wrong. They're confused."

Matthew looked his daughters in the eyes, going back and forth.

He sensed the black shadow creeping in. The urge to run towards it, to swing the Ark and force it away went through his mind, but he knew he must stay calm for the girls to stay strong. He couldn't divide the group. "I can see some of the bad things that you can't, so you'll have to trust that we'll keep them away. The bright gold pieces we're carrying, they will help protect us. Those bad people might charge the building. They might act crazy and mean, but they can't get past these pieces."

"Like Ursula? She's crazy and mean to the Little Mermaid," Beth said.

Matthew gave a soft laugh. "Yes, those people are acting like a sea witch. And I need you two, and your cousins, to stay in the middle of us. Just like the muskoxen babies. If you're strong, then the adults will be strong too. Okay?"

"Matt," Zech called out. "You see it? Cause I'm sure starting to feel it more and more."

As Matthew caught his dad's eyes, his father read the grim expression on his face.

Zech began positioning the group.

Beth held up a fist. Lyn soon copied her as the two girls pretended a mean face. Matthew winked at his girls, remembered how his grandfather's winks always made him feel special.

"You heard him, kids," Zech said, catching Noah and Joy's attention.

"Yup!" the two older cousins said in unison.

"It's here. All around us." Matthew pulled out his Ark. "Circle up, everyone. Arks on the outer edge!"

The group quickly fell into a pair of concentric half-circles. The kids in the middle against a brick wall, with Zech, Mary, and Millie around them as they huddled down. While the outer half-circle included five spread out pairs: Luke and Lucas, J and Ashley, Mark and Grace, Jimmy and Paul, and Matthew and Liz.

"The demon is here. Arks out!" Matthew screamed. He looked across the circle and realized one pair didn't have an Ark. Jimmy and Paul. The same pair that Terrence's illusion killed through the monitor at the jail.

"Paul, Jimmy, fall back," Matthew shouted as everyone held up their guns.

"Let 'em come!" Paul shouted back, inching forward as Jimmy stepped back.

"You don't have an Ark! Guns won't–" Matthew screamed, but it was too late. As Paul aimed for the shadow, Matthew saw it clutch his leg. The muscle and flesh of his calf shriveled and turned black.

Paul screamed in pain as the group watched in horror. The shadow pulled Paul's leg forward, ripping him off his feet like a shark throwing a wounded seal.

"Dad! Ark!" Matthew shouted to his father. Zech turned to Jimmy.

Jimmy was ready. As they locked eyes, Zech tossed his Ark to his fellow church elder. Jimmy caught the piece and, without hesitation, he bent down and swung before Paul's leg.

Matthew saw the darkness release, but Paul's leg remained damaged. Jimmy pulled Paul back into the half-circle, giving the Ark back to Zech. Lucas and Luke shifted to fill the space. Mark and Grace also side-stepping to even out the gaps.

"Hold. It can't get past the Ark," Matthew said.

After Jimmy broke the shadow's hold on Paul, the demon swelled in front of the group.

"J!" Matthew called out. "It's right in front of you."

J was now closest to the rotunda doors with Ashley at his side. After seeing the life sucked from Paul's leg, J slung his rifle over his shoulder and held his piece of the Ark out with two hands. His knuckles were white as he tried to steady his hands.

To everyone in the group, J appeared to be in an invisible, reverse tug-of-war style fight, but Matthew saw the dense black cloud leaning into him. The dark force concentrated on J, trying to break down the first line of defense.

"It's talking... to me..." J struggled to say through gritted teeth as sweat broke out on his forehead. His body shook, and a moment later, he dropped to one knee. His posture weakened by the second.

Ashley jumped in to support him. She put her arms around him and squeezed.

"I'm with you!" she pulled him up. J slowly rose with her support, but the Ark drifted lower as his arms fell. The golden piece only protected his lower half. J's head remained exposed.

Matthew saw the dark cloud shooting out strings of black at J's mind. His head dipped as if being hit by a boxer's jab. His face contorted as he took the spiritual blows.

"No!" J screamed into the void. "He loved my father! You killed him. Zech loved him!"

Like Rocky Balboa refusing to give up in the face of over-whelming blows, J leaned into the cloud. Ashley prayed at his side, giving him the strength to weather the storm.

But as J leaned in, Ashley became the target. Dark clouds shot out against her, taking her strength.

"We have to help them," Matthew said to Liz.

Ashley dropped, holding her side, and screaming in pain like an arrow struck her midsection. J bent over to help her, but an invisible force knocked him back. He fell over her.

Matthew instinctively moved to J, Liz staying at his side, but he didn't get three steps before hearing his father call out. Matthew looked back, and to his dismay, the demon instantly capitalized on the open hole. The darkness shot through the gap and went for the children, Zech holding his Ark and standing his ground as the shadow leaned on him.

Matthew grabbed Liz's hand and moved back into position, cutting off the darkness impacting his father.

J held up the Ark over Ashley and knelt above her.

"Keep praying," J told her through gritted teeth. They regained their defensive position.

The demon now tested each pair, slowly pushing each back as they tried holding their ground. Methodically, the darkness prodded, testing for weaknesses.

Matthew nearly lost his footing as he felt a swing from the darkness, like a bat trying to break his ribs. The Ark protected him, but the physical force knocked him a step back.

"I won't believe that lie! In Jesus's name, I won't believe your lies!" J screamed, his voice growing hoarse.

"It's talking to him," Liz said.

"It's breaking us down," Matthew said as his eyes darted around, trying to think. His body tensed as it prepared for the next strike.

"No, Matt, it's *talking* to him!" she reiterated. Matthew looked at her confused.

"Just like Ashley is praying, we can talk too!"

"You're right. We need more prayer," Matthew said.

Matthew looked over to his brothers. Mark and Luke overheard and started. Grace and Lucas following their lead. Mark caught Zech's eye as their father joined in.

"Everyone, pray!" Zech shouted from the center of the group. The inner circle, six more people, began to speak to God, asking for deliverance from evil, for strength to overcome, for God's will to be done.

The five Arks brightened within the holder's hands. The light pushed back on the shadow.

Zech's voice boomed, as if intensified by a deep, spiritual power from within him.

"Lord, let us come together to protect each other. Only *you* can save us from this evil. We rest in *your* mercy Lord, and know that if we go, we can rejoice to see *you* in Heaven. If *you* keep us alive through this torment, we'll continue to do *your* work. Together, we work for *your* kingdom, here on Earth. As you said through Paul in the letter to the Philippians 'For I can do everything through Christ, who gives me strength.' We can do anything through *you*, who gives us strength!"

Together, Matthew thought as all five Arks glowed like burning torches. He felt stronger from the prayer and as he looked around, he could see the others standing up straighter with more confidence.

"We can't do this alone," he said.

"No way. All together," Liz agreed as she wrapped her arms around his and continued to pray. She looked back and saw their two daughters, holding onto their grandmother, also praying. A giant smile erupted on Liz's face. She closed her eyes and prayed from the heart, letting the Spirit guide her as she spoke to God for their deliverance.

Matthew felt stronger as Liz grasped his arm and prayed. He looked out into the darkness, noticing it pulled back.

"It's backing up. Keep praying!"

"I might not see the shadow, but I see them," Luke said as he looked out the glass walls. "They're coming!"

The mob outside was now moving toward them. Some walked, gradually building speed as others broke out in sprints.

"Hun, are we really going to shoot these people?" Liz asked in her husband's ear.

"I don't want to, but–"

Guns raised around the room, pointing at the mob.

"Hold! They're stopping," MIllie cried out.

She pointed to the people who stopped cold at the boundary of the drop-off loop right outside the doors and glass walls of the rotunda.

"Yay!" the kids behind her celebrated.

Matthew looked closely at the mob. The darkness still washed over their expressionless faces. They crossed over the entire parking lot but stopped at the last stretch of pavement before the concrete leading up to the doors. The drop-off zone blacktop rested like a black moat curving around the church, holding back the advancing army.

Behind the mob, colored lights flashed, illuminating nearby trees as a caravan of police came into the parking lot.

"It's about time," Paul tried to stand up from one knee and hobbled over on his damaged leg to get a better look.

"You called the cops?" Matthew asked.

"Of course. I'm not bringing all these weapons out to defend my family, only to end up in legal trouble like Isaiah. The authorities will know we acted in self defense!"

Multiple cop cars and two vans pulled around the crowd, who seem to flow away from the cops in unison, then fill the space like water. The vehicles came to the drop-off zone and the officers piled out.

"Let's hear it for the boys in blue!" Paul pumped his fist.

"Thank the Lord," Zech said as he stepped up, laboring through pain, to his friend.

The cops stood in defensive positions with their guns trained on the family in the church.

"Something doesn't look right here," Jimmy said, trailing off. "Their faces..."

"Forget their faces. What about their guns?" Mark said as he knelt down, pulling Grace down behind him.

Matthew saw the men in uniform, now surrounded in the darkness. The family's prayer pushed back the dark shadow, but now it changed strategies. The officers' expressionless faces matched the mob behind them.

Matthew saw the darkness grow around the officers, and their hands tighten on the firearms.

"Take cover!" Matthew screamed, but before anyone could move, the police opened fire.

The family ducked and fell to the ground.

Matthew prepared to feel the deathly sting of bullets rip through him. He pulled in Liz, wrapping an arm around her as they hid behind the Ark. He heard glass panes shatter and crash to the ground. But miraculously, he didn't feel the bullets.

Tentatively, he looked up. Countless bursts of light coming from the glow of the Arks deflected the bullets.

He remembered the one flicker of light in the hotel room when Terrence fired on him. The light deflected the bullet just enough to miss his forehead. But now, illuminated bursts were all over them, surrounding the Ark and protecting the family like a giant shield of light.

Matthew turned his head, looking back at his father. Zech remained in prayer, as did Mary and Millie, as they huddled in front of the children.

"Give it back to 'em!" Paul screamed as he pulled up his semi-automatic and let bullets fire. J was the second to open fire, and soon someone from each pair of the outer half-circle was firing. Even Liz, holding up a shotgun, aimed and shot at the enemy outside.

They ripped apart the glass and aluminum wall in between the two warring parties.

Matthew watched the darkness ebb and flow in the melee, as if enjoying the carnage. But he also noticed something else: None of the police or the crowd behind them fell.

"Stop!" Matthew shouted. He repeated himself multiple times, trying to get his voice heard over the deafening shots.

Eventually, his side stopped firing.

"We can't hit them. It's protecting them."

"As the light protects us, the darkness protects them," Zech said.

Matthew caught his father's eyes and nodded.

"Can we wait them out?" Luke asked.

"No. I don't think so," Lucas said. "I think the question is, how long can they wait us out?"

The enemy stopped firing, and the policemen stood up, blending into the mob behind them. Then the group of possessed parted, like water shifting and reforming once again.

As the closest row and the police side-stepped, Terrence came into view. The group behind him closed ranks and stood behind their puppet master.

Pale white where once olive skin covered his face, his eyes were now black pits that seemed to bleed oil. The black liquid spread like a cancer around his face, unholy veins of black intertwined through his skin.

To Matthew, Terrence looked like a black hole. A bottomless void that engulfed all signs of life and love.

Their enemy stood impatiently, a snarl across his face.

"I don't think he's going to wait for anything," Mark said.

"We must stick together. No one alone!" J shouted. "In the prison, he sent waves of men at us. The Ark was the only thing to repel them. Stay close and swing hard! We'll eventually get out of this."

The group nodded as they stared out at the demonic figure and the army behind him.

Together, yes, but where will we go? Matthew thought to himself.

"We can't just let them come in waves," Matthew whispered to Liz.

"Don't talk like that, Hun. We'll pray, we'll keep praying. We'll make it," she said as she glanced back at her children and then back at Terrence.

Matthew looked back at his girls, too, but his mind went back to the prison and how close the flood of prisoners came to engulf them.

They'll see us ripped apart. We can't wait and pray, he thought.

He looked from his girls to scan the group. His father, Zech still visibly in pain as Mary, Millie, Paul, and Jimmy stood around them.

Then Matthew looked at the outer circle, his brothers and J. Those closest to him, all his loved ones, were ready to fight and die, if need be.

We can't just wait and pray, he thought again.

He noticed J's face look up. Others in the group also looked up, a surprised expression coming over them.

"Matt, you seeing this?" J asked.

Matthew turned his head towards the possessed crowd. The concentration of darkness around Terrence that spread like a fog through all his mindless followers came together. It rose like a tornado, a thin wiggling line that expanded as the darkness fed on its followers. The worm-like line expanded quickly. A storm cloud stretched up and across the sky as it took on a new shape.

"I do... Do you?" Matthew asked.

"I see it..." J said. His jaw dropping.

"So do I," Liz said in his ear. "Is that...?"

Its body took shape as it had in J's dream. A thin line formed a worm in the sky. Soon, the worm took on the head of a snake as the body grew thicker. Then, massive wings shot out and blotted out the light of the sky. The darkness formed a giant dragon.

"Dinosaur," Lyn said in amazement from behind her grandfather.

"Dragon," Zech said behind them.

"*The* dragon," J said. He braced himself, holding out the Ark in one hand and Ashley's hand in his other.

The enormous dragon stretched its wings that covered the horizon like its own demonic skyline.

The beast descended upon them, its mouth snapping, stretching its jaw for the impending feast.

The dragon roared towards the front of the half-circle, towards J and Ashley.

J held up the Ark with two hands, and Ashley's arms held J. They both prayed, bracing themselves with a firm posture, yet they slid back as the roar of the dragon sent a darkness at them. Like a battering ram striking J's Ark, they held on as their feet squealed across the tile floor.

Terrence raised his hands, as if evoking a greater effort, and the dragon roared again. Another blast, a supersonic black ball hit J and Ashley, lifted them off their feet and sent them backward. The two crashed into the group guarding the children. Matthew's heart sank as he heard his girls scream.

"We can't just wait and pray," Matthew said aloud now, instead of just thinking to himself.

The dragon leaned back and lifted his head to the sky and roared a black cloud that rose like a breath on a snowy day. The darkness rose into the sky then fell on the possessed people around it. It snapped its jaws, sucking in the black haze but taking more than it spit out.

Portions of the followers that surrounded the church fell.

"It's gaining power from all the smaller demons. It can feed on the people forever," Matthew said.

He turned to Liz, a confused expression on her face. "We can't stand here alone. We must bring the Arks together."

Liz looked up at the growing dragon and reluctantly nodded.

Matthew squeezed the Ark in his hands, then glanced around the room. His loved ones all looked up at the dragon. Each person in their remaining pairs held their Ark.

"Fall back!" Matthew shouted as he and Liz moved back toward the smaller group centered on Zechariah.

The group fell into a tight circle, everyone within a couple of feet of each other. The tighter half-circle of stood shoulder-to-shoulder. Matthew and Liz reached down, helping J and Ashley back to their feet. Mary and Zech turned back to check on the girls, Grace and Mark calling out to Noah and Joy as they gave each gave a thumbs up and continued praying. Paul and Mille stood at the sides of the inner circle, their weapons at the ready.

"We stand together!" Zech said in a firm, reassuring tone.

But as J struggled to stand, he dropped to one knee and caught Matthew's eye.

"It's your dream," Matthew told J. "He tried killing all of us, and now he's blotting out the sky. One-by-one he'll kill us."

The dragon flapped its enormous wings. The roaring air picked up pieces of glass shards from the gunfight and whipped through the large room like a wind tunnel.

Luke grunted as he stepped back and felt his arm. Blood quickly seeped out of a razor-like cut from a piece of glass.

"Keep praying! Push it back!" Zech shouted above the raging wind.

Flying pieces of glass caught Lucas and Mark. Mark dropped to one knee, a red line through his shirt as his skin opened from his left tricep, along his shoulder, and up to his neck. Lucas jerked his head back and put a hand to his ear. Blood trickled down the side of his head.

With every prayer, the blackness was pushed back, but with every pause in their speech, even during a breath, the darkness took its shot. One-by-one, the deadly wind sent tiny, razor-sharp missiles into the group. They each covered their heads and slunk back, praying less with every slice on their forearms, legs, and heads.

Grace held up her husband Mark, helping to hold up his Ark as his arm weakened. He stood a moment with her support, but soon she curled over and held her side. Mark's Ark fell to his side, and the two dropped.

"It suffocates out all the lights from the sky," Matthew said.

J shook his head, refusing his best friend's words.

"Then, the waters come," Matthew screamed to be heard over the raging wind.

"No," J mouthed as he shook his head again.

Matthew nodded.

"Yes," his solemn expression unchanged as he held out his hand.

"No," J said again. His eyes grew watery as he clenched his jaw.

Matthew turned to Luke. "Brother, I need your Ark!"

Luke slid back, Jimmy at his side, and both were already down on one knee, bleeding all over their arms. Matthew saw Jimmy's large scar across the side of his head. The scar he'd received in the first battle at Isaiah's side over fifty years ago. It was open and bleeding, as if the darkness sought the wound to uncover horrible memories of the past. The story of Isaiah and Jimmy defeating their first evil was a story Matthew would never forget.

"You sure?" Luke said to his brother as he held his Ark.

Matthew nodded, and Luke handed him the piece. "I got your back, brother."

Matthew nodded, then turned to Mark.

"Mark! Your piece?" Matthew shouted.

Mark and Grace were both hunched over and noticeably in pain. At Matthew's signal, the pair slid back on the tile, now next to Luke. Mark locked eyes with Matthew and grabbed his brother's arm. Matthew could see him losing strength, but Mark's eyes were still blazing. He shined determination to never give up.

Mark handed the glowing piece to Matthew. Grace and Mark slid back through Zech and Mary. They went to Joy and Noah and held their children. The family of four prayed like spiritual warriors.

Jimmy and Mark fell back, too, behind Zech, and prayed with Mark and his family. Lucas took note and slid into the group, placing his hands on Mark and Luke as he prayed.

Matthew held three pieces as he turned back to J. He held out his hand for J's piece.

"No," J said as he stood. "You can't."

J moved up to confront the dragon in Matthew's place, but the wind threw up glass that peppered him as soon as he took his first step. Glass sliced his legs, ripping his pants as spurts of blood shot out into the wind, but J pressed on into it.

"J!" Matthew shouted.

"Jeremiah!" Ashley shouted as she grabbed at his arm.

The police snapped to action, pulling their guns and unloading without hesitation. Previously, J and Ashley curled behind his Ark, but now alone and standing tall, J was exposed.

Three bullets struck him in quick succession, each sending a red mist into the black cloud. The first hit near his hip, stopping his forward progress. The next struck his arm, forcing him to lean backward as the Ark lowered, nearly falling from his hand. With the Ark away from his midsection, the last bullet penetrated his upper chest. Red mist flew into the black haze of the whipping wind as J fell backward.

"NOOOOO!" Ashley screamed as she pulled J's body back into the group.

J coughed, struggling to breathe as she put her hand under his head.

J looked up at her, his eyes holding hers as tears ran down her face.

Matthew slid to his side. J's eye left Ashley and met Matthew's.

Matthew could see the pain in his friend's eyes.

"It hit his lungs," Ashley said frantically as she tried to press down on the wound. J grabbed her hands, looking at her with sad eyes as he accepted his fate. She shook her head, but his hands calmed her as tears formed in her eyes.

J turned back to Matthew.

"You'll die," J said softly. His eyes now filling with sadness. "I can't let you..."

He coughed and blood pushed out of his chest.

"You must," Matthew said. He held his hand out.

J's hand shook, unsure.

From the side of their vision, another hand came and rested on J's chest. It pressed on Ashley's hand, adding more force to J's mortal wound.

"You must," Liz said as tears rolled down her cheeks. Her other hand went to Matthew. She squeezed his shoulder with all her might. Her look told Matthew that she knew the dream.

J finally lifted his Ark and handed it to his best friend. He knew the next part. Matthew brings light to the world, giving it new life, but at the cost of his own.

Liz turned and hugged her husband, pulling back his face and kissing him. She looked into his eyes, her eyes now pouring out tears. Then she let go and made her way back to their girls.

Matthew looked up, his brothers at his side and J below him. They nodded reassuringly. His father and mother beyond them, seeing the scene and smiling at their son. Past his parents, his two daughters grabbed ahold of their mother, but their eyes stayed fixed on their dad.

"Stay behind Grandpa!" Matthew shouted in a deep, firm voice that split the sounds of rushing water growing behind him. "Behind the Ark, keep praying. Together!"

He found his daughters' eyes one last time. With a smile, he winked at them, just as his grandfather always winked at him.

He squeezed J's arm and spun around to face the darkness behind them.

The dragon was a tidal wave that overtook the landscape. It rose hundreds of feet, blotting out all the people, even Terrence. The shadows below the dragon were like black waves in an ocean, a sea of darkness. Above the sea, the dragon remained, a tidal wave of death.

The beast exhaled a black plume as its eyes set upon Matthew. Its shoulders rose as it prepared to send another shockwave.

Matthew felt the heat from the giant's dark breath. As the monster grew, its breath heated. It sent another breath from its snout which singed his hair as he felt the air around him sizzle.

"Matt!" Zech called out. "There's so many!"

Matthew turned back and nodded to his family. He saw his wife and daughters hold each other as they prayed.

The dragon took in a deep breath. It pulled in parts of the tidal wave underneath it as it prepared to fire on Matthew.

Matthew looked down; four pieces of the Ark in his hands. Through the four pieces, he saw a vision of the full Ark of the Covenant in his hands. Two wings stretching out on each side towards the middle.

He kept watching as the picture in front of him turned from the Ark into a tomb. A giant stone slab over a stone coffin. The pieces of the Ark were still wings, but no longer golden. Each pair now seemed to be made of light around a perfect human being-like figure that sat on top of an open tomb.

The covenant.

The promise.

The resurrection.

Matthew took in the picture, then slammed the four pieces together in his hands. A great blast of light went out from him, shoving away the black atmosphere of the dragon. Where all the possessed people were, Matthew saw the full picture of the demons possessing them. Ugly and snarling, each looked bloodthirsty. A towering demon, their leader, stood above them all. At the feet of the dragon, the demon that possessed Terrence towered over all others in a suit of black armor that covered charcoal-like skin. A ten-foot sword in one hand, a six-foot spiked mace in the other.

"There are so many..." Matthew said as he looked over the demonic army. He heard the demon over Terrence growl in fury at the light emanating from the church.

Then Matthew felt bursts of flickering light grow all around him. The light grew and expanded into the black sky above him. It flickered across the horizon, drawing battle lines in front of the dragon as it roared. The beast was forced back a step.

Matthew looked up to the heavens and saw the sky split open. Brilliant light emerged out of the darkness as heaven's warriors raced forward.

"There are many, but don't be afraid," Matthew said, "because there are more of us than there are of them."

Matthew stood to his feet.

Then he took off, sprinting towards Terrence and the dragon. An army of angels followed overhead, battling the demons below.

Chapter 49

Order from Chaos

"The largest dragon protects the most valuable treasure," Zech said as watched Matthew race into the crowd. Liz held her arms out over her girls as she watched a glowing light surround her husband as he ran into the battle.

The dragon flapped its wings, but the bursts of light around Matthew knocked aside the tiny pieces of razor-sharp glass as the wind swirled. The police opened fire, sending a barrage of bullets toward him. But again, flashes of light, like a million firecrackers popping on a dark night, came to his defense.

Matthew kept running.

The demon above Terrence pointed his sword forward as the dragon roared in unison. The army charged forward. Each possessed person ran, a demon on their back charging like evil calvary whipping the horses below. The mob below the dragon built the foundation of the tidal wave, the sea of darkness, that rushed at Matthew like a giant battering ram.

Matthew charged toward the void, holding the four pieces of the Ark. It fused together into one piece, and it gave an overwhelming and unexplainable sensation of confidence and love. The earthly outcome of the war left his mind. His only goal: victory for Heaven's army. He thought of the angel battalion charging behind him to combat the sea of darkness. He felt the love from the Ark clothe him like armor and the Ark itself a massive sword to combat Terrence's weapon.

As he rushed into the void, from overhead, a giant V-shaped light shot ahead of him and plunged down. Within the bright light, he saw winged warriors covered in light. Their swords, shields, helmets, and breastplates all appeared to be made of a perfect, gold-like substance. Yet, their skin shined brighter than any of their glorious weaponry. The attacking party slammed into the opaque tidal wave of possessed humans. Like an arrow cutting flesh, it split the group. Dark shadows and pieces of light exploded from the collision.

The light ripped through the mass of demons, cutting a hole for Matthew. The hole went straight at a figure below the dragon's belly: Terrence. He stood, staring at Matthew as the giant, death-like warrior spirit towered above the man's physical body. Matthew saw the fiery red eyes within the living shadow. They appeared hungry.

To either side of Matthew, shining lights from above dropped in to reinforce the initial arrow of angels that broke apart the dark waters. The lights sparkled as swords cut into the shadows all around, sending possessed people and their demons flying backward. With every slash of their swords, a burst of light protected the boundary of Matthew's journey. Walls of black fought back as enemies rose around him. More shining lights came in to fight back against the wall. The initial cut into the waters now formed a canyon-like tunnel, like a parted sea. The path led Matthew straight towards Terrence. He ran at the dark warrior and the dragon towering above.

Matthew felt like he was flying as he barreled forward. Bursts of light continually formed a protective boundary from attackers, bullets, and stray shadows.

Beside him, Matthew noticed more warriors of light. As he ran, they flew, creating a group of charging light with him at its head. He noticed the giant, winged warrior of light. The bright light should have blinded him, but instead, the brilliance that blasted away any approaching demon was gentle to his eyes. The angel at his side was closer than the others, directly on his right hip as it charged forward. He was much larger than Matthew, easily eight or ten feet tall, and seemed to help Matthew run as he flew beside him.

Matthew caught the warrior's eyes. They were a of perfect light set in the brilliantly bright skin, yet he could make out the angel's face. A half-smile flickered at the edge of the angel's mouth, then he winked at Matthew. The love of his grandfather, of his entire family, and of all these angels pulsed through him.

The love of God powered him forward, into the belly of death.

The giant shadow over Terrence charged at Matthew and his defenders of light. The evil beings all around synchronized their attacks to blot out the light in front of them.

Immense jaws opened and descended on Matthew as the dark warrior carried Terrence's body forward. The sword, mace, dragon's jaw, and a wave of the possessed slammed into Matthew and the charging angels.

Zech, J, and the rest of the family lost sight of Matthew during the melee. They watched the dragon's head descend and shoot forward.

The dark shadows blasted into the sky along with brilliant rays of light, and the family saw it all. The collision was like an explosion within a mudslide, both light and dark hurtling out from the carnage.

The blast threw the mob to the ground. They lay motionless as the dragon broke apart, the dark clouds evaporating as the bright lights dissipated into the air.

As the dust settled, bursts of light moved across the family. The shining light found their wounds and danced across the open flesh, healing the skin, and leaving scars in its wake. Mark moved his arm, staring at the scar now stretching across his shoulder. J's entire body flickered with light as the bullet holes from his hip to his chest and the slashes across his legs healed.

In their amazement, they looked up, past each other, to see that the countless bodies of the possessed didn't move, and neither did Matthew's.

Chapter 50

Inside Death

Matthew felt like he was lying in a comfortable bed, halfway between dreaming and waking up, unsure if he should open his eyes to risk ending the dream. It was all dark, quiet.

Yet, the peaceful silence around him seemed to will him awake as his mind woke up. He opened his eyes to see magnificent light all around him. He wasn't in a warm bed, but in the middle of the parking lot. Exactly where his body fell, lifeless, only moments ago.

He looked around. His family and friends were like fog. A mist that formed their bodies, like a cloud of dust illuminated by an inner light. The color of it was familiar. The same glow of the Ark.

The misty forms of his loved ones barely moved, as if in slow motion, as they came towards him. His father, mother, J and Matthew's brothers, Ashley, Lucas, Paul, and Jimmy. They all stared towards the ground at his feet, but he didn't worry about their gaze. Liz stole all his attention.

Where the others walked, she ran to him.

He watched her run in slow motion, one step taking seconds. A look of horror filled her face and he could see her mouth open, screaming. Her tears overflowed and trickled from the sides of her almond-shaped eyes. The peace he felt in the silence now broke, like his heart, as he saw her sorrow.

Her eyes looked down as she slid, her jeans tearing on the concrete.

She slid into a body at Matthew's feet and put her hand under the head, holding it up and burying her weeping face in it. She felt for a breath, for a heartbeat, then lifted the neck and pushed in breaths of her own life into the motionless body. Her efforts to save the life of the motionless body blocked Matthew's view.

But he didn't have to see it.

He knew.

In his peripheral vision, he saw the legs he stood on. He didn't want to focus on them, knowing that once he saw, then he'd truly wake from the dream and face reality. If he saw it, he could never unsee it.

Tears rolled down his cheeks as he watched his wife repeatedly try CPR. J stepped forward, his body renewed and wounds healed. He knelt beside the body opposite of Liz. With two firm hands, he began pumping on the heart, alternating a few pumps after every series of breaths.

The body didn't move.

J and Liz were still like a thick mist to Matthew. He looked up at his other loved ones, and then at the scattered bodies all around him. There was an obvious difference—no internal light in those lying motionless, but Liz and J, along with the rest of the family, had a light inside them that glowed.

Matthew continued to resist looking below his legs, now picking his head up. He saw his father take his mother's hand. She grabbed Luke's hand, and he took Mark's, then Lucas stepped in and soon everyone held hands, forming a half circle around the body, enclosing it as much as possible while still giving Liz and J room.

Zech started the prayer, and soon everyone was praying vigorously. It all continued to unfold in slow motion as Matthew looked down and saw J lean back, still on his knees. He pulled his arms off the body and wiped his eyes. Matthew saw his friend's red and puffy eyes.

As the group prayed, their inner being, the brightness from deep within their core, glowed brighter. It made the dust-like mist that formed their bodies grow fainter, but the light grew stronger. As they prayed, their physical bodies became harder to see.

Then a new light caught Matthew's attention. As his loved ones prayed around him, beings of light took shape around him. Giant men and women, easily two and three feet taller than Matthew's six-foot frame, stood around him. Their armor was a perfect gold-like substance and their skin like an infinite number of burning filaments. Each inch of their skin was like the center of a light bulb stretched and made into a patch of light.

As Matthew's family continued to pray, their light minimized their presence but ignited the surrounding giants. More definition and features arose in each unique being. Faces formed as their lights grew brighter.

One angel stood close to Matthew, a sword of brilliant light rested at his side. Matthew looked at the man and, as the face formed, he saw a smile. It was the angel at his side when they charged the dragon. As Matthew caught the light-filled eyes, he looked down. Not knowing why he hid from the perfect face, but finding himself looking straight down at what he was previously avoiding: the legs of the body below him. His legs.

The feet he stood on disappeared in the midsection of his body lying below. Liz wrapped her arms around his lifeless chest. Matthew could see, even in slow motion, his wife, the woman who rarely cried, convulse as she wept. Beth and Lyn broke away from their grandmother and joined their mother. Liz reached up and pulled them in above Matthew.

With Liz's movement, the face looked straight at Matthew.

He saw there what he already knew.

The body was his.

His spirit stood above his lifeless body as the physical world faded away. The glowing light of the angels, the giant men and women all around him, and their brightness overtook his vision.

"Well done," a voice came from the nearby angel. Matthew now held his stare, looking up at the immense being.

"Who are you?" Matthew asked.

"We are the King's guard, and we proudly fight for the throne. We thank you for leading this fight." The angel bowed his head.

Matthew opened his mouth, but no words came out. The being of light smiled, as if delighted by Matthew's inability to speak.

"The King accepts all into his family. At least all who desire to be there. We fight and follow all the royal family."

"Royalty?" Matthew said.

The being nodded his head, the hint of a smile now growing broad. The angel's expression showed an underlying joy that screamed happiness as Matthew spoke.

"You're..." Matthew tried to say.

"We are the King's Guard. The Royal Guard, if you will. We fight for the King." He leaned down, his head level with Matthew's, "and we fight for anyone in the Royal Family. We fight, and defend, for you and yours, Matthew Light, because *you're* in the royal family."

Matthew remained silent, telling himself to remember everything around him.

"The red-eyed demon, and now this dragon, and the one above Terrence, who... What are they?" Matthew asked.

The being's smile turned to a frown as he looked across the battlefield. "Fallen comrades."

"You saved me from the darkness, the sea of darkness, from my dream. I remember lights, a slashing and flash of lights that beat the demon back. And again, in the hotel, you helped me save my family. And again here," Matthew motioned to the church, "you've saved me repeatedly."

The angel nodded, then he looked toward one of the woman warriors nearby. The giant, feminine angel stood above Liz.

"You chose well," she said in a Scottish accent as she looked down at Liz, then back to Matthew. "She prayed all night. Wouldn't stop. Made my job easy."

"Made all our jobs easier," a massive warrior above J said.

"Amen," another said as he stood above Luke.

"Hallelujah! Love fighting for some prayer warriors!" an angel-woman said above Aunt Millie. The angel above Aunt Millie turned and high-fived a magnificent-looking angel above Mary.

A smile broke across Matthew's face as he saw the two angels laugh.

"You received the gift of sight, Matthew," the angel closest to Matthew said. "And what you see, you must say. Speak truth."

Matthew nodded and then looked over the battlefield. "What will happen to all these people? To Terrence?"

"The King will decide," the angel said in a solemn tone.

Matthew sensed a sorrow in his voice.

After a pause, Matthew turned and caught the angel's eyes once again. "Is my grandfather with you?"

"He is," the angel nodded, "just as he is always with you." The massive hand pointed to Matthew's chest.

"Keep praying, young Matthew. Speak out and act. You make our job easier," he said as the bright beings faded.

Matthew wanted to call out to the angels, but he held his tongue. He wanted to ask more about Terrence and the surrounding bodies, but mainly he wanted to know about his family.

"It is *His* will, Matthew Light. And you have served it well. Well done," the angel said. He looked at Matthew and winked.

Without another word, the heavenly bodies faded away, and Matthew's view went black.

Chapter 51

Bump

"Girl!" Liz shouted from the curb. She ran towards Ashley with open arms, her eyebrows raised and jaw dropped in an exaggerated expression.

"No way," Liz said as she hugged her friend and felt Ashley's belly. "You knew before you left, didn't you?"

Ashley smiled and shrugged as she felt the baby bump. "I had to wait to tell you in person. Once we knew for sure."

"Well, a six-week honeymoon in Europe? I can understand coming back with a priceless souvenir like that," Liz said.

Ashley laughed, and Liz opened the passenger door for her.

"Well done, my friend." Liz playfully elbowed J before dashing back to her open driver-side door.

"Hi, Liz," J said playfully as he picked up the two large, rolling suitcases. He slid them into the back of Liz's black SUV.

Engines and squeaking tires echoed in the airport arrivals pickup area around them. The group closed the door as Beth and Lyn jumped up and down in the center row of seats.

"Girls! Back in your seats," Liz checked her mirrors and pulled off the curb.

"So, first tell me, was the super extended honeymoon worth the wait?" Liz said as she shot a sideways glance at Ashley in the front passenger seat. Ashley turned to catch her husband's eye.

"Absolutely," J and Ashley said in unison. A smile creeping across their faces they couldn't contain.

"Uncle J," Beth said, "I made you this!"

She handed J a thick cross made from popsicle sticks and glue, each layer of sticks painted a different color of the rainbow.

"Oh, thank you."

"I made this!" Lyn chimed in and held out a white piece of paper with various shapes and colored scribbles close, but not quite, inside the lines.

"Thank you so much! See that, Hun?" J motioned to Ashley. "I get presents on my return."

"And this is for Aunt Ashley!" Beth and Lyn said as they held up boxes of chocolate and candy.

"What?" J shouted. "She gets candy?"

The girls laughed as J grabbed his face and pretended to scream.

"Thank you, ladies!" Ashley said. "And don't worry, we have wonderful surprises from Europe and the Middle East. Just wait until we get home."

The girls screamed with excitement.

"You two sure you want to come over? I understand if you want to go home first, especially after being gone so long," Liz asked.

"Oh, my own bed! How I miss thee?" J said as he feigned falling asleep. But he was too tall for the headrest and his neck curled over the cushion.

"We had some magnificent hotels and bed-and-breakfasts. We're good to come over for a couple of hours," Ashley said as she touched her friend's arm.

Liz smiled, knowing Zech, Mary, Aunt Millie, Paul, and Jimmy were all waiting.

"Did you all see Grace and Mark, or Lucas?"

"We did," J replied. "Spent a couple days with each. I can't believe how quickly their ministries are growing."

"Hey, have you heard of an Agent Bowers?" Ashley asked Liz.

Liz shook her head. Ashley glanced back at J as they both smiled.

"What?" Liz asked.

"Just Mark," J said. "He thinks he's a super spy now that he's talking to that Brit in INTERPOL. Him, Lucas, and Luke are all on a group text he calls *super-secret agents.*"

"And I think J is jealous," Ashley leaned in and whispered.

"Oh, I am not!" J shouted from the back seat. "But I'm just saying, you can't nickname yourselves *super-secret agents.* Matthew wouldn't have stood for that!"

"Totally jealous," Liz said to Ashley.

J grunted and rolled his eyes.

"It's okay to be jealous," Beth whispered to J as she patted his knee. "It happens to me sometimes, too."

"Thank you," J whispered to the young girl.

Thirty minutes later, the girls were sprinting from the SUV, racing to hold open the door for Uncle J and Aunt Ashley. Zech came out and beat them to it.

"Hey, Grandpa!" Beth said as Zech hugged his granddaughter.

"And how's my favorite pastor? You refreshed and ready to lead the next twelve sermons after your sabbatical?" Zech joked.

"Twelve?" J said as he hugged his mentor. "Maybe two."

"What? I figure you could handle the next quarter while I get my sabbatical." Zech smiled at the girls. "But you're right, after being gone that long, I'm never letting you on my stage again." Zech slapped J's shoulder.

"I knew it. I knew it." Aunt Millie turned to Mary as they stepped outside and saw Ashley's bump. "I told you, didn't I?"

"Was it really *that crazy* of a prediction?" Mary said. She moved forward and hugged J and Ashley.

"Now, I know this one was tight-lipped on names until those babies popped out," Millie pointed at Liz, who shrugged unapologetically. "But what you thinking? Boy name? Girl name? Do you know the sex yet?"

"If it's a boy..." Ashley looked at J.

"It'll be Matthew," J said.

Ashley nodded and then looked at Mary and Liz. The three came together and hugged.

"Matthew?" Lyn belted out. "That's my dad's name!"

"That's kind of the point," J said as he picked her up and carried her into the house.

Jimmy and Paul stood up from the dining room table and greeted the couple.

"Euchre, already?" J asked.

"Just had to beat our newest congressman. Let him know civilians still hold the power," Jimmy said.

"You act like I'm opposing the second amendment," Paul joked. "And I'm the most honest politician you've ever seen."

"That's a relative term," Jimmy said.

"Congrats on the election," J hugged Paul. "I still can't believe that interview went viral and set your campaign off."

"When an entire operation gets exposed for treason, I suppose millions of views from folks pushing back on unconstitutional Capitol Hill can still win a seat!" Paul said as he puffed his chest.

"Oh, sit down," Zech hollered at his friend. "Get this election nonsense off my table and deal me in. Mary?"

"Nope." Mary directed the woman and girls away from the table as they chatted on the couch. J, Paul, Jimmy, and Zech stood around the table.

"Well, I guess it's us four. You forget the game already?" Zech motioned to J.

"I'll own these two like it's my job," J said as he sat down.

"Hey, speaking of new jobs." Jimmy said. "I have to say, I heard from the architects over on Division Street. They're impressed. That boy is doing some good work. They ain't never raved about a consultant like this. He calls out everything in their design, and for the better!"

"One of your boys get a new job, Jimmy?" J asked as he tried taking the cards from Paul.

"Nope," Zech interjected with a smirk. "One of mine. Started his own business."

As if on cue, the front door opened. Beth and Lyn lit up and ran to the front of the house.

"Daddy!"

Epilogue - Isaiah's Last Ride

Isaiah drove around the corner and parked on the side of a nearby street. It had a view of the intersection ahead. He would see if the van headed north, toward the Storage Yard. The leader of this van had mentioned the docks.

Isaiah was right to warn Paul. Terrence must have worked it out that if he could not find the Ark at the church or Zech or J's house, he would go to the Storage Yard. Terrence might already be there. If the gas station stop was unexpected, then the van would head north, right through this intersection and the city's port area.

Isaiah took a deep breath. He felt his age. His body was tired and his mind weary.

He could turn the car around and return home.

He could also try the police again.

But he did neither. Isaiah sat and watched the traffic lights change colors in the intersection before him. He closed his aging eyes. The wrinkles filled his face.

He prayed for God's protection and wisdom.

He prayed for God to hold his Rebecca tight. He missed her, yet felt joyful that she had returned to Jesus, had returned home.

He prayed for God to be with Zech, with Luke, Mark, and with Matthew and their families. He prayed for J as he dealt with the newly reopened wounds of his father's loss. For J to find his wife and to find a greater understanding of himself. For Matthew to continue helping the church in this time of need.

Finally, he prayed that God use him, Isaiah, for His Kingdom.

He prayed for strength.

For wisdom.

For courage.

As Isaiah opened his eyes, he saw the van continue north toward the Storage Yard. The men had figured out how to start the van. As it drove past Isaiah's line of sight, it seemed a darker black than it had before. As if the blackness of the paint was more than just physical, more than just pigment reflecting light.

It had a sense of death to it that pulsed from the van.

Isaiah no longer felt tired. In contrast to the van's blackness, he now had a soft, warm glow about himself.

He felt refreshed.

He was ready.

Pulling away from the curb, he approached the intersection, and turning right, he followed the van. As he gave a few car lengths, he felt tiny bursts of light around him, as if his skin and the surrounding area in Jimmy's car were sparkling in the fading sunlight. He glanced up in the rearview mirror and caught his reflection. His skin was glowing, just like the golden piece of Ark he'd passed down to his son.

From the corner of his eyes, he saw a similar light around his car. Looking out, there were beings of light flying alongside his car. They wore golden armor and their skin shined like the brightest sun, yet somehow their light didn't blind him.

The angel at the driver's side door looked at Isaiah. They locked eyes. The giant winged being of light motioned for Isaiah to look ahead.

Isaiah's vision went forward to the black van. The aura of black around the vehicle grew exponentially since it had gone through the intersection. Isaiah could see a towering black figure, its demonic head sticking out of the top of the van as a black cloud swirled around the vehicle. The darkness grew as it sped forward.

"Ready for one more ride?" the voice spoke to Isaiah.

Isaiah looked back at the angel at his side. "It's good to see you again."

"You as well, Isaiah Light. It's been our pleasure serving with you. Well done."

Isaiah nodded.

"I'll miss them," he said, thinking of his loved ones. "Be with them?"

"Always."

Isaiah looked at the billowing black cloud growing in the van. He turned back to the angel and winked at him.

The angel smiled and winked back.

The End.

***

Thank you for reading Light of the World, Book 3 in the Light of the Ark series.

I hope you enjoy this book and the entire series.

Have Feedback?

Tell me through a review or email me: jamesbonkwrites@gmail.com. **I love hearing from you**.

Free Preview

Interested in more?

Keep reading for a special preview of the stand-alone prequel to the Light of the Ark series, featuring Isaiah Light.

JAMES BONK

ISAIAH LIGHT

and the

SEA of DARKNESS

A LIGHT OF THE ARK SERIES PREQUEL

Michael's Gift

Chapter 1

Isaiah struggled to catch his breath.

Sweat and blood rolled down his face, dripping off his nose into the hot sand that now caked his hands. The last kick had forced all his air out as he gasped to bring it back. Pushing up, he slowly moved off the ground.

"Go ahead, GET UP!"

TTTHHUUDD

Another kick came hard and fast to his midsection and searing pain remained where his ribs were cracking.

Raising one hand to protect his head, he saw Jimmy, his closest friend, lying motionless twenty yards away, blood pooling around his arm and head where two deep gashes were opened.

Jimmy needed medical attention, and so did Isaiah.

The attacker switched back and forth from kicking to pushing with the bottom of their shoe, using it to shove Isaiah. He pushed at his head and shoulders, moving him closer to the busy road ahead of them.

"I knew this day would come," the voice standing over Isaiah said.

TTTHHUUDD

Another kick now came to the head. Isaiah's arm absorbed part of the blow, but the impact to his skull left him dazed as if a grenade went off nearby and stunned his senses.

"You just had to keep asking questions about Joan, then Gary, and then Barbara. You just couldn't accept the answers."

The voice was muffled in Isaiah's ringing ear.

Isaiah felt so naive. All this time, the common thread of all the hurt people. It was right in front of him, but he didn't see it.

He'd underestimated the evil in the world. He thought those involved were looking out for the kids, keeping their interests in line with their own.

How wrong he had been.

This wasn't human nature or self-preservation. This was evil in human form.

It was preying on the young adults of the community. Who knew how many bodies it racked up as it fulfilled its pleasures. There were seven that the police knew about, maybe more they didn't. And now Jimmy and Isaiah were being added to that list.

TTTHHUUDD

Isaiah winced at the pain. He had to stand up. He had to help Jimmy. He couldn't let this evil go on. He had to return to Rebecca. She would be next on the list if he didn't survive.

He struggled to get to his feet as another kick hit his midsection.

TTTHHUUDD

"You want to get up? Go ahead, GET UP!"

Another kick came, not giving Isaiah a chance to get to his feet. Toying with him. Pushing him toward the road.

As he guarded his head against the blows, he realized his Bible was underneath him. He had it when the surprise attack first hit Jimmy and then turned to Isaiah before he could respond. He unconsciously held on to it, protected it, and now still had it through his struggle.

The ancient artifact held in the book's bindings glowed, catching Isaiah's eyes.

If he died, he would never be able to talk to his father about it.

Isaiah knew too much for his attacker to let him live. He was too much of a threat. And Jimmy now knew as well, so he was now in the same boat as Isaiah, floating on the sea of darkness.

If Isaiah couldn't fight back, he would be killed, and the attacker would finish Jimmy off, then move on to Rebecca.

Another push from his attacker's leg, inching Isaiah closer to the busy highway road ahead. Trees and overgrown shrubs blocked the view of the road but the sounds of engines roaring past filled the air as they inched closer.

His eyes caught the Bible again.

In the scramble of the attack, he instinctively protected the book, but as his senses dulled from the kicks, he now saw the glowing light. The light took all his attention. The blows came harder and faster; he was now on the last patch of dirt before a drop to the shoulder, hidden from the cars as they sped past.

"Still can't GET UP?" Tim shouted as he raised his elbow.

Isaiah didn't hear the attacker scream at him or feel another rib break as an elbow dropped on his back, snapping bone.

He was being pulled off the ground so he could be thrown into the road. The busy road with the deceiving turn. The same turn that nearly took Gary's and Barbara's lives.

As the attacker pulled Isaiah up, his Bible and the warm glow gave him strength.

His resolve sharpened.

He had been protecting the book. Protecting the millennia-old glowing gold piece of cherub wing that was hidden in the bindings.

In the chaos of the moment, the book seemed to speak to him. To teach him what he never grasped on his own.

He had been protecting the book, but he was never meant to protect the book.

The book was meant to protect him.

It was his weapon against the evils of this world.

The last seven days were his education, his preparation for the coming fight.

Seven Days Ago
Chapter 2

Isaiah was twenty-eight years old when his father, Michael, decided it was time to pass on the Light family secret.

The year was 1962.

"Son, I want you to have this," Michael said to Isaiah, holding out the worn green family Bible.

"Dad...?" Isaiah said slowly, questioning his father.

The dark blue 1945 Dodge pickup sat running behind Isaiah as his wife, Rebecca, patiently waited in the front seat.

"I wanted to give it to you years ago, but..." Michael paused as his eyes watered.

Isaiah was taken aback. He had seen his father cry but only on rare occasions, and never while saying good-bye to his son. Michael hadn't even blinked when Isaiah and Rebecca moved away from their backwoods rural town to North Florida nearly ten years ago.

Michael was of average height but held a strong presence and seemed to have authority over any room he walked into that made him seem taller than he was. His defined jawline typically held a stern face that Isaiah saw too often during his childhood. Michael rarely needed to punish the young Isaiah for whatever mischief he had gotten into, only to flash his son the stern look and Isaiah knew he had been out of line. However, at times when Michael allowed it, a bright smile would highlight his jet black hair. Michael's smile would beam brightly as he closed every Sunday's service. He led a small, local church and ended his messages the same way for over three decades: "Go in peace, to learn and to love as Jesus would." Michael would say his closing line as he looked to his wife and Isaiah's mother, Leah, and both of them smiled ear to ear.

Michael's black hair had gradually turned salt and pepper and now was nearly all bright grey. His smile and grey hair framed his watery eyes as he held the family Bible out to his son.

"I wanted to give it to you ten years ago, but...but..." The pause was unlike Michael and seemed an eternity to Isaiah.

"There was so much I wish I could teach you, son. But I think...*we* think." Leah stepped up behind Michael and put her hand on his shoulder. He continued, "We think you need to experience it for yourself before I talk to you further about it."

"Dad," Isaiah said, confused and unsure.

Rebecca noticed Isaiah's confusion and stepped out of the truck behind him. Isaiah sensed her, and like Leah gave Michael confidence, Isaiah was bolstered by his wife's presence.

Isaiah reached out his hand to grab the Bible.

In all his time of learning how to lead a church from his father, Bible studies, and devotionals, Isaiah realized he never actually held his dad's Bible before. It was either in Michael's arms or in the top drawer of his dresser. He never left it out, never forgot it at church or on the kitchen table. It was always in his bedside dresser or in his hand.

As his hand unconsciously extended to take hold of the book, Isaiah felt a sensation he never felt before.

His hand flinched as he felt a sudden pain shoot through it, as if pieces of his hand were running from each other, twisted and pulling on a microscopic level within the internal chaos. The brunt of it lasted only a moment, but as he took hold of the book, the pain lit up his whole body like being plugged into an outlet, and a remnant of the feeling lingered within each cell of Isaiah's body.

As the intense pain reduced, a warm feeling took hold. It was a loving, welcoming, pure feeling. Isaiah lost every other sense in his body as he felt the loving warmth take hold of his hand. He felt as if the book was now holding him instead of him taking hold of the book. The welcoming feeling flashed through his body, just as the pain did, but held longer and deeper, finding a home deep within his core.

Rebecca's hand was on Isaiah's shoulder as he held the book, and with a soft tremble of her hand, Isaiah knew she felt the sensation he did.

Isaiah opened his eyes wide, looking to his father without knowing how to respond. His large, hopeful eyes highlighted an otherwise expressionless face.

Michael smiled and released the Bible into Isaiah's full grasp.

***

The Bible sat between Isaiah and Rebecca on the four-hour drive home. The front of the fixed-up pickup truck felt brighter, as if there was a new glow coming from the holy book and illuminating the couple.

They were visiting their hometown in rural Georgia for a somber event: Joan Auferetur's funeral. Joan was nineteen and lived in the North Florida area not far from Isaiah and Rebecca. Her parents made a similar move as Isaiah and Rebecca, going from rural Georgia to the growing beachside area of North Florida. They lived across town but would come by the Light's church to attend holiday services and stay in touch. Before graduating, Joan attended their weekly youth group and even transferred to the local high school as a varsity swimmer, winning regionals in her junior and senior year and placing top three in states. She also loved to hike and explore, finding solace in nature.

However, one weekend, she left for a hike and never came home.

Her body was found by another hiker seven days later.

Her death shook the local community as well as her small hometown when it hit the papers.

Joan's parents didn't believe the accident story and suspected foul play. When the police wouldn't reopen the investigation, they took their frustrations to the papers. It wasn't like her to go alone or be unprepared but with a lack of evidence and no witnesses, it appeared a tragic accident of falling off the trail and hitting her head on the rocks below. Her parents' frustrations with the lack of investigation ultimately led to their choice to have her buried in their hometown.

As Isaiah and Rebecca drove home, they were quiet for nearly two hours before starting to talk. They didn't talk about the Bible—as miraculous as the feeling was, they seemed to have an unspoken understanding—and Isaiah didn't think he could describe it if he tried. They were more speechless than anything on the subject of that new sensation.

Their conversation started with Joan and shifted to their church and that night's upcoming youth group. The group had grown slowly and steadily in its early years but had seen a spike in attendance in recent years. The increase in attendance coincided with the church leaving Isaiah and Rebecca's home and expanding into a nearby high school gymnasium for Sunday service. The youth group was still hosted at their house every Wednesday, and participation quickly increased as attendance rose in Sunday service.

Isaiah and Rebecca moved to the North Florida coast from rural Georgia ten years ago after getting married. They first met in the church, specifically Isaiah's father's church during a youth group session. They connected immediately and over time built a shared passion for educating the next generation, especially teenagers going through the difficult transition to adulthood.

Isaiah and Rebecca's bond was forged quickly when both were bullied for voicing their opinion on religion, particularly for loving God's people. During Isaiah's history class, he commented on the harsh treatment of African Americans during the Civil War and likened it to the Jews in Egypt before their exodus. The comment stirred up another boy in the class, who took offense and blamed "those negros," as the boy put it, for the deaths of family members generations ago in the Civil War. Isaiah responded sharply, telling the other boy that his family had no morals, and if they'd enslaved blacks, they likely would have been Nazis if they lived in Germany. A fight broke out and both boys were suspended from school and left with black eyes.

World War Two had ended only five years prior and many kids in the class still held fresh wounds from relatives or parents in the war. War-related comments only magnified the racial comments. The civil rights movement was bubbling but still years away in the 1950 Jim Crow south. Isaiah's comment fired up others in the class, and when a young Isaiah returned from suspensions, he now faced five angry students shouting at him before the teacher could get back control of the class.

Gossip in the small town school spread quickly and Isaiah's comments didn't take twenty-four hours to turn him into a negro and Jew lover. Soon after, he was being called a fairy and pansy. His father's church was his only solace, and even there, he got the sense his peers were merely quieting their insults instead of rebuking them.

Isaiah and Rebecca had met a few weeks earlier and had only been on one date. Rebecca could have easily been scared away or left Isaiah during the incident, but she sided with Isaiah and defended his comments. She was soon labeled with similar names amongst the other girls.

The name-calling blew over within a month or two as the other kids found another topic of destruction, but more than ten years later, the feeling of being an outcast because of their beliefs still fueled the couple. Youth group was an important outlet for both of them to give a safe and secure place for young Christians to meet, make similar friends, and learn about the world.

Most importantly, just as God informed Elijah of seven thousand other believers around Israel in 1 Kings, Isaiah and Rebecca wanted to remind the kids they were not alone.

As Isaiah and Rebecca returned home and unpacked their bags from the trip, Rebecca brought up an issue Isaiah had been trying to avoid.

"Do you think Gary will show up tonight?"

Isaiah stopped and thought.

Gary Freed was a junior at the local high school and his family had been in the church for five years, with Gary attending youth group every week. His parents were also engaged and active in the small church, usually being the first to volunteer in organizing community efforts and potlucks.

A few months back, Rebecca was elated to hear that Gary and Barbara, another longtime youth group attendee, had begun courting. Their friendship was turning into a young romance for the adorable couple. Meanwhile, Isaiah was hopeful that Gary would take up a leadership role in the youth group.

Gary was also quickly becoming the big man on campus. He had all the traits of a well-rounded, respectful young man combined with strong academics and athletics. He took over the starting quarterback job as a sophomore when the first string quarterback was injured and performed far above expectations. The town was abuzz for his breakout junior year for the recent fall season, but the team underperformed and everyone seemed to be deflated. Being the newly hyped QB and then having led the team to a disappointing season, Gary took much of the blame on his shoulders.

Gary had still attended the youth group and Sunday service each week with his family during the season. Isaiah was proud of the young man, noticing that he still had a good attitude and work ethic during the adversity of the rough season.

But soon after the season ended, Gary stopped coming to youth group. A couple of weeks later, his family stopped attending church altogether.

Isaiah remembered Gary bringing a warm and confident presence to the entire youth group. He prayed for the boy to return.

Rebecca's question lingered. "Do you think Gary will show up tonight?"

"I hope so," was all Isaiah eventually replied.

That night, Gary returned.

But not the Gary they remembered.

Books By James Bonk

Light of the Ark Series

1. Light of the Ark

2. Shadows of the Ark

3. Light of the World

- Isaiah and the Sea of Darkness (standalone prequel)

More Fiction

- Christian's Look Back at Life

Stay up to date on new releases and email exclusive content:

https://hello.jamesbonk.com/signup/

Acknowledgements

Thank you, Lord. None of this is possible without you.

My wife and daughters, for dealing with the extra time my mind spent in this world.

Leonard Petracci, for coaching me along this journey (*and for anyone who likes the Young Adult Sci-Fi / Urban Fantasy Genre, check out his work, especially the Star Child series*).

To Pastor Russ and my Life Group brothers at Southpoint Community Church, for helping me think through these topics via sermons and weekly discussions.

Photographer, Author Picture and Cover Model: Alicia Bonk (https://aliciabonk.com/)

Cover Art Designer: Jelena Gajic (zelengajic@gmail.com)

And a special thanks to the Beta Readers whose time, effort, and thoughtfulness improved this story:

- Maureen H.

- Zanese D.

The Author

J ames Bonk writes Christian Fiction to develop his own faith and as a ministry. He lives in the North Atlanta area with his wife, two daughters, and fluffy Chartreux cat, Porkchop. When he's not writing, he's usually swimming or building forts with his girls!

His Light of the Ark book was the #1 New Release in its category upon release, with multiple five star reviews from adults and young adults alike.

Besides writing, parenting, and being a husband, James Bonk is a supply chain leader and business intelligence professional. He has a BS in Mechanical Engineering, MS in Industrial Engineering, and an MBA. He previously held his Professional Engineering license in Industrial Engineering.

Find out more at and get access to all his books at: https://store.jamesbonk.com/

You can also find James by searching James Bonk Author on your favorite platform or following the below links:

- Goodreads (https://www.goodreads.com/author/list/219 97660.James_Bonk)

- Facebook (search *'James Bonk Author'* or go here: https://www.facebook.com/people/James-Bonk-Autho r/100092204034685/)

- BookBub (https://www.bookbub.com/profile/james-bon k)

The Author - James Bonk

Made in the USA
Columbia, SC
12 May 2025

57739902R00241